A Modern Day
Sexy *Cinderella* Story

JENNIFER MILLER

ISBN: 978-0-9894074-8-9
Copyright © 2016

Cover Designer: Robin Harper, Wicked by Design
Formatting: Elaine York, Allusion Graphics, LLC

For Jake,
my real-life Prince Charming.

Prologue

Six Months Ago

Knee deep in clothes when my phone starts ringing, I regret my impulsive decision to clean out my closet. I wonder if climbing the Matterhorn resembles the feeling I have as I move to get my phone. Catching my foot in the neckline of some random cast away garment, I stumble and almost fall on my face. Righting myself and cursing under my breath, I snatch my phone from my dresser and answer breathlessly, "Hello?"

"Hi! My name is Tiffany, and I'm looking for a Miss Gabriella Barrie, please."

"Yes, this is she," I respond absently looking at the small round solitaire engagement ring sitting erectly on my finger startled at the realization that it wouldn't be my name for too much longer. The thought makes my stomach twist uncomfortably and I place my hand on my tummy trying unsuccessfully to knead the pain away.

The voice on the other end, obviously astute to my distraction, reorients me. "Uh, hello…hello…Hi, Gabriella! Like I said before, my name is Tiffany. I'm calling from Fairytale Vacations – where it's our job to give you a happily ever after! I'm so excited to let you know that you've won a complimentary all inclusive vacation to an exclusive resort in Cabo San Lucas, Mexico."

"Seriously? A vacation? That's the best you've got? Very funny. Katie put you up to this right? It's not funny," I tell Tiffany or whatever her name really is with a mixture of disbelief and annoyance. I've never won anything in my life.

"Um, no. I'm not sure who Katie is," she says and I can hear the confusion in her voice, which brings a moment of pause. "You attended a bridal expo last month and visited our booth," she states. The completely overwhelming experience comes crashing through my memory like a tidal wave. I had reluctantly attended the event at the insistence of Jeremy's mother Mariel. Hundreds of vendors were all crowded into a small space handing out samples, taking my name, number, and email address for all kinds of things from a free limo ride, wedding cake, even a wedding gown. Mariel was insistent that I participate in every available give-away – she even had pre-printed labels with all of my personal information to enable quick entry. The whole experience left me with handfuls of contacts, and several ideas, but more unsettled about the wedding details I wanted than when I arrived.

"Yes, I remember the expo." *Do I ever.*

"Great! Well we drew your name from over ten thousand entries, and you have won an all expenses paid trip to Cabo San Lucas, Mexico for two!"

"Well…wow. That's amazing!" I reply feeling speechless and shocked.

She laughs lightly, "I'll send you an email with details on how to book your vacation, all the resort information, other activities that are available for you to schedule, as well as vouchers for the restaurants on site and the day spa."

"That all sounds…incredible!"

"It really is. All you need to do is decide when you want to go and then arrange your flight accommodations with us – easy peasy!" She says excitedly and I quietly snort at her expression. "Well of course, you'll probably want to buy a new swimsuit or two. Or heck, go crazy and get a new wardrobe," she says laughing at herself.

"Well this is really great timing actually. My wedding is coming up soon and we were still trying to work out honeymoon details.

I guess this settles that." I can't help but feel excited about going to Cabo - I've never been to Mexico before. My mind is already spinning with visions of myself lying in the sun, walking on the beach, enjoying a massage at the spa, and sneaking kisses from my new husband on the beach at night as we bask in the moonlight while listening to the ocean beat against the shore.

"That's great, but just so you know, the voucher is for two people - *any* two people. So if for some reason you decide to do something else for your honeymoon… or for any other reason… you can use it for anyone, as long as you are one of the users. And you have a year in which to use the package."

"Thank you so much, this is really great. Jeremy, my fiancé, won't believe it!"

"You're welcome. Congratulations. I just need to verify your email address, please."

"Sure," I reply and give her the information.

"Okay, I'll get that email confirmation sent over. Congratulations again, and may all your dreams come true."

Chapter 1

Present Day

My vacation started off as a way to escape. I needed to get away and wanted relaxation, but most importantly, I wanted to have some much needed and overdue fun. Where better to get that than a place offering plenty of sun, sand, and the healing powers of the ocean? And I would not do it alone - I'd have my bestie by my side; the person who knows me best and loves me most. How lucky I am to have such a meaningful friendship with her. I knew this time away with her would help heal the cracks of betrayal my heart was carrying. If I were lucky, my wounded pride would also be restored. And god knows I needed a saturating reorientation to the single lifestyle after being in a committed relationship for three years. Or at least I was committed. What I didn't expect now, two weeks later, was to be returning home more broken hearted than I was when I left.

Walking away, well I guess it's more like sneaking away, from the man I somehow managed to fall in love with over the last week, feels impossible. After returning my rental car and checking in for my flight home, an overwhelming urge to bend over at my waist and scream runs through me. I want to rant and rave at the unfairness of falling for a man that can never be mine. At having a stepmother from hell that's in part influencing my decision to leave. For not being brave enough to say goodbye to his face. For letting my heart shred into so many pieces I wonder if it can ever possibly find its way back together again.

Fate is a sick and twisted bitch and I'd really like to give her a nasty catfight. I'd totally pull her hair, scratch out her eyes, kick, and fight dirty. That bitch fate deserves it.

The feelings are so visceral that it takes everything I have to keep them reigned in. Yet, somehow I manage. Barely. I keep it together as I check in my luggage and obtain a boarding pass. I exude a false calm as I go through security, removing each item I'm carrying to be inspected, take my shoes off and wait patiently for my turn. I even manage a smile when the customs agent greets me and I get randomly selected for a more detailed search of my items. The official pulls everything out of my carry-ons, almost making me laugh at the look on his face when he sees the results of my hurried packing. He opens things and peers inside like I might have contraband hiding. In lipstick tubes? Geesh. Finally, he concedes that I am harmless and stamps my passport while ushering a sigh. What? He's disappointed? I continue to keep it together, though I swallow repeatedly to keep the emotions from being emitted. Proceeding to the gate area, I search the corridor for the nearest restroom, rush inside, lock myself in a stall, and finally cry unrelenting tears.

My cries and sobs become howls at some point. Not intentionally; but I produce babbly, high pierced sounds like a dying animal. I become aware of this because a few people knock on the door to ask me if I'm okay. One asks if there's anything she can get me, or anyone she can send in after me. It's nice of them and I appreciate the kindness. But it also further humiliates me. I manage to utter syllables meant to tell each I'm fine, but I'm not sure the message is clear. Perhaps it is betrayed by the immediate resumption of wailing. Grabbing a handful of toilet paper, I blow my nose loudly, dab at my face, and try my best to quit crying, knowing that it's not helping or changing anything. Logic, however, gives way again to emotion. I try another rational approach. There was no other option. Leaving this way is easier – simpler – and the right thing to do. Saying goodbye in person would have broken me beyond repair.

Especially if I saw in his eyes that my leaving wasn't as hard for him as it was for me. There's no way I could face the, "thanks for a great time," line I'd been likely to receive – not when for me it was so much more than that. Tears set in yet again. Where do they all come from?

I'm being ridiculous – I know this. I've told myself repeatedly that any kind of relationship or legitimate feelings for someone after a mere week is ridiculous. I need to simply be thankful for the time we had together, the fact that he helped restore my confidence and made me feel beautiful and cherished when I needed it most. I need to move on – to get back to my life and remember this time with fondness. If only my heart – and wherever these tears get formed - would listen to my head.

"Gabriella Barrie, please proceed to gate 18C. Again, this is the last call for Gabriella Barrie. Please proceed to gate 18C. Your plane is leaving."

My eyes widen at the words I hear through the intercom. How long have they been calling me? *Oh my god!*

I claw at the roll of toilet paper to clean up my business. How could my bladder have had anything to empty after all of the water I used in tears? And what timing. Fate – you really are a bitch. I take another large bunch for good measure since I don't have any tissues. I jump up and lift my undies and jean capris over my hips and begin fumbling with the buttons. In my haste, my fingers decide to quit working properly and I fumble like an idiot. It doesn't help that the buttonhole always seems too small for the button and I struggle every time I wear these. With a curse, I give up and tug my zipper up and leave the button for later. I'll fix it when I'm on the plane. Grabbing my things, I spring through the open stall door, hurriedly wash my hands, and dry them on my pants as I make a mad dash for the door.

Maybe it's no surprise that running through the airport as fast as you can while simultaneously trying to keep your pants up is not an easy thing to do. Maybe later I'll laugh about what a hot mess I must look like right now. Huge bag over my arm, wild hair flying about my face, a hand at my waist holding up my pants while my other hand wheels a bag behind me that keeps toppling over. Heavy beads of sweat form and begin to fall from my red swollen face and I feel trickles of perspiration making a mad dash down my backside. I'm the only person alive, late for her own flight while sitting *in* the freaking airport. How long was I in that restroom anyway? Clearly, it's a black hole in there. These are travel hints they should tell people.

Leaving my pants undone was clearly a mistake. With each slap of my feet on the ground, I can feel my zipper sliding down tooth by tooth. My jeans get looser and looser around my waist. Gripping them tighter, I continue to run, muttering apologies as I bump into other passengers and almost take a woman with a small dog out. Seeing the gate ahead, I move faster and yell to the worker at the door, letting go of my pants, I start waving my arm in the air hoping to attract her attention.

"Wait! Please! I'm here!" I yell, feeling panicked, my breath coming in pants. She smiles kindly when she sees me, which is more than I deserve considering I've likely held them up. "I'm so sorry. So sorry. Lo siento," I add for good measure considering I'm at the airport in Mexico. Handing her my boarding pass, I watch her scan it before she looks up. I'm not sure what she sees in my face, but there's kindness in her eyes as she gestures to the door.

"It's okay," she says, her Spanish accent thick, "Go. Vamos." She tells me with a smile and gives me a wave. Tossing her a quick, "Thank you!" over my shoulder, I run down the jet way toward the plane's door.

"Hi," I tell the exceptionally pretty flight attendant breathlessly as I get to the door. My breaths are ragged and I feel slightly dizzy from the chaos.

"Gabriella Barrie?" she asks as she takes in my appearance, her gaze resting at my hand where I'm once again clutching my pants that now sit a bit lower than my waist, before returning to my eyes.

"Yes. I'm so sorry I'm late. I was in the restroom for a long time." As soon as the words are out of my mouth, I feel my cheeks flush. "I mean, not because I was going to the bathroom all that time. I mean, I guess I did pee. But that's not what took me a long time. It was because I was sad. Crying. Men, what are you going to do?" She continues to stare at me, and it increases my discomfort. Clearing my throat, I shrug, "Uh, thank you. Thank you so much. Sorry again," I tell her feeling like a complete fool and apparently unable to just shut the hell up.

She smiles tightly, "Please find an available seat. Fortunately, our flight isn't full."

Nodding, I turn away from her and flush deeper when I see the passengers in the front have heard every word I just babbled. Lifting my head and faking confidence I don't feel, I pass them, making my way down the aisle, looking for a seat. I carefully avoid the eyes of other passengers, their ire and annoyance palpable due to waiting on me. Part of me feels like I should grab the intercom phone and make a formal group apology. Lifting my chin, I try to roll it off my shoulders and see a row that has only one woman sitting in the aisle. She's smiling widely at me and she's the first kind face I see. "Hi. May I please sit here?"

She smiles, "Of course, dear."

"Thank you." Reaching across her to set my purse in the seat I've claimed, I swing my carry-on up to the open overhead bin. There's plenty of space available, but my soft sided bag is stuffed and doesn't slide inside easily. Hoping it's pushed in enough, I try to close the bin, but it won't latch. Even when I give it an extra slam and a few pushes for good measure. With a sigh, I let the bin open back up, then start shoving and pushing my bag roughly with both hands in an attempt to rearrange its contents to get it back a couple more inches. Feeling additional penetrating stares of passengers and the flight attendants alike compound my frustration.

"Ugh," I yell and look around for an airline attendant for help. "Excuse me," I call to a blonde one down the aisle a bit. She is poised in a selfie pose, twirling her hair around a finger while she speaks to an attractive man. He's smiling at her and I realize she not only didn't hear me, but it's going to take a miracle to get her attention. Rolling my eyes, I turn back to my bag and start shoving it again, harder this time, both hands beating against it in annoyance as continuous beads of sweat fall down my nape. It's immovable.

With a curse I yank it out, turn it around, and give it another hard push. At the same time the bag finally slides back into position, I feel my jeans slide down my hips and a ceremony of gasps fill my ears.

With embarrassment I realize I could be partially mooning my fellow passengers behind me. Quickly lifting my pants, I will myself to believe that no one actually saw anything, but must forego the masquerade, clearly aware of the definition of their gasps. Under my lashes, I glance behind me to see one woman looking away, her shoulders shaking in what I assume is laughter. Laughter at me. The sight causes my face to flush redder, which is a feat given that I know I'm already bright red. Another woman, older, catches my eye and then touches her forehead, sternum, and each of her shoulders in the sign of the cross – likely saying a quick prayer to cleanse my soul or to protect her from me. A quick glance to the row behind them finds me meeting brown eyes of a man who looks to be around my age - mid twenties. He grins widely at me, and even winks. Why I'm regarding their expressions I do not know – it's like I've been paralyzed. Shaking my head as if to wake up from this nightmare, and turning hastily, I scoot past my row companion hitting my leg on the armrest on the way. Falling into my seat, I struggle to fix my pants, then buckle my seatbelt across my lap. With a sigh I turn to look out the window as feelings of total mortification and humiliation wash over me warring with the brokenness I'm already struggling with today. Funny how earlier I didn't think this day could get any worse.

As if on cue, tears start streaming from my eyes, and I'm sniffling in no time. I pull the seat back toward me in hopes that an unused napkin resides there but seeing none, reach for my purse, rifling through looking for a tissue in what is likely to be a vain attempt, lucidly aware that I threw the toilet paper I had grabbed in the bag that now resides above me – what was I thinking? A tap on my arm gets my attention and I turn to see the woman next to me holding out a tissue. With a shaky smile I take it from her and wipe my nose, "Thank you." She hands me another.

"Of course, dear. Are you okay?"

The simple act of kindness, the concern in her voice, and the fact her salt and pepper hair, dark eyes, and soft smile reminds me a little bit of my beloved aunt, makes the tears flow faster. "No, not really," I respond honestly.

"Do you feel like talking about it?"

Twisting the tissue in my hands I force out a laugh, "It's a long story."

"Oh honey, we have nothing but time."

She isn't wrong; we have a long flight ahead of us. Still. Turning my head to the right at the crazy thought of spilling my guts to a stranger, I begin to shake my head no, but something stops me. Truth is, I feel like I want to tell her. She's someone that has no idea who I am or anyone I might speak to her about. Baring my soul to her is more than intriguing, it feels necessary, and safe. Maybe she sees that I'm considering it because she smiles warmly at me, "Who knows, dear, maybe talking to me will be like confiding in your very own Fairy Godmother, and I'll be able to help make your dreams come true."

Laughing softly at the mirth in her eyes, I sniffle, "Well, that's a nice thought. If only it were true."

She smiles and holds out her hand, "My name is Faye, love. And you are?"

"Gabriella, but my friends call me 'Ella'."

"Well, Ella, will you please tell me why you're so sad?"

I begin shredding the tissue in my hand and I watch as the pieces fall like snow into my lap, "I don't even know where to begin."

"Well that's easy, love. At the beginning of course."

With a nod and a small smile, I take a deep breath, and begin.

Chapter 2

Two Weeks Ago

When I was a little girl, Cinderella was my favorite princess. I loved watching her dance at the ball in the arms of Prince Charming – it's still my favorite part. Even though it was a cartoon and not an animated version like we have today, you could clearly see the love in Cinderella's eyes, a small smile of happiness upon her lips, and even a look of stunned disbelief at times on her face. Looks that told me she couldn't believe how happy she was and that she was dancing in the arms of her love.

Looking at my reflection in the mirror, taking in the vision, I focus intently, desperately searching for a look just like that princess in blue. But, there isn't even a hint of a smile upon my lips or a trace of a twinkle in my eyes. Instead, there's uncertainty, desperation, and perhaps a twinge of fear. I'm wondering for the hundredth time if I'm doing the right thing. Am I sure that I want to walk down the aisle? Is this really the man that I want to be with for the rest of my life? Is Jeremy my real life prince? Are these thoughts normal to have on my *actual* wedding day?

Fidgeting with my veil, I purposefully take some deep breaths; hoping doing so will calm my nerves. Closing my eyes, I try to picture my doubts as dust particles that simply blow away with each, and every, exhale. I give up when it feels like I'm closer to hyperventilating than calming down. I'm trying to avoid a tiny voice in the back of my mind that's screaming, "RUN!" It seems that ignoring it is only making it get louder and louder. It's telling me that I'm about to make a mistake. A huge, gigantic mistake.

When Jeremy proposed marriage, saying "yes" just seemed to be the appropriate response. We knew one another in college and were casual acquaintances initially. His father worked for mine and I knew who his dad was, but Jeremy and I had never officially met before. We didn't begin dating until he attended a work function with his father that I was also attending; we gravitated toward each other and hung out for the evening, spending hours talking. We never quit spending time together after that and our relationship developed from there. He met my stepmother and stepsister and I saw his dad again, met his mother and his brother. My family loved him, his loved me, and most of our friends always made comments about how perfectly matched we were, and I wondered if maybe they could see something that I didn't. I knew that I loved Jeremy, but lately I'd been questioning if I was *in* love with him.

I enjoyed spending time with him, but I always felt like something was missing. I never felt the passionate, fiery love that I've read about and saw in movies. But, I know that those kinds of feelings are fictional. It's silly to base real life on some fairy tale and so I pushed them aside and told myself I was being unrealistic. So, when he proposed, regardless of my hesitations, I agreed to become Mrs. Jeremy le Pieu.

"Just say the word."

"What?" I ask startled out of my thoughts. Turning to my best friend, and maid of honor, Katie, I smile at her appearance. She looks beautiful in the rose hued strapless dress I selected for her that compliments mine. The tulle skirt flares at her waist and stops at her knees. Her dark hair is piled on her head and her lips are painted the brightest pink. However, one look in her eyes shows me they are full of worry.

"I said, just say the word, and we will make like Julia Roberts in *Runaway Bride* and get the hell out of here."

I start to laugh at her joke, but find myself wondering if I could do it? Could I walk away? I know she's not kidding, all I have to do is give her a nod of my head and she will make it happen.

What's worse? Marrying a man I'm unsure about and living a potential unhappy life, or disappointing people that will eventually get over it?

She takes my hands in hers, "Ella, no one knows you better than I do, and I know you aren't happy. I know you are just doing this because you think it's the right thing to do. I know given everything you've been through that settling for mediocrity is easier than being alone, but I'm begging you, one last time, don't do this."

Biting my lip, I look deep into Katie's eyes and see her sincerity. There's no judgment, no abomination, only concern and a desire for me to follow my heart. Taking a deep breath, I squeeze her hands, and give her a tiny nod. She expends a sigh of relief, "Thank god. Okay, here's what we're going to do-" before she can continue, the door opens, freezing us both as if we were already caught in the act of running.

When we see who walks in the door, we probably shouldn't be surprised. I mean really, why wouldn't they try to ruin today like every other day they're a part of? Katie and I both exchange a look that screams, "What now?"

My stepsister, Jackie, decked out in head to toe black is closely following behind my stepmother Angelica who's also wearing black and topped off with a black pillbox hat with a small veil that covers her eyes. They are quite the duo. I can't decide if they've confused my wedding for a funeral, or if they are mistaking New York for London. Either way, they both look ridiculous.

To say there is no love lost between us is an understatement. I'm surrounded by a family that's anything but mine. My mother passed away from breast cancer when I was a little girl. My father grieved for years and while I know he missed her every day, we made the most of a life with just the two of us. I had a content and wonderful childhood. It was full of love, laughter, and beautiful memories of the three of us together as a family before my mom died, and more of my father and I after her loss. My father doted on me, and while I missed my mother, I never lacked love and affection.

Katie came into my life in the fourth grade, just before the loss of my mother. We bonded over our mutual love for dancing and the color pink. I never felt sad that I was an only child, because in my mind, Katie has always been my sister. I felt like I had an almost perfect life. So, when my dad started dating, I had a hard time initially, but quickly tried to understand his need for a woman's companionship and conversation. I was thirteen and was determined to show my maturity at the situation even though part of me hated it. I didn't want to share my father with anyone – I'd gotten too used to the two of us. When I was introduced to the woman that would become his wife, Angelica, it was easier than I expected to push the jealousy away because his happiness was far more important. I was kind, polite, and did my best to welcome her and my new stepsister, Jackie, into our lives.

Right from the get go, there was no love lost between Jackie and me. Anything and everything we could have argued about – clothes, boys, TV shows, school activities, friends – you name it, we did. Inevitably, we did our best to avoid each other unless we were forced to spend time together with our parents as witness.

When my father died unexpectedly from a heart attack a few years back, all bets were off. I no longer cared about getting along with either of them. Overnight they had become greedy bitches from hell. When they found out my father had not only left me money to pay for college and a trust to take care of myself, but that he also gave me controlling interest in his company as well, they were livid. I didn't care. I was off to college anyway, eager to meet the requirements needed to take my rightful place as head of his company, and I didn't have time or patience to deal with them.

If it hadn't been for Jeremy, I wouldn't even have invited them to our wedding, but at a weak moment, he talked me into it. He reminded me that as we began a new chapter in our lives it was time to let go of the past and to start fresh from our wedding day forward. I wasn't so sure I agreed, but went along with his preference to invite them anyway. Clearly, that seems to be my MO where he's concerned. From the look on both of their faces, I'm regretting giving into his suggestion.

With a sneer upon her lips, Jackie spits, "So, this is really happening then? You're marrying him?"

"Excuse me?" I ask at the same time Katie says, "What the hell do you both want?"

My dear stepmother says nothing, but Jackie spits, "I'm not talking to you," to Katie before turning to look at me once more. "You're seriously going through with this?"

My brow furrows and while I'm definitely not going to go through with this, I still don't understand why she's asking, "Why are you asking me that? What are you doing back here?"

She shakes her head, "That bastard. He didn't tell you, did he?" She looks at Angelica, "See? I told you he hadn't told her." Angelica's lips somehow manage to purse even tighter.

"Tell me what? What are you talking about?" I throw up my hands, "You know what? I don't care. I'm kind of busy here. Leave," I tell her knowing I need to get the hell out of here now and the longer she delays my escape, the more impossible sneaking out is going to be.

"Jeremy and I have been having an affair," Jackie blurts. "We have been for quite some time."

My mouth falls open and my stomach twists painfully making me gag. Katie reaches out and grabs my arm, her fingernails painfully digging into my skin. I may be ready to walk out on Jeremy, but that doesn't mean I'm not still shocked and hurt by the bomb that just dropped.

Katie recovers first, "What the hell are you talking about? This is low. Even for you," she snaps at Jackie.

"It's true," she hisses. "Fact is Jeremy doesn't love you. He only wants to gain access to the business. I wouldn't even be telling you this if I didn't have to. But, he's hoping that by marrying you, he'll get to eventually run your father's company and push you out."

"He can't push me out of my own company," I state thinking about the marketing company I manage that's become my pride and joy. I love what I do, love that my father loved it as well. No one is taking that away from me. No one. I'll die first.

"Maybe not, but you weren't signing a prenup were you? He can certainly take you to court and make your life hell down the road. If it came to that. Or maybe you'd be so in love with him and his little act that you'd sign over controlling interest to him? Regardless, you can't tell me that Jeremy wasn't going to get a primo position within the company. He has it all planned out and he wants to leave you with nothing."

Jeremy's been working at the company since I took it over. I love my job, love coming up with creative and innovative ways to help our clients promote and market their dreams. Playing a role in helping them share their dream with the world, to realize that dream, well that's just an amazing experience. Plus, I'm damn good at it.

"And what?" I ask her. "You're doing me a kindness by telling me because you care about me? Because of our sisterly bond? Seems to me you both have more to gain by not telling me a thing." I scoff while gripping Katie's hand tighter in my own. Nausea washes over me at the thought of Jackie and Jeremy together and I do my best to cover it up. *Jackie and Jeremy. Jeremy and Jackie. Isn't that cute? Their names even go together. Gag.*

"No," she snaps. "I don't really care about how this makes you feel at all. I regret he let it get to this point, such a waste of time and money, but I have no choice now but to take matters into my own hands."

"Do you want me to say 'thank you'? Because if that's what you're waiting for, feel free to hold your breath."

"Why should she even believe you? How do we know you're even telling the truth and not just trying to be a bitch on her wedding day?" Katie asks.

"Don't believe me. I don't care. Or I can show you the photos I have on my phone of us together. Just…don't go through with this," she says as her hands touch the front of her stomach and she caresses it. In that moment, her words register. She doesn't have a choice but to tell me, and I know why. This isn't just about her anymore.

"Oh my god," I state feeling sick. "You're pregnant." Katie gasps, and the look on Jackie's face is a mixture of apprehension and triumph. Angelica's face shows only glee and malice. Clearly, she's only here for the view. I almost laugh. Does Jackie think having an affair with an almost married man and getting pregnant with his baby deserves some kind of reward? Does she think I'd be grateful to her? The smirk she sports on her lips makes me want to smack it off. With a toss of her long hair, she spins on her heel and stalks out of the room, my dear stepmother following. Both of them walking away from the damage Jackie's actions have left behind.

Chapter  3

Katie and I remain frozen, staring at the door Jackie slammed behind her. Words lie on the tip of my tongue, but are unable to form completely. I begin taking stock of my emotions – surprise, check; betrayal, check; anger, oh absolutely. Part of me expects tears to well in my eyes and screams of anguish to emit from my throat any second. I wait for them to run like rivers down my face and to burn from my throat, but they don't come. There are no tears for the wasted years, months, hours and minutes I wasted on a man completely undeserving of every second he was with me. So much wasted time, wasted moments and memories. But there are no tears, at least not yet.

Forming sentences continues to elude me, so I remain quiet. My gaze falls upon a clock on the wall and my mind can't help but marvel at the way time continues to pass during moments that feel like life stands still.

Katie receives clarity before me, and when she turns to me, her eyes capturing mine, I see the anger there, burning like an inferno. "There is absolutely no way you are not leaving here with me, right the hell now," she practically spits each word. "It's best friend code or some shit. Best friends shall not let each other marry a rat-cheating bastard that impregnates her wicked stepsister with what will no doubt be the spawn of Satan. I'm sure it's a commandment or something."

Nodding my head absently, I whole-heartedly agree, and as she's speaking to me, another flood of anger comes over me. It's as if I'm kindling and the rage churning in her eyes grabs hold of my dry branches and sets them aflame. Before I know what I'm doing, I've grabbed my bouquet of white lilies and am out the door of the dressing room, making my way to the large room we've rented and decorated for our wedding ceremony.

Halting at the sight of the large wooden doors before me, I picture the betrayer I'm seeking behind them. Like a lion hunting prey, all I can think about is getting at him, and tearing him from limb to limb – physically, emotionally – it doesn't matter as long as I make him bleed.

Out of nowhere my wedding coordinator, Brenda, pops up in front of me startling me and halting my steps. When she gets a look at my face, she flinches and visibly gulps. I've got to admire her bravery however, because it doesn't keep her from asking her question, "Ella, what are you doing? You aren't due to walk down the aisle for another," she glances at her watch, "three minutes. You're early. You can't go yet."

I start to tell her there's been a change in plans, but instead, I nod my head and turn to Katie. She takes me aside and acts like she's giving me a hug, her lips close to my ear, "What the hell are you doing? We need to go out the side door right there," she gestures with her head. "We can tell Miss Commando over there that you want some fresh air before you walk down the aisle. Once we're outside, we can take off. My car is parked right there."

I can feel myself smile, but it's all teeth, something predatory, "He's not getting off that easily."

She backs up and her wide eyes meet mine, "Ella-"

"It's okay. I'll be fine. Just walk down the aisle as planned, okay? I'll handle the rest."

She reluctantly nods, but I know she doesn't want to agree. It's a testament to our friendship that she trusts me and does it anyway.

She knows when to push, and she knows when to back off. "Please tell me you're going to march down that aisle and kick him in the balls in front of everyone before you turn and walk out."

Despite my fury and shock, she still manages to make me smile – just a little. "Just be ready with your keys in hand, okay?"

She clutches my hand, "Always. I'm always ready for anything you need."

"Katie, it's time," Brenda says, tapping Katie on the shoulder. Katie looks at me hesitantly and I can tell Brenda wants to ask me what's wrong, but I force a smile and give Katie a nod, silently telling her to go, that I'm fine.

With a look over her shoulder, she turns and disappears through the doors. I concentrate on my breaths while I wait. Inhale. Exhale. Inhale. Exhale.

The fact that I've got no one to walk me down the aisle today is blaringly obvious. I'd give anything for my daddy right now. A pain in my heart at the thought takes my breath away and makes the back of my eyes sting. He would be livid right now. He'd walk down the aisle and rip Jeremy apart with his bare hands. He'd whisk me away, do anything to try to make me feel better, but all I'd want is one of his bear hugs that I miss so much it hurts. I wish I could cry on his shoulder, and hear him tell me that everything will be okay. But he's not here, so all I can do is think of him and hold him in my heart knowing that doing so will give me the strength to get through the next few minutes.

"Ready?" Brenda asks with a smile. I clear my throat, throw my shoulders back, and give her a nod that she returns before opening the doors. Immediately the string quartet we hired to play the wedding march sounds in my ears. Taking another deep breath, I do my best to put a small smile on my lips, lift my head, and confidently walk down the aisle toward Jeremy. My eyes immediately find him standing at the end of the aisle sporting the stupid grin I used to think was cute upon his face. My steps falter, and I consider turning around and bolting right there, but then I catch sight of Jackie in the crowd. The look she's wearing of surprise that I'm walking down the aisle, keeps me moving forward. Looking back to Jeremy, I see a frown upon his brow as he looks to where my gaze had gone and looks back and forth between Jackie and me a few times. I quickly think that he looks like one of those dog bobble heads one might see in the back of an automobile and I momentarily feel the corners of my lips turn up in a grin. Simultaneously, I catch a last look from Jackie and can feel her anger as I pass, her gaze burning into me.

When I arrive at the large arch we are to be married under, Jeremy reaches for my hand and I give it to him, trying to push back the nausea that twists at my tummy and moves up my throat at his touch. When the music stops, the officiate begins to speak and my mind spins making me feel momentarily that I'm outside of my body watching this train wreck. I force myself to calm, and wait for the right moment.

I can feel more than hear Katie shifting behind me no doubt wondering what the hell I'm doing, the tension between us palpable. I mentally implore her to hold tight. When the time finally comes for our vows, we had planned on reciting traditional phrases of love, honor, and obeying. When Pastor Ben asks me to repeat after him, I look at him briefly, "Actually, I have my own vows I'd like to speak if that's okay?" Jeremy looks surprised and squeezes my hands while raising a brow. I force a smile, "I know I'm throwing you for a loop here, but I find that I have more to say and would like everyone to hear how I really feel."

He smiles a little and nods encouragingly. I can almost see cockiness in his expression, anxious for me to praise him to the crowd. It makes me angrier and something must flash in my eyes because suddenly, his eyes show apprehension and I can't help it – I smile wickedly.

Laughing without humor I begin, "Oh, Jeremy, I know I've taken you by surprise with my change in plans and believe me, I don't expect you to come up with your own vows too at the spur of the moment, don't worry. Besides, I'm sure I'll leave you speechless." The crowd gives a chuckle and Jeremy fakes wiping sweat from his brow playing up to the guests. Asshole.

"As I stand here today, looking into your eyes, seeing the smile upon your face, flashes of the last three years pour through my mind." I pause, "I've learned that love is so many things. It's putting your partner before yourself. It's giving your words meaning by making sure your actions back them up. It's showing the person you love in big and small ways alike how and why they matter to you. It's wanting them by your side always, and finding yourself missing them when they aren't. It's making dreams together and doing everything you can as one to achieve them. It's thanking god every night that he gave you someone that shows you what it means to love, honor and cherish them. It's having a lover that takes you to the moon and back with a word, a suggestion, a touch, and a stroke. It's not always easy. In fact, it can be hard, and sometimes brutal, but there's always beauty to be found in the pain. There's beauty in the simple joy of being lucky enough to have and love each other." Jeremy smiles at me, and squeezes my hands in encouragement nodding to my words like he's thought the same things too. Yeah right.

My fingers and toes have gone numb. My heart is frozen. Tears clog my throat, but I push past them to get through this. "And today, as we stand here before family and friends, I want them to know, that those are things that I've *never* had or found in you." The room gasps and I hold tighter to his hands when he tries to pull away from me in surprise.

"Maybe we tried to force something that was never there. Maybe all you ever really cared about was getting control of my father's company like Jackie told me today." I force myself not to look in her direction. Not yet. "Maybe it's because you were too busy fucking my stepsister to really give us a chance, I really don't know. I do know that I'm not blameless. I should have listened to myself when I was concerned about the lack of spark, or how sometimes I was more relieved when I was alone and you were away than sad because I missed you." Then I smile nastily, "Or maybe all the orgasms I've had to fake over the years and your selfish tendencies in the bedroom should have been a huge clue that we were doomed." I swear I hear some snickers in the crowd. Jeremy's face flushes with embarrassment and anger. Part of me can't believe that he's still standing here, but perhaps he's frozen in place. Shocked at what's happening. I can only hope. He deserves it and so much more.

"All I know is that I certainly wish that it didn't take my stepsister Jackie telling me moments ago that you've been cheating on me, and that she's pregnant with your baby to come to this realization. I guess though if nothing else, I can thank you because through loving me so *horribly*, I was able to learn what true love really is."

Turning to the crowd, my gaze meets Jackie's horrified one, "Jackie, go ahead and stand up. Let everyone get a good look at Jeremy's whore." She remains seated and looks to Jeremy for help, "It's okay, don't be shy. I want everyone to see the woman that is carrying the baby of the man that I was supposed to be marrying here today." I almost laugh hysterically as she actually stands. Jeremy's parent's faces are painted in dismay and it's the only thing that gives me pause. But I push it away, emotions to deal with another time. My very own wicked stepmother from hell looks embarrassed and yanks on Jackie's hand trying to get her to sit down.

Turning back to Jeremy, I realize I am ready to end this. "The worst mistake I ever made was agreeing to marry you. I've had doubts from the beginning, and I should have listened to my heart. Really, Jackie," I say turning to her again, seeing she's once again seated, "I owe you. I owe you from keeping me from making a *huge* mistake."

Turning back to Jeremy, I vehemently say, "Don't call me. Don't come near me ever again. If all of this didn't make it clear enough, allow me to say it succinctly, we are done." I spit emphasizing each word.

I take a step back and he immediately lunges for me, grabs my arm and says desperately, "Wait. Please listen."

Jerking away, I spit each word, "Don't. Touch. Me."

Walking over to Jackie, Katie at my back, I toss her my bouquet. "Have at it. I mean, everyone is already here and dinner's paid for. Have a great life. I hope you two are very happy together. Hopefully the sex is better for you than it was for me," I fake a disgusted shudder, "Good luck with that." I turn to face him one more time and say "Oh, and I would be prepared for the Board to decide that your performance is lacking and fire you. So you might want to start working on your resume during the weeks you had requested off."

I walk away, Katie at my side hearing Jeremy behind me bellow, "Ella, no! Don't do this. It isn't true. I don't know why, but she's lying. I've never even touched her!"

Jackie starts screaming at him and the guests becomes louder and louder with their disbelief over what they've witnessed. A few of the company's board of directors are here and staff I work with – the shame and embarrassment is almost stifling, but I force myself to raise my chin anyway and keep moving.

Suddenly, I'm whipped around, Jeremy's fingers digging into my arm and I know I'm going to be bruised. "You are not leaving until we talk about this." I bare my teeth at him, rear my fist back and let it fly straight into Jeremy's face. His nose explodes with blood and some of it splatters onto my dress - fitting really. Shaking my hand from the pain, I open my mouth to say something nasty, but close it again. There are so many things I could say, so many things part of me wants to say, but sometimes quiet speaks louder than any words of hate could. And Jeremy, he doesn't deserve any more words from me.

Turning to Katie, I don't have to say anything. She comes to me, puts her arm through mine, and we walk out, side by side.

Chapter 4

I'm suffocating. My dress feels like it's five sizes too small and all I can think about is getting the damn thing off. I'm clawing at it, trying to free myself. I need it off my body.

Now.

Every second it remains on I feel like it gets tighter and tighter. It's a reminder of the mistake I almost made today and part of me feels like the faster I get this off, the quicker I can erase it from my mind, from my life. It's a mistake I almost willingly walked into, even though I knew better. Even though I had doubts, fears and worries. Even though I had uncertainties and reservations for quite some time, I kept ignoring them and pushing myself anyway. Why did I do this to myself? Why?

My dress is strapless and tight to my body. Lace covers me head to toe, and like a sick mockery of my dark and twisted emotions, my veil shimmers in the light. It shimmers with promise and hope and beauty. I'm a vision that's supposed to represent love, happiness, new beginnings, commitments and promises. I almost laugh hysterically at the sight. It's all an illusion because when I look deeper, past the façade, all I see is hate, ugliness, lies, cheating, and brokenness.

I can't get it off fast enough. "Please," I implore of Katie, "help me get it off."

"It's okay. I'm here," Katie murmurs over and over again as I continue to paw at myself trying to get at the buttons. She never tells me to stop. Never tells me to hold on. She just rushes to help me as quickly as possible. When the first few come undone, I whimper at the feeling of being released from my prison. My whimper quickly turns to a cry of relief when it finally slides down my body. Katie takes it and shoves it into the corner and returns to stand before me, her eyes looking into mine briefly before she wraps her arms around me. The love and concern I see in her eyes, makes my own fill with tears. Looking over her shoulder, I find my reflection staring back at me. There's so much sadness there, and it finally makes me break. A sob I'm unable to stifle makes my chest ache, and Katie holds on tight as I sink to the floor, and curl over myself and just…let…go.

I'm angry at myself, angry that I didn't allow myself to see what was clearly in front of me. I'm devastated that I didn't love myself enough to know that I deserve more. That I was willing to settle for a love that was mediocre at best. Part of me held onto hope that time would change things, and that the missing elements from our relationship would take root and grow in time. On top of those emotions are feelings of embarrassment, but more than that, it's the overwhelming fear that I'm not enough. That Jeremy clearly didn't find happiness with me either. While I know in my heart that this is for the best, and I feel thankful that I didn't just make a huge mistake, I struggle with inadequacy and pain. The pain feels unbearable. And Katie? She just holds me through it all while whispering words of love and support in my ear.

After a time, I finally get control of my emotions and am able to stop the tears. My sobs have long since turned to sniffles. Katie pulls away from me, wiping the wetness from my face, paying no heed to the fact I've left a teary mess on her own dress. "What do you need? What can I do? Do you need to punch something? Eat something?"

Katie takes hold of my hand and gives me a tug helping me to my feet. Shaking my head in confusion, "Why am I so upset? I don't understand." I look into her eyes and confess, "I was about to walk out anyway," I whisper. "I was standing there looking at myself in the mirror and waiting to feel…something. Anything. I wasn't going to go through with it, so why am I even crying? I feel so stupid."

Taking my upper arms in her hands, she turns me to face her, and waits for me to look into her eyes instead of at my feet. "Because what he did hurts. Because the decision you made isn't an easy one. It's hard, and brave, and strong. But that doesn't mean that you don't have a right to grieve over the end of something you had wished to be different. Accepting the loss of a dream is hard. So, regardless of how right the decision is, it doesn't mean you aren't allowed to be hurt and angry by his and Jackie's betrayal."

"I don't think I've been in love with Jeremy for a long time – if ever really. I think I was simply going through the motions and kept thinking everything else would come eventually. That love isn't some fairytale where everything is happy all the time. Love is hard, and it can hurt, and it can be both a poison and a balm to your heart and soul. And I thought that this type of love was all that I deserved, even if greater love is available for others."

"No. Love, the right kind of love, should never be a poison. And you're right, it isn't always a fairytale, but that doesn't mean it can't also be wonderful even when it isn't. And you deserve the best of loves – never something less than optimal," she says.

That manages to get a small smile from me, "And how would you know miss single and loving it?"

"I had wonderful examples."

"Yes, your parents," I nod.

"Yes," she agrees. "And yours."

Her words encourage a small trickle of tears to escape their prison and move down my cheeks, but I nod, "Yes. I want a love that's passionate, fun, honest, safe, and happy. I want to fall in love with a man that encompasses all of those things – not just the idea. I want the real deal, not merely a hope or wish of what it might become. I want a love like my parents had."

Katie smiles, "And don't forget great sex."

This time I laugh, "God yes. And great sex. I deserve that. Jeremy...well, let's just say it could have been better."

"Oh god, if we are going to talk about shitty sex, let's break out the alcohol."

With a laugh we head to the kitchen to do just that. Looking around, I take in all the moving boxes I packed over the last few weeks in anticipation of moving to Jeremy's place. All boxes I need to unpack now. Sighing at the thought of all the wasted work, I can't help but feel grateful that I insisted we wait until after the wedding to move in together. It certainly wasn't for his lack of asking me over and over, but because I didn't want to leave Katie high and dry before I had to. Plus, I wasn't exactly thrilled with moving into Jeremy's place. Sterile décor, monochrome color and in desperate need of a woman's touch, it wasn't my ideal place to visit, let alone live, but we hadn't yet found another home to move into. That wasn't because we hadn't looked at everything and anything listed for sale, but because we could never agree on a place. Or a price. Anything I liked he had a problem with and anything he liked, I found lacking something. And he wanted to spend more and buy larger than me. It was a nightmare; neither ever willing to compromise. I'm thankful now. And why I didn't take that as a huge clue that there was a problem I'll never know.

Katie rummages through the cupboard and takes out a couple shot glasses and the bottle of tequila we keep hidden in the back – just for emergencies. She pours until there's no more room at the brim and we have to be careful as we lift them to our mouths so we don't spill. Downing mine and slamming the glass back on the counter as a wordless request for a refill, I revel in the burn. She obliges and after a few more times I'm feeling nice and tipsy. When a smile graces my lips she nods like she's completed a mission.

Thinking of her holding me while I lost my shit, being there for me today, offering to help me get the hell out of dodge, and everything after that, my heart warms. "Thank you for being my best friend," I blurt.

Her brows lower into a frown, "You never have to thank me for that."

"Of course I do. I don't ever want you to think I take our friendship for granted."

"I don't think that. Ever."

"I'm lucky that you were there for me today."

"I'll always be here for you. Always. Never doubt that."

"Until we're old and gray?" I ask her. An old promise we always ask one another.

"Until we are old and gray," she confirms.

Looking around at my apartment again, replaying the day's events in my mind, I feel at a loss. "What the hell do I do now?" I ask Katie, not really expecting her to have an answer any more than I have one for myself.

"Well. You could start by getting some actual clothes on."

At her reply I look down at my white lacy strapless bra and thong. I was so desperate to get my dress off, it didn't occur to me that I'm practically naked now. Suddenly, the fact I'm sitting at the kitchen table bare assed well on my way to getting drunk strikes me as funny and I start to giggle. "Not exactly what I expected to be doing right now in this get up," I confess.

Katie's laugh joins mine, "I'd imagine not. But hey, at least you don't have to worry about faking an orgasm on your wedding night." And then we begin to laugh at her comment. The ridiculousness of the situation combined with the alcohol coursing through our systems makes tears fall from our eyes.

Our laughs are immediately cut off when we hear banging at the front door. Our eyes cut to each other in surprise. Our looks clearly asking the other if they heard that too. We remain frozen our heads slightly cocked to the side and I almost laugh at how we must look.

When it remains quiet, our bodies visibly relax until there's another pounding on the front door, and this time there's a voice to go along with it. "Ella! Ella, open up the door! Let's talk about this."

A sick heat made up of dread and disbelief runs through my body, twisting in my gut, making me wretch. My eyes, no doubt big as saucers look at Katie and she stares back at me. By silent agreement, neither of us makes a sound, hoping he'll assume we aren't home and will leave.

"I know you're in there, dammit. Both of your cars are here. Answer the door. I'm not leaving until you answer the door. Talk to me. Please. Please talk to me," he says, his demands turning to pleading. He sounds desperate to speak to me, but all it does is make me angry. What is he thinking? That I'll forgive him? That I'll be okay with the fact he got my stepsister pregnant, and what? We can work it out and I'll be a stepmom to his kid? Um no. I can't believe he even has the balls to be at my door right now.

Walking to the door, ready to yell at him, I stop when Katie grabs my arm. "No! Don't you dare open that door," she whispers harshly.

"I'm not," I shake my head. She holds onto me for a moment longer, but then nods and lets me go. Walking to the door, I keep it closed but yell loud enough to be heard through it, "Go away, Jeremy. I have nothing to say to you. I can't believe you would even come here. Leave."

"Ella, please I'm begging you. Open the door. Let's talk about this. It isn't what you think."

"Are you serious? Oh thank god! So you mean your dick just accidentally found its way inside of Jackie? How stupid do you think I am?"

"Just hear me out."

"No way in hell. How could we possibly work this out? Go away. You made a mistake coming here."

"Fine," he growls. "I will give you tonight, but I will be back here every single day until you talk to me. I'm not giving up on us."

"It's not going to work. Just go away. We're done. The fact that you could even think anything differently is ridiculous. Leave," I say sternly, "And don't come back."

"We'll see. I'll get you to talk to me eventually."

His words make anger rush through me fast and furious and I have my hand on the doorknob ready to open it and scream in his face, but once again Katie is there. She places her hand on my shoulder and the small act is like ice water on a burn, I instantly calm down and am able to realize that the last thing I want to do is talk to him, look at him, hear anything he has to say.

Dropping my head between my shoulders, I take some deep breaths calming myself. Then I sink to the floor once again. This is becoming a really shitty habit. "What am I going to do?" I ask not really expecting an answer.

"We should leave," Katie says.

My eyes whip to hers, "Wouldn't that also be known as running away from my problems?"

"No, I prefer to call it problem avoidance – at least for a little while. Getting some distance so you can think and breathe without having to worry about him breaking down the door will be a good thing."

I think about it for a minute then look at her again, "Just leave?"

"Why the hell not? You won that trip didn't you? It's all in your name plus a guest. You're already packed and ready to go." She shrugs like it's the simplest thing in the world, "And since I know you'd prefer to have someone with you for a little while, I will volunteer." She laughs and shrugs, "Let's get the hell out of here."

"You would do that? For me?"

She rolls her eyes, "What kind of question is that? Will I be there for my best friend and go on a vacation to Cabo San Lucas where we can get drunk, get tans, and reintroduce you to the single world? But most importantly, where you can find a little peace and heal in the process. Please, where do I sign up?"

"You can get the time off work without issue?" I ask, not quite ready to believe her yet.

"I already took a few days off for your wedding, and you know Sally will give me a couple days more considering the circumstances," she says talking about her boss at the insurance claims office that she's worked at for the last few years. Her boss is a doll and loves her to pieces. "I'll call her in a few minutes to make sure. Let's check the airline first and make sure there are seats open on the same flight you're taking."

"My vacation is two weeks, but I guess I don't have to stay for that long," I say thinking out loud.

"You don't have to, but you may want to. We can start off spending time together and then we can play it by ear from there. You may not be ready to leave after a few days, maybe you would like some time to yourself as well."

"True," I tell her, my mind turning with possibilities. Looking at her with a smile, I stand and head to the stairs leading up to our rooms.

"Where are you going?" she asks.

Stopping I turn to her with a smile, "Do you want help packing or what?"

She smiles and we run up the stairs. While I pull out her leopard print suitcase and start getting clothes for her, she grabs her laptop to book a flight and calls her boss. As I grab a few of her favorite bikinis, I picture us lying by the pool, margaritas in our hands, laughing, relaxing and most importantly forgetting. Sounds like the perfect medicine.

Chapter 5

Present Day

"Katie sounds like she's a wonderful friend to you," Faye comments with sincerity.

"She is. We've been best friends since we were eight. I can't imagine my life without her. I hope I never have to."

Her eyes turn serious a line appearing between her brows, "We should all be so lucky to have friends like that. I hope you cherish her."

"I do," I reply honestly with a nod of my head for emphasis. "I have no doubt that she knows how much I love her."

She smiles, "That's good."

I find myself smiling back and something inside of my chest eases. She has a soothing quality about her and the pain in my heart seems to ease a bit while talking to her. I'm not sure what it is about her that's so calming, but I'm thankful for it.

"We had a great time together," I tell her with a small laugh thinking about our week together in Cabo. When Katie returned home after a week, I did elect to stay for the second week after all. It was a week that was so amazing that thinking about it makes a gamut of emotions wash over me. Happiness, excitement, fondness, passion and sadness all in a rush so fast it makes my head spin.

"She's not with you now, so I assume you did end up staying longer?"

"Yes, you're right. I didn't intend to before we left. Part of me thought that time alone would be too hard emotionally and I didn't want to end up crying in my margaritas over my life. The funny thing is, I didn't do a whole lot or mourning over my combusted relationship with Jeremy. At the beginning I had a few things to work through, but then, it was like I was able to let go. There's nothing I can do about what happened; dwelling on it wasn't going to change a thing. Maybe I should feel guilty about how easy it was to move on, but I think it's a sign of just how wrong being with Jeremy was." I shrug not really having any other words to explain what I feel. I mean, how much should a person mourn a relationship they weren't completely happy in and never should have let go on as long as they did in the first place? I don't think there's a manual about that.

"And you realized that being alone while on vacation wasn't so bad after all?"

My cheeks flush and I look down, absently scratching my nose, "Um, well, not exactly." Glancing at Faye, I see amusement in her eyes.

"Oh?" she asks raising a brow.

"Well, I didn't exactly spend that week alone." I wait for her face to reflect judgment or disgust when she realizes exactly what I'm getting at. My breath stalls and I look at her worryingly, partly confused as to why I care what she thinks, and partly wondering why the hell I'm telling her any of this to begin with.

"Well honey, I didn't think so. A woman doesn't board a plane from a beautiful place like Cabo San Lucas crying for any reason other than a man. So, get on with it. Do tell me more. Starting with when you and Katie arrived, of course."

My breath comes out in a rush and I laugh softly reveling at how much I adore Faye already considering I've just met her. "Yes, ma'am."

Chapter  6

When our plan lands we begin a crazy experience at the airport going through customs and retrieving our luggage. Before we reach the destination given to me by the resort to obtain our shuttle, we have to weave our way through a maze of people offering god knows what. It's confusing and rather intimidating as some people are pretty aggressive, but we find the driver of our shuttle and settle in for a ride that reveals the countryside and non-touristy part of the city. The drive passes quickly. I feel the tightness in my shoulders begin to give way on the ride, but the minute our shuttle pulls through the security gates of our resort in beautiful Cabo San Lucas, I feel my entire being start to relax.

Passing security where they ask my name and make sure we are on the list of check-in's, our shuttle comes to a huge resort entrance. To my surprise, instead of pulling in, we continue past. Looking out the window, I see huge homes set in semi-circular patterns high up in the mountains and a large number of southwest-looking brightly colored buildings below. Lodging spreads out over what looks like many acres. Continuing, we capture sight of lush flower gardens, welcoming pools, a large fountain, and golf carts moving all throughout the property, driven by hatted men dressed in light khaki colored clothes, clearly transporting guests to and fro.

As our shuttle continues down a long road, I see ahead of us, at ocean level, another large resort. It sits alone at the bottom of the mountain and it's easy to tell even from this distance how amazing it's going to be. Cabanas garnish the ocean's edge where blue ocean water laps the sandy shore. Excitement builds and my foot starts tapping in my impatience to arrive.

From the moment we walk through the glass doors of the lobby to check into our room, our mouths are agape in wonder. The pictures I'd seen of the resort definitely did not do justice. The lavish, yet tastefully adorned lobby is shaped in a circle, with an opening between eleven and one o'clock that reveals a breathing taking view of the ocean – its beauty as far as the eye can see. The white caps of the water keep winking in and out of view, and the smell of sea and salt is potent in the air. The lobby emits an appeasing aroma of lavender and something else I can't place. The combination is divine and I can't help but take a deep breath, close my eyes, and imagine the stress of the previous day rolling off of me in waves and evaporating into thin air.

I feel a small twinge of sadness when I overhear the cute couple clearly in love checking into their room before us say they are here on their honeymoon. Knowing I'm supposed to be here on mine as well makes my eyes sting with unshed tears. I sniff and clear my throat hoping the action brushes the impulse away. As if she knows my thoughts, Katie catches my eye and smiles widely. The wonder and excitement of the few days we have together clear on her face. I can't help but smile back, feeling thankful for the distraction. Looking forward to spending some time in an amazing place with my favorite person, makes the sadness fade away.

As soon as we get to our room we make a joke about the huge king size bed. Unfortunately, they were unable to switch us to a double, but it's okay, the bed is massive and we will easily be swallowed up into it with plenty of room on either side of us. I still tease Katie that I'd like to be the small spoon and she the big one.

After we finish checking out the room, oohing and aahing at our ocean view, the towels folded into perfect fish, the plush robes in our closet and the multitude of toiletries available for our use, we immediately dig our swimsuits out of our luggage. Not even taking time to unpack anything else, we excitedly change, grab magazines, our kindles and sunblock, and get our booties to the pool.

A couple hours later, I'm lounging next to Katie, sucking down my third, or maybe it's my fourth, margarita. Happily feeling the buzz of alcohol, especially since I'm drinking on an empty stomach, we are enjoying the view. The pool sits at ocean level and the only thing that separates us from the beach is plexiglas that has been perfectly placed at the outer edge. It helps mute the sound of the wind and ocean, and likely would protect the pool from any gusts of dust if the wind would pick up, but does nothing to obstruct the gorgeous view.

Our resort is adult's only, so the pool while hopping, doesn't include excited screaming children running around. Waiters and waitresses constantly move around chairs either taking food and drink orders or delivering orders to guests. Katie and I just ordered fish tacos– because yum.

"It's like a Mariah Carey video," Katie says at my side. She's on her tummy, feet kicking in the air behind her, rocking her fuchsia and orange bikini. Her shades are on the top of her head and she's looking out toward the ocean.

"What is?" I ask, adjusting the top of my royal blue and white bikini wondering if I should put on more sunblock.

"Those beds on the ocean."

"Oh, they are so romantic," I sigh happily looking out to the cabanas she's referring to. There are four of them and they are large four-poster beds literally sitting on the beach halfway between the pool and the ocean. They are gorgeous. Dressed with white linens and teal and tan pillows, they are adorned with gauzy white drapes that can be pulled – along with the darker shade- for privacy. The drapes billow in the wind creating a pretty picture and longing fills my stomach making it burn. "I bet Jeremy and I would have rented one of them."

"No you wouldn't have because you were never going to go on a honeymoon with Jeremy," Katie states her sunglasses lowered on her nose so she can glare at me.

"True. I just can't help but think about it I guess." Looking toward the beds again, I let out another sigh. "I just can't help but think about sex while looking at those things. Hot, clawing the sheets, sweaty, screaming orgasms kind of sex."

Katie laughs, "You mean the kind of sex you *didn't* have with Jeremy?"

I gasp, "Hey!" I tell her a little miffed she would use what I've told her against me at the moment.

"Just sayin'. You know it's true."

"Too true." The admission makes me think of something and I cringe knowing exactly what Katie will say when I confess. "Katie," I whisper, "I need to tell you something," I swear that sounded like I slurred it.

"What?" she says too loudly back.

"Shh!" I tell her, flailing my hand in a shut up gesture.

"Why are we having to 'shh'?" she asks eyes wide repeating the same flailing gesture I just made.

"Because I need to tell you something personal."

"Okay," she whispers back hesitantly, and I laugh when she blindly uses her lips to find her straw and keeps missing. "Shut up," she says with a roll of her eyes knowing I'm making fun of her.

"I almost…" I pause reconsidering this topic of conversation.

"Almost what?"

"I almost gave up my butt for Jeremy."

Katie immediately lets out a shriek and sits up straight almost spilling her drink. Her sunglasses fall from the top of her head into her lap and she looks at me with her jaw wide open, "No!" she gasps in horror.

"Yes," I nod solemnly.

"No!" she repeats herself.

"Yes!" I nod again emphatically and take some large swallows of my margarita as if it will drown the shame.

"Why?" She asks, "Why would you do that? I just don't understand! We've talked about this. We should make a no butt sex pact or something. I think it's another commandment. Best friends shall not let each other succumb to butt sex."

"You have a commandment for everything."

"For good reason! Look what you almost did! Again I ask you, why?"

"Well," I shrug, "I told you that our sex life was lacking. He kept bringing it up and I guess I thought maybe it would help."

"Butt sex is never the answer," she says louder than comfortable.

"God, Katie! Keep your voice down!" She giggles and signals our attractive waiter from across the pool. He nods at her with a wide smile and heads on over. "Hi Juan, may we have two more margaritas as soon as possible, please? It's a margarita emergency. An emergarita," she says with a laugh and I can't help it, I giggle. I think maybe we should consider quitting the margaritas actually.

He smiles and laughs, "Uh-oh, sounds serious." He walks away to place our order and her eyes track him lingering on his firm ass.

"Looks to me like you're thinking about doing something with *his* ass," I say watching her head tilt to the side and wondering what the hell she's thinking.

"Oh, please. I can appreciate a nice ass, maybe even want to give it a nice bite, but that doesn't mean I would ever consider giving up my butt. That's completely two different things."

"Never?" I ask.

Her eyes narrow slightly and she slides her sunglasses down her nose to make eye contact with me, "No!" She slams down her empty margarita glass on her thigh for emphasis, "What were you thinking? It's exit only, Ella!" She makes a gagging sound which makes me laugh out loud. "So gross."

"Do you think everyone has your opinion?" I ask.

"You mean *our* opinion? No, of course not." Her eyes rove around the pool and settle on a couple. "Look at them," she gestures casually. A man and woman lie side by sound in their loungers. The woman is lying on her stomach, her cheek resting on her arms as she looks at the man next to her. He is talking to his companion while his fingers trail down her back, over the curves of her ass and back up again. They are completely lost in each other. "I bet you they partake – probably have a bondage set and everything. I bet you he was more experienced and he's been teaching her all kinds of things – maybe in his very own red room. They only have eyes for each other and will probably pack up and leave here soon so that they can go fuck like bunnies," she tells me.

I laugh at her mini story. Katie and I enjoy people watching. We come up with elaborate stories for our subjects, trying to top the other with our creativity. It's silly and makes us laugh.

"What about them?" I ask my eyes following a woman wearing a cute black and white suit with a sarong tied around her waist and designer sunglasses perched upon her nose. She's got a beach bag on her arm and her man is trailing behind her, following as she selects chairs for the two of them. She waits for her companion to arrange the towel on her chair for her, and then makes a few adjustments herself before sitting down. Removing her sarong from her waist, she folds it before putting it in her bag, doing the same with the t-shirt of the man she's with. She takes out sunblock and after spraying it all over her body she leans back, rather stiffly, and appears to close her eyes.

"Not in a million years," she tells me.

"I'd have to agree. They probably schedule sex in their calendar. Twice a week, like Tuesdays and Thursdays. She takes her birth control like clockwork and probably has a list of places that are okay to kiss and places that aren't. Sex is probably considered messy and while he doesn't agree, he likely gives her a lot of 'yes dears'."

We giggle at my made up story based on nothing other than appearances and then I laugh harder, "I'm probably totally wrong and they are animals in the bedroom and just reserved in public."

"You're probably right," she agrees with a laugh.

Looking around the pool once more, my gaze settles on a group of men that just arrived. They each grab a towel from the cart of fresh, clean, towels for guests and they are all holding beers in their hands and are laughing. Every single one of them are shirtless and it's like a freaking abs parade. "Holy hell," I breathe out a little breathlessly and Katie murmurs her agreement. They are all ridiculously attractive. One man breaks away from the rest after he removes himself from a headlock another guy had him in. They are laughing and he puts his fists up jokingly telling his friend to 'bring it'.

He finally turns and moves to a seat not far from us and throws his towel into the lounger claiming it as his. The top of his body is concealed by an umbrella. He begins wobbling the heavy base back and forth in an effort to move it out of the way. His muscles move and flex under his skin and I treat myself to a long look. Starting at his sandal clad feet, moving up his muscular calves that flex with his movements, and head right on up and stop for a moment at what I can see of his muscular thighs. I find myself immediately wondering what the hair on his legs would feel like rubbing up against mine. I imagine our legs tangled together, one of his strong hands stroking my body, while the other is tangled in my hair. The thought makes the hair on my body stand on end.

Moving my eyes up further, I stop and almost blush at the large bulge he's showing off at the front of his shorts. My nipples tighten at the sight, and when he turns around and I get a view of his tight bottom, I can't stifle a soft groan. As he moves his shorts tighten against him leaving no imagination to the roundness underneath.

"Oh, yeah." Katie says drawing out the word as her eyes likely take in the same view as mine.

"Any story I would come up for him would include myself in it," I tell Katie and she grunts her agreement.

My eyes continue their journey as he turns around once more having finished his task and his stomach and chest make my breaths come faster. I've never had such a visceral reaction to someone before and I bite my lip to try and calm myself down. This man was made for sex. Forget a six pack, he's sporting an eight pack and they look like they are chiseled from stone. His hard pecs frame the flat discs of his nipples and I imagine running my tongue over them. Under his navel is a small trail of dark hair and I almost groan again thinking about where it leads, but lick my lips at the thought instead. His biceps are large and his shoulders broad and when my eyes finally move to his face, I suck in a breath when I find his eyes on mine.

His eyes are crystal blue, and rival the beauty of the ocean at his back. His longer dark hair blows in the wind, a strand escaping from the rest and brushing against his high cheekbone. I find myself jealous of a strand of hair. His full lips curl up into a seductive smile and I can't help but think how unfair it is that a man that looks like that is unleashed upon the women in this world. I don't know that I've ever found a man beautiful before, but he certainly is. With a smirk, he pulls his sunglasses from the top of his head and puts them on. He turns his head to one of his friends and says something, making them both turn back and look at me.

"Wow," I say to Katie not able to tear my eyes away.

"Oh my god, Ella. Do you know who that is?"

"Who? You know him?"

"That's the actor Asher Charming."

"What? No way." I tell her finally breaking eye contact to look at Katie. She's nodding her head, eyes big and wide. Looking at him again, watching him laugh with his friends while at the same time looking at the menu of food selections, I think of the many action movies I've seen Asher in and try to find the resemblance. It's there, a little, I think. Maybe it's the alcohol making my memory fuzzy.

"That's totally him," Katie says emphatically.

"What are the chances that Asher Charming would be staying at the same resort that we are?"

"I don't know, but let's thank the sex gods because with any luck we'll get to look at that during our entire stay."

I let out a sigh of pleasure, "No kidding." Letting my eyes fall on him once again, I find that I need to cross my legs when I take in his wide smile. "I don't know, Katie. I gotta tell you, I would totally consider butt sex for him."

"Oh my god," she says and laughs and I join her laughing loudly. I about die when he turns toward me brows raised with a smile getting larger by the second. My neck and throat flush with heat and I look away quickly, my stomach burning with embarrassment. "Please tell me there is no way he heard that."

"Uhh. Okay. Sure. There is no way he heard that," she says to appease me. "You weren't louder than you think you were at all."

"Oh god," I mutter, a nervous giggle escaping me.

"Come on," Katie says and stands.

"What are you doing? You're ready to leave?"

"No, we're going to go take a selfie with Asher. I'm posting this shit on Facebook."

"No way. I'm not going over there!"

"If you don't come with me, I'll call him over here."

"You wouldn't."

She just stares at me and I make a sound of annoyance. "Fine. But you so owe me for this."

She smiles and I stand and we make our way over to Asher and his group of friends. They're laughing again, but it dies down a little when they see us standing there. I turn my head and look at the pool feeling embarrassed and stupid. Katie on the other hand, smiles widely and totally cocks her hip out in her signature flirting move. "You're totally Asher Charming aren't you?"

I can't help but look back toward Asher, if that is indeed who he is, and feel myself flush deeper when I find he's lost the sunglasses and is looking at me again. As our eyes connect, I forget where I am for a moment. I'm lost in blue and don't ever want to be found. I feel tingles all over my body, and massive butterflies in my tummy. Unfortunately, someone clears their throat loudly and it startles me from his gaze. When I look toward Katie she's smiling as she looks between the two of us.

He nods and smiles, "Yeah, I'm Asher," he says, his voice raspy and as sexy as he is.

"I knew it!" Katie says making people laugh with her enthusiasm. "Can I please have a photo with you?"

He hesitates, "Well, I would, but I don't really want anyone to know I'm here if I can help it."

"Oh, I won't share it until I get home. I don't have international service anyway, and sorry, you're hot, but I'm not about to spend fifty bucks just to post a photo of you on my social media accounts."

Asher laughs, "Fair enough."

Katie goes and stands next to him and I stand awkwardly, still not having said a word. A friend of Asher's takes Katie's phone and when I look back at Katie and Asher they are both looking at me and I realize Asher said something. To me. "I'm sorry, what?" I ask, feeling like the biggest fool in the world. But he only smiles, "Get in here for this," he demands with a smile and I wordlessly walk to him. He wraps his arm around my waist and everywhere his skin touches mine feels magnified. I swear I hear him suck in a breath and

I look at his face, seeing him looking down at my breasts. I try hard not to push them out so he can get a better look – I'm not ashamed to admit I've got some good tits. He pulls me until my hip is touching his and we all smile for the camera. After his friend takes a photo, Katie happily thanks him, and I know it's not my imagination that his touch lingers on my skin before he lets go.

Asher smiles and nods and makes Katie promise again that she won't post it. "Are you guys here vacationing for a while?" He's looking at me, but for whatever reason I can't find myself able to respond. Clearly I need some more alcohol for bravery or something. I absently look around for Juan our server, as I nod my head and Katie answers for us. "Yes, we are here for a week, Ella is here for two."

He looks at me again, and smiles. "Well, I'll see you," his gaze lingers on me, "both of you around."

"Yes you will!" Katie says excitedly and once again I nod my head like I'm mute, but at least I manage a smile, thank god.

With a little wave, we walk back to our seats. Fortunately, Juan returns to us at that moment with fresh margaritas and the fish tacos we ordered – the perfect distraction. We continue to enjoy our time at the pool, making up more stories for our people watching game and indulging in celebrity gossip. All the while my gaze keeps returning to the sexy man down the way from us the rest of the afternoon.

Chapter 7
Present Day

"Uh, sorry," I flush all the way to the top of my head, "I guess I momentarily forgot I was talking to you and not Katie. I'm pretty sure you didn't need the details of umm… well… you know." I look down in my embarrassment, unable to meet her eyes.

Faye throws her head back and laughs, bless her. She has a great laugh too. The kind that makes you happy and you can't help but laugh along with her. So I do, albeit hesitantly at first.

"I think I'd very much like to spend time with you and Katie," Faye tells me with merriment twinkling in her eyes.

"I don't know. You'd probably be horrified," I tell her with an honest smile finally returning my gaze to her face.

"Oh honey, I doubt that. I may be quite older than you two, but that certainly doesn't mean I'm ignorant to some things." And just like that, I flush again. "So, it seems like the vacation was just the thing you needed. Katie was right. It sounds like the two of you had some fun."

"Somehow we always manage to laugh and have fun. No matter where we are or the circumstances surrounding us."

"I can tell," she smiles again. "Now, tell me. Did you ever see that young man again?"

"Young man?" I ask, even though I know exactly whom she's talking about. It's just I didn't expect her reference to make my heart stutter in my chest.

"Yes, I believe you said his name is Asher Charming."

"That's right."

"So, it was the actor?"

"Yes, it was."

"Well tell me, did you see him again? Talk to him? It sounds like he took your breath away at first sight."

"You have no idea," I tell her shaking my head a little at the memory.

"Well don't stop now. Tell me what happened next!"

Chapter  8

Less Than Two Weeks Ago

"Oh my god, I don't believe it!" Katie yells while staring at her phone.

"What?" The two of us decided to go outside the resort for lunch and walked in and out of various souvenir shops along the road to our destination. In front of a storefront Katie stopped to take selfie's in a huge sombrero that had grabbed her attention and then pictures of us in various poses.

"That picture we took with Asher?" she asks as if I could forget. She teased me forever over the way I acted in front of him. I told her I hated her, but then she bought me another margarita so all was forgiven.

"What about it?"

"This." She turns her phone toward me and I see that all of our heads have been chopped off. My mouth falls open, I look at Katie's face and see how annoyed she looks and so I double over at the waist and start laughing. "It's not funny! Who the hell doesn't know how to take a picture?!"

"Apparently they didn't believe you when you said you wouldn't post it."

"I'm totally going to hunt them down and demand another one."

"I'm sure you will, I'd expect nothing less," I tell her with a laugh. "What about this? Does this say, 'you were supposed to get married and didn't'," I ask Katie while holding up a little trinket using it to distract her.

She rolls her eyes, "No. It screams, 'I went to Mexico and instead of having fun shopping with my best friend, I had a pity party'."

"Hey!" I react immediately in self-defense at her comment, but then sigh. "Actually you're right. I don't know why I said that."

"Because you're still angry, that's why. I'm not saying you shouldn't be, I'm sorry if I sounded inconsiderate of your feelings. I just hate you wasting any more time on that piece of shit."

"Yeah, he really is a piece of shit, huh?"

"Totally. Which is why I actually sent him a flaming pile of poo in the mail."

My words stutter on a laugh, "What?"

"Yep. Before we left, I ordered a pile of shit to be sent to his front door."

"You're kidding."

"No, I'm not. There's actually an online company that provides it. You get to choose the amount and even get to pick the kind of animal it's ejected from too. And the inside packaging kind of disintegrates when it is removed from the outside container. I swear you can order anything on the internet."

"Get. Out." My mouth is hanging open and I'm staring at her in both awe and surprise.

"I'm serious," she shrugs as if sending someone literal shit in the mail isn't the tiniest big deal.

Rushing to her, I throw my arms around her while laughing. "I have the best friend in the whole world."

"Hell yes you do," Katie agrees squeezing me back in return. "The only thing better would be if they offered to somehow take his picture while he opens the extra large package, but unfortunately, we'll just have to imagine that ourselves."

I'm bent over at the waist laughing so hard tears are falling from my eyes. I can only imagine Jeremy's horror. Here's hoping he drops it and gets it all over himself, making a huge mess and carrying the smell for days. So gross yet so awesome.

"This is cute," Katie says while pulling a very beautiful dress in gorgeous shades of blue from a rack. A woman hurries over and offers to take it off the hanger for her, so she can try it on. She shows her all the ways it can be worn. "How much?" Katie asks. She and the woman bargain for the best deal and then Katie says, "Sold," when it reaches a price she's willing to pay. Everything is a negotiation here. Several times we've picked up items to ask the price and put it down because we don't want it that much, to be told a different, and lower, price. Katie gets a serious look on her face and will barter back and forth like nobody's business. I'm a bit shyer about it, feeling like I'm taking advantage of the hard work they've put into making their wares. I'm afraid to offend them by suggesting too little.

With her purchase in tow, we head to the next store and browse. I have my eye on a blanket. I'd love to bring one home, but haven't found the perfect one just yet. Although several places have been willing to offer me the 'best deal'.

"How do I not feel like a complete loser?" I blurt out, finally giving voice to the thing that's been bothering me.

Katie looks at me, her face showing her confusion, "What are you talking about?"

"Jeremy cheated on me, Katie. Hell, I told you myself that our relationship left a lot to be desired, but *he* cheated on *me*. I wasn't enough for *him*. He had to go and get off with my *step* sister because he wasn't getting what he wanted from me. How is that not humiliating?"

"I understand that it's upsetting."

"It's more than upsetting," I mutter.

She continues as if I hadn't spoken, "But you knew that something wasn't right in your relationship, so much so that you were ready to walk out even before you heard that little gem of news. Did you really think that he didn't feel that there was a problem too?"

"Actually, no. I thought that he was getting everything he wanted out of our relationship. I didn't see this coming at all."

"Don't beat yourself up over it, Ella. It doesn't mean that something is wrong with you or that you aren't good enough. It only means that you both weren't right for each other. He's a speed bump in the road to your greater destination. That's all."

"Yes, I suppose you're right. It's just bugging me."

"I get it. You were blind-sided, but you know very well that your whole heart hasn't been in this relationship for a while if it ever truly was and so it makes sense that something like this would get by you. On some level maybe you didn't care enough to know."

"I think I'm afraid this will happen to me again. God, can you imagine? I don't want to be made a fool."

"You have to let go of that, and you need to let go of him. He's not worthy of your time, thought, fear, consideration, nothing. He deserves none of it. He wasn't right for you. You know I love you, but I've seen that for a while. You know there's a reason why he and I never totally hit it off. I just couldn't see how he was right for you."

"You're right. The thing is I've had a chance to think a lot the last few days -obviously - and it has hit me hard - how much I didn't really love him. How much I was settling. Why would I do that to myself? Why would I just hold onto something that wasn't real so tightly, not willing to love myself enough to wait for something more? Something better?"

"Maybe because you've spent so much of your life alone first losing your mother, then your father. Things have been a rollercoaster and I think part of you just wanted some damn stability - to not lose one more person in your life. And I don't think you could be the one to allow that to happen. It's one thing when life does it to you. It's altogether something else when we do it to ourselves. But doing it for ourselves is healthy. It's been a good lesson for you, Ella. One you are sure to grow from. So, please, stop beating yourself up over this. Let it go. Let him go. He doesn't deserve you."

"I'm not holding onto him. He doesn't deserve to be held onto."

"Are you sure about that? You're asking questions of yourself that you know the answers to. I'm not saying that after only a few days you should be over a relationship that lasted three years, and please don't get me wrong, but taking the blame for his actions isn't right. That is totally on Jeremy. He should have manned up and talked to you and made the right decision. But he tried to have his cake and eat it too. He was a jerk. That's on him."

"A relationship is two people," I remind her.

"Yes, yes it is, but even though you didn't feel like things were where they should be or how you wished for them to be, you didn't go and look for it somewhere else. *He* did that."

"Maybe I should have spoken up and said something sooner."

"Maybe you should have. And maybe it would have made a difference, but maybe it wouldn't have. Personally, I don't think it would have. Want to know why?"

"I already know why," I tell her while picking up a cute salt and pepper shaker set of a man and woman wearing sombreros. "Because he never gave me that boom feeling."

"That's right. There was no boom."

"I wonder if someone will ever make my heart go boom." A brief flash of Asher crosses my mind and how I felt when I saw him for the first time. Feeling silly, I push the thought away with a shake of my head.

"I think so, but in the mean time, how about we find someone that can make your vagina go boom."

"Katie!"

"What? You're a single woman again. A single woman that's had shitty sex at best for three years. Let's get someone to rock your world, make you go boom, you deserve it."

"I don't even know how to be single again."

"Oh please. Stop talking like you're some old woman that's been married for twenty-five years and just got divorced. It's time to party again, live it up, have fun, make some memorable mistakes that you can learn from later."

Laughing, I can't help but find myself intrigued at the prospect. "I wonder if Asher Charming is single," I ask jokingly. Okay, maybe not so jokingly.

"According to *Sexy Talk* magazine he's one of the top ten sexiest bachelor's in the world right now."

"Oh god, I forgot if anyone would know it would be you. You're such a celebrity gossip whore."

"Yes, yes I am," she says with no shame.

We walk into another store that has a ton of pottery pieces to choose from. I gravitate toward large chip and salsa bowls and look through the stack. "This would be a cool souvenir."

"They're cute, and practical," Katie agrees and she helps me pick out a beautiful bowl that's hand painted bright yellow, red and orange. It's vibrant and fun. And the little shop gives it to me for only fifteen dollars.

"Anything you want to do for your last couple days here. I can't believe time has already gone by and you'll be leaving soon," I tell Katie. Since Katie could only stay a week I fully intended on returning home when she did, but Katie talked me into reconsidering and taking some time for myself. I was hesitant, not wanting to be in a foreign country on my own, but the resort is safe and some time alone does sound nice.

"Let's go out to dinner tomorrow night. That restaurant on the property looks like a good choice. All the windows facing the ocean, the water running around it and all the candles they have lit at night. It looks beautiful."

"I like that idea," I agree. "We can get all dolled up too, it will be fun. What about tonight?"

"I'm game for whatever. We can hit the pool or maybe hang out by the fire pits."

Charming

Later that evening, with my brand new throw blanket in shades of ocean blue, teal and white, thrown over my lap, Katie and I sit on a couch next to a fire pit that's only steps from the sand. With the breeze coming off the ocean, it's a little chilly, but between the blanket and the fire, we're comfortable. Each with a glass of merlot, we sip our wine happily while staring into the fire. I'm not sure if it was all of the walking earlier or the ambience, but we are quieter tonight. I've been a bit pensive, my thoughts straying from introspection, to reflection, to contemplation. The world is really my oyster, as the saying goes, if I choose. I stop all of my wandering thoughts and try to absorb the atmosphere around me and just live in the moment.

The resort is full of people, but it's not at all crowded tonight. There are other people around the pit too, but it isn't loud by any means. Rather people speak in low voices and quiet whispers. Husky laughter drifts on the air to my ears making my toes curl. My eyes roam looking for the source and rest on none other than Asher Charming across the lick of the flames. He's sitting next to a guy and they're talking and laughing about something. The sight of him makes a thrill run through me, and my heart skips a beat. He's simply gorgeous. I feel like a stupid love struck fan, but who could blame me? It's impossible to look away from how the wind is blowing his hair and how the light of the fire manages to both light up one side of his face, while casting the other side in shadow. It's breathtaking. Or rather he is. He looks both approachable, and mysterious.

"You know…talk about the perfect way to jump back into singledom," Katie tells me following my gaze to Asher.

"Oh yeah right. Because *The* Asher Charming, action actor extraordinaire, one of the sexiest men alive, would totally want to hang out with some random chick on vacation from New York."

"Hey, stranger things have happened you know," Katie says. "And hell, just think about the stories you would be able to tell your grandchildren some day."

Her comment makes me laugh and I'm surprised when suddenly Asher's eyes meet mine across the fire. I wonder if somehow my laugh managed to have the same effect on him. Don't I wish. I can't help but smile softly at the thought and I swear that his lips twitch with amusement back at me before I move my gaze away.

Not long afterwards, Katie and I decide to head back to our room and I swear I can feel his gaze burning into me as I walk away. Likely wishful thinking.

Chapter 9

Wiggling my hips, I slide my dress for the night up and pull the zipper into place at the side. Spinning to face the mirror, I do a quick inventory. My blonde hair is loose around my shoulders, flowing in soft waves. I went with a smoky eyed look on my lids that makes my gray eyes look striking, soft pink colors my cheeks, with pale lips to finish off the look. My gray maxi dress is cut low in the front and the fabric crisscrosses under my breasts before it flows down to my feet. Slipping my feet into nude sandals completes the look.

Katie and I stick to our plans of yesterday and made reservations to eat dinner at the restaurant located here on the resort this evening. We heard some guests at the pool raving about it today and that confirmed our choice. We'll critique it for ourselves. It has a semi-formal dress code, but I'm glad we chose to go to the trouble because damn, I look good tonight. I can't help but smile at my reflection in the mirror. Dressing up has made me feel confident and beautiful which is a nice feeling given my low self esteem lately after everything with Jeremy - or as Katie has started calling him, 'fuckwad'.

Walking into the bathroom, Katie stands next to me and slides lip gloss over her lips. I admire how beautiful she looks in a flowered bohemian style sundress that falls off one shoulder and belts at her waist. The hi-low dress emphasizes her curves and she looks fantastic. She smacks her lips when she finishes glossing them and turns to me. We each give the other a thorough evaluation and smile. "Beautiful darling," I tell her with a wide smile.

"Oh, no, no, no, *you* are beautiful darling," she replies as we giggle and air kiss.

"Til we're old and gray?" she asks me.

"Until we're old and gray," I confirm. "We're going to be the sexiest old ladies in the nursing home."

"You know it!"

"We'll rob everyone blind at bingo because they'll be too busy looking at us to pay attention to their boards."

She laughs, "We'll be the queens of bingo."

"You ready?" I ask glancing at my phone to verify the time before putting it into my small clutch. I've been carrying mine wherever we go because I have international service. Katie brings hers for the camera, but we left my number with her family and my assistant in case of emergency.

"Ready."

We head out of our room and down the hall toward the main part of the resort. We don't have far to walk, the restaurant is located smack dab in the middle of the property, all the rooms surrounding it in a semi-circle. We arrive just in time for our reservation, and smile as we're escorted to our table, passing lit candelabras on the way. The décor is all dark wood, which works strangely perfect against the light backdrop of the sand and ocean. The part of the restaurant where diners are seated is a half circle with floor to ceiling windows all around. We luck out and get a table that sits us mid-center of the large window, with access to a magnificent ocean view. Additionally, we've arrived just in time to see the sun begin to set, casting colors of gold, yellow and orange throughout the sky that reflect off the water making it look like it's on fire. It's breathtaking and before we even glance at our menus, we spend a few minutes silently taking in the view and taking a few photos.

Katie and I peruse the menu and each order extravagant meals of lobster and shrimp with baked potatoes. My mouth already waters at the thought. "Not to bring something up that will sour your mood, but have you thought at all about Reveal Design and Marketing and how you're going to handle everything when you get back?"

And just like that, my watery mouth dries up like the Phoenix desert in July. "As far as what?"

Katie sighs and leans closer, "You know what. Your bitch of a stepmother is likely working behind your back even as we speak to do what she can to work her way into the company."

"She can try all she wants. Even if she works her way in, she would have one hell of a time trying to push the CEO and owner out."

"I know that Ella, and you know that, but that doesn't mean that the damn woman isn't going to try."

"You're right, but I'm not about to waste my time worrying over what may or may not happen."

"I like this side of you," she says with a soft smile, "but who are you and what did you do with Ella?"

Shrugging, I can't help but feel a little defensive, "I don't know. I guess being here, after everything, it's just... hell... life is short and you know we can think that we do everything right and sometimes the shit still hits the fan. Life- and horrible people like her - are going to do what they're going to do. I'll be damned if I'm going to be so distracted that I become blind to the life that's worth living right around me because I'm too busy worrying about all of the what if's, or trying to be this perfect person that I'm not. I'm so over that. Or at least getting over that. This week has taught me that, if not anything else."

We pause as our food is set before us and we each take our first bites. I close my eyes in happiness at the taste of everything and do my best to not shove it all into my mouth as quickly as possible in my excitement. "Anyway," I pause, taking a sip of my wine, "maybe it's this place. Maybe it's everything with Jeremy," Katie clears her throat and I roll my eyes, "Fine, fuckwad," Katie smiles happily when I use her term. "I don't know what it is, but I do know that I have an amazing assistant, and April will let me know if she gets wind of anything going down at work."

"Yes, that's true. April's great."

Nodding my agreement, we continue to make small talk and order more wine as we finish our meals and enjoy the ambiance around us. As the wax from the candles falls lower, the sun completely sets casting the ocean in darkness. Glancing at the beach, I notice fires start appearing as fire pits come to life. The murmur of conversation and music starts filtering into the restaurant each time someone opens the door. People are walking back and forth and it seems as if an event of some sort is taking place. "I wonder what's going on down at the beach?"

Katie shrugs, but the waiter that's filling our water glasses answers my question. "There's a party on the beach tonight for guests. They have one every Friday evening and everyone is welcome to attend. You should go, it's always a lot of fun. They have a bar, dancing, fire pits on the beach and games."

"Oh, sounds fun," Katie says.

Nodding, I agree, "We should check it out."

After we finish our dessert of raspberry crème brûlée we do just that. I feel like I should be rolled out of the restaurant, I'm feeling pretty full. "Walking off the food I ate is a good idea," I groan.

"Definitely," she agrees rubbing her full belly making me laugh.

"How about a walk on the beach before we join the festivities?" I ask her.

"Sounds perfect."

We each remove our sandals before walking closer to the water. Even though the sun has set, the moon casts silver and white ribbons on the inky black water while bright stars twinkle in the distance, offering a dazzling reflection. Lifting my dress and keeping handfuls in my hands, I stand still and close my eyes for a moment and simply feel. I smile as the breeze kisses my face and whips my hair about my shoulders. My ears become alert to the lapping waves beating against the shore as my tongue slides across my lips, tasting the saltiness. My feet dig deeper into the sand, reveling in the feeling of the grainy rocks between my toes as the swirling sand brushes against the tops of my feet.

"Good evening, ladies," a gentleman dressed in a resort uniform says to us, interrupting my meditation. "Please don't wade out any further into the water. Stay close to the shore. The tide comes in quickly. We want you to remain safe."

"Thank you, we'll be careful," we promise, smiling and nodding as we move past him eager to continue our walk. As we make our way along the shore, the party sounds decrease, now merely reaching our ears in intermittent waves. The further we move away, the less it competes with the natural environment, until all that remains is the sound of the ocean. How is it that this sound – the captivating, intoxicating, rhythmically lapping waves and crash of the surf as the tide plays tag with the shore - can soothe one's soul so completely? It's both ever changing and constant. Never-ending. Tranquil. I feel myself relaxing and…settling. A peace washes over me I haven't felt in years.

After walking several more feet, I come to a stop again and gaze out at the water, continuing to feel moved by its magnanimous and majestic presence. I let it speak to my soul, I let it metaphorically wash away the stain felt on my heart related to Jeremy. Life changes, presents challenges, can be amazing or painful, but there's something comforting in the fact that the ocean always remains the same. It's always here. It's deep and ever lasting and I find that it grounds me. It's peace and comfort when life feels anything but.

"Beautiful isn't it?" Katie asks startling me from my thoughts.

"It really is. I know it sounds weird, but something about it makes me feel… makes me feel…"

"I know," Katie says. And I know that she does.

Standing side by side we remain still and simply breathe. I allow the smell and the view to wash over me, to heal me. Tears come to my eyes and my heart lifts. I feel happy. Moving closer to the water, I lean down into the sand and with my finger write Jeremy's name. Then I stand back and wait for the waves to come and wash over it, watching as it disappears under the water's wrath. Leaning down again I write betrayal, then I write sadness, and then the date of our wedding that wasn't. I watch each and every time as the water takes them all away. With each disappearance it feels as if those memories and moments hold less weight; that the definitions of each are washed from my heart and soul. After the last one I look up and find Katie's eyes on me. She wipes away a tear and when I smile at her, we laugh in unison, and I feel lighter than I have in days. Sensing my lightness of spirit, she walks to me and embraces me in a loving, meaningful way.

We make our way back up the beach and to the party and stop at the beachfront showers. We wash the sand using both the tall, huge showerhead and the lower one at calf height. The water is freezing and we each squeal at the temperature. When finished, we quickly head to the pool and grab towels from the cart, eager to dry the water from our legs before putting on our shoes and heading to the party. It too is on the beach, but at least we won't be encased in wet sand.

The first thing we do is head to the makeshift bar. We each order a shot and make a toast, "To new beginnings," I say.

"Cheers!" Katie says.

We laugh and signal for another round right away. This time she raises her glass and says, "To the single life. Because this girl is going to remind you how great it is to be single once again."

"Here, here," I laugh and swallow the liquor savoring the burn as it slides down my throat and warms my tummy.

She grabs my hand after leaving cash on the bar for our drinks and hauls me onto the beach where several people are dancing. We waste no time moving to the middle of the crowd. Putting our arms above our heads, we begin moving and swaying to the music. Several guys come up and grab hold of our hips and dance with us. Katie and I laugh and entertain them for a bit, before moving away or closer to each other. All the while we laugh, smile, and proceed to do one of our favorite games. We spot someone in the crowd that is dancing and mimic their moves. The other person has to guess who we're imitating. The game is funny because mimicking someone else, and not moving naturally, makes our moves choppy and silly and we look ridiculous. Giggles continue to overtake us.

The constant laughter makes my bladder scream for release and I point at the bathrooms silently telling Katie where I'm headed. She gives me a nod and elects to stay and dance some more. Hurrying to the bathrooms, I wait for only a couple minutes before I find release, wash my hands and move back to the party. Stopping at the bar, I grab margaritas for Katie and I, but when I return to her, I find that she's made a friend on the dance floor. And I use the term friend loosely – she's grinding all up in his business and I'm pretty sure a margarita from me is the last thing she would care about at the moment.

With a smile I make my way back to the bar, set her drink down, and take a seat. Most people are walking along the beach, dancing, or sitting by the multiple fire pits. Many stand around talking. There are plenty of seats available at the bar. The atmosphere is electric. Everyone is relaxed, just wanting to have fun and there is much laughter in the air. It's impossible to not get caught up in the feeling and I find that a smile curves my lips. Taking a drink of the tart margarita, I close my eyes and enjoy the feeling of the beach breeze in my hair and the sound of laughter in my ears.

"I swear I'm not giving you a cheesy pick up line when I tell you that you're beautiful."

Opening my eyes, they widen when I see the husky voice I hear is not only talking to me, but that it belongs to none other than Asher Charming. Smiling before I even realize it, my thoughts leave my mouth, "I'm not sure if I should believe you."

"Oh, well it's totally true," he says while setting his drink on the bar and sitting beside me. An internal part of me wants to scream Asher Charming is freaking sitting next to me, but I reel it in, knowing that he's a person just like me. One hell of a sexy person though, because hot damn the man is fine. Wearing jeans that are well worn and clearly a favorite, he's also sporting a white button down shirt that's been rolled up to his forearms. The white emphasizes his sun kissed skin and makes his blue eyes blaze. "If I were using a pick up line it would have been something like, are you a fruit because honeydew you know how fine you look right now?"

"Oh god. Now I believe you. And do you actually get girls with that line?"

He laughs and my body responds in a way I've never felt before. My nipples tighten and I cross my legs and squeeze them together tightly because I'm tingling in places that shouldn't be tingling from a mere laugh. This is ridiculous.

"No, and I can't imagine why because come on, it's a good one." I laugh again and shake my head in disagreement. "Even though we took a picture together, I guess I never formally introduced myself."

"Yes, it's true. You're rather rude."

He smiles and gives me a look at his perfect white teeth, "You know, if I were less of a gentleman I could point out that you didn't introduce yourself either."

"Good thing you're a gentleman then."

"Yes, good thing." He holds out his hand to me, "Asher Charming, and you are?"

"Gabriella Barrie, my friends call me Ella. So, you can call me Gabriella."

He laughs, "Beautiful name for a beautiful woman."

"Okay seriously, you can stop now." He laughs and his eyes twinkle. I'm downright mesmerized.

"Noted," he says. "Tell me, what do I have to do to get to Ella status?"

"Hmm, well I guess you can start by buying me a drink."

"Done," he says and asks what I'm having before ordering then turns back to me after placing the order with the bartender. "Where is your friend?" he asks looking around. My heart falls and I think that maybe he's interested in Katie and I don't like the way that disappointment feels. Pointing toward the dance floor, I stifle a laugh when I see Katie. "She's dancing with a new friend." Dancing is being kind. She's practically having sex in her clothes. Wrinkling my nose, I shake my head at the downright indecent way she's grinding on some guys leg. There should be a warning label floating above her head or something.

Asher laughs, "Well, she happens to have made *friends* with one of mine."

"Oh yeah?" I ask raising a brow, "Jealous?" I ask and then want to slap my hand over my mouth in shock that I said that out loud, but I refrain.

"Not even a little bit. Truth is, I actually knew where she was. I've been watching the two of you for a while."

"You have?"

"Yes."

"Oh," I reply not sure what else to say.

"I was trying to get the courage to approach you."

He needed courage to talk to me? Seriously? So I tease him, "And that line was the best you could do after all that thinking?"

He throws his head back and laughs and I enjoy the sound. "Anyway, don't worry about your friend-"

"Katie."

"Katie. The guy she's with is a good guy."

"I'm not worried. Katie can handle herself."

"What about you? Can you handle yourself?" Asher asks me with a smirk and seriously, the urge to jump into his lap, straddle his hips and have my way with him is ridiculous. No wonder he sells millions of tickets to his action movies. *Note to self – slow down on the drinks. Or not.*

"Absolutely," I tell him and he laughs, then hands me a drink. Clinking his glass with mine he says, "To the night ahead." I nod and take a drink. He opens his mouth to speak, but before any words leave that beautiful mouth of his, Katie chirps, "Hi!"

Turning to her in surprise, I see she's standing next to the man she was dancing with and her eyes are wide as she looks from me to Asher a few times. Smiling and laughing softly, I say, "Asher, allow me to formally introduce you to my best friend, Katie. Katie, you've met Asher."

Katie smiles widely and cocks that hip of hers again. I narrow my eyes wanting to tell her to knock it off. "You owe me another photo. Where the hell is that friend of yours anyway? I need to teach him how to take a photo correctly."

Asher looks at me in confusion, "What happened?"

"She's mad because your friend cut all of our heads off."

Asher laughs, "I promise we can take another one together. Cool?"

"Alright then," Katie agrees.

Asher gestures to Katie's dirty dancing partner, "Mick, this is the beautiful Gabriella. Her friends call her 'Ella', so you can call her Gabriella." He says and I swear there's a little bit of possessiveness in his look and tone. Mick looks at Asher and smirks as if he's in on some secret joke that Katie and I aren't aware of.

"Hi, Ella," Mick says with emphasis and a laugh, "Nice to meet you."

"You too," I reply, "and don't worry. Asher has to call me Gabriella too."

"What? No way. You said I could call you Ella if I bought you a drink."

I slam back the rest of my jack and coke and smile, "I said you could start with one drink." He laughs and turns to order me another.

"Ella, can I steal you for just one second?" Katie asks me and I nod, excusing myself.

"I will eagerly await your return," Asher says and I giggle. I freaking giggle. Oh my god.

As soon as we are out of earshot, Katie turns to me, "Oh my hell!" she whispers with a smile.

"I know. He just came up to me and started talking not long before you came up." And interrupted I want to say. What is wrong with me? Maybe Asher isn't the only one feeling a little possessive. Which is insanity – I have no right, no claim – nor does he.

"That's Asher fucking Charming," Katie says and her eyes are a little unfocused making me laugh.

"Yeah it is," I say with a shrug.

"Oh please, you can't tell me you're not freaking out."

"Sure I am a little. On the inside. But whatever, I mean he's just a guy. A guy I'll never see again after tonight. May as well enjoy it."

"That's my girl," she says and then a wicked grin curves her lips, "Speaking of enjoying it...."

"What?"

"Well, Mick and I kind of hit it off. He asked me if I want to leave and go get drinks somewhere. But, I don't have to go. I shouldn't. I don't want to leave you; I'm being stupid. What am I thinking?"

I grasp her upper arm, "You are being stupid, but not because you're considering going with Mick. I don't need a babysitter. Go. Have fun. Enjoy it. Please. You're not here much longer and my god, you've catered to me enough the last few days."

"Cater? Ella, you know better than that."

"You know what I mean. Please go, seriously. I'll be mad if you don't. I'll be fine. What's the worst that can happen? And I'll see you in the morning."

"The morning?" she asks brows raised.

"Well yeah. I'm totally counting on you getting lucky, then telling me all about it." We laugh and walk arm in arm back to the guys. She and Asher tell each other goodbye and she gives me one last look as she leaves. I nod telling her without words that I'm fine.

Asher and I look at each other and smile again. "So," I begin, "What is *the* Asher Charming doing in Cabo San Lucas? Shouldn't you be on a movie set somewhere?"

His brow raises, "You've seen my movies? I was surprised you and Katie recognized me."

"Really? Who doesn't know who you are?" I ask and I swear his face flushes. "You're face is usually plastered all over the movie theatre. How many Jack Danger movies have you done now?" Jack Danger is the action movie character he's played in a series of movies about a hit man employed by the government to go on secret assassination missions.

"Well I want to know about *you*. You didn't answer my question – have *you* seen my movies?" he asks again.

"I've seen your movies," I tell him with honesty and now I know there's no doubt. He's definitely blushing and I can't resist pointing it out. "You're blushing."

He shrugs and smiles and it's incredibly endearing, "I don't know that I'll ever get used to that."

"Seriously? You've been in how many movies now? You have to deal with screaming crazy fans all the time."

"Seven, four of them Jack Danger films. But, that doesn't mean it ever stops being surreal. And I think that the moment it does, I won't want to do this anymore because I'll be an ego inflated asshole."

We each take a sip of our drink, watching each other out of the corner of our eyes as we do so. I almost smile, every cell of my body tuned into his. I notice every movement, every blink of his eyes and twitch of his fingers. "A bachelor party."

"Excuse me?"

"You asked why I'm here in Cabo. My best buddy got married and we've been celebrating. When they decided to get married here they invited guests to make a vacation out of it. It's been a bachelor party, wedding, and honeymoon vacation. I'm here to attend everything – well not the honeymoon."

"That's cool."

"I'm his best man in the wedding." I nod my head not sure what else to say. The wedding talk for once isn't making my stomach drop or sadness surface and it's a relief that makes me smile. "And you?" he asks.

"Me?"

"Yes. What brings you here?"

I think about my answer, not sure what I want to say. If anyone would understand wanting privacy it would be him I'm sure. I settle for a small truth instead of full disclosure, "Bad breakup."

He nods, "You know…I can help with that." His voice drips with sex and suggestion and it makes my body tingle. Everywhere. Shivering at the feeling, my mouth falls open as I gasp wondering if he just propositioned me and why the hell I'm screaming '*Yes! Yes! Yes!*' in my head.

No doubt Asher would give me one hell of a rebound, that's for damn sure. Before I can give it anymore thought, he lifts up his finger and calls, "Bartender! We need some shots over here!" He smiles at me and somehow I return it, but my body deflates in disappointment. Immediately on the tails of disappointment, I internally freak out because I realize I totally want to have sex with Asher Charming.

Chapter 10

Present Time

"What can I get you to drink?" a cold voice asks me.

The flight attendant looks at me expectantly with a plastic looking smile on her face. Her hair is pulled back in a bun so tight the corners of her eyes pull back just a smidge; it has to be giving her a headache. Maybe that's the reason she's wearing a pinched expression every time I look at her. Or maybe she was accidentally mooned along with the rest of the people near my seat. If so, I was certainly judged and found wanting given her frigid attitude. Oh well, that just means I smile widely at her when I answer. "I'd love a diet coke, please."

Nodding she makes a note on a pad of paper then looks at Faye for an answer, "I'll have a water, thank you." When she moves on to another row Faye turns to me, "Is Asher just like the character he plays in those action movies of his, Jack Danger?"

I can't help it, my head falls back and I laugh. "Wait, so not only do you know who he is, but you've seen his movies too?"

Another laugh almost bursts from me when she actually rolls her eyes at me. "Honey, what did I tell you? I'm older, but I'm not dead. I've seen his movies. Have you?"

"Yes," I nod. "And I guess I would say both. He is and isn't like Jack." Talking about him makes his face appear in my mind - his dark hair, chiseled cheekbones most women would kill for, the slope of his slightly crooked nose, the only small imperfection he has. If I concentrate hard enough I can see his eyes too although my memory doesn't do them justice. They're so expressive it's really no wonder he's an actor, he can say so much with a look. My heart automatically aches with longing and I take a deep stuttering breath to try and ease the discomfort in my chest.

"I'm guessing if you spent time with him, and seem upset that it's over, that he must have been a nice young man?" Smiling and nodding at Faye, I know she's trying to continue the conversation and encouraging me to share more. Even though I don't know her well I have no doubt if I elected to quit talking, that would be fine with her, she's simply being kind. Curious a little, no doubt, but her mannerism and style of communication is encouraging and enabling rather than invasive or inappropriate in any way.

"Yes, he was more than nice. Being with him was strange at times, a bit surreal, but it also felt…right. It was odd how comfortable I was with him too. Almost as if we've known each other forever."

"A bond like that between two people is special. It almost sounds like you were meant to be together." Looking down my eyes well with tears. I hate how easy they come. "Well get to the good part, honey. Did you sleep with him?"

Gasping, a laugh bubbles up my throat, "Faye!"

"Do I have to remind you again?"

"No! I know! You made it clear before – you have eyes and hormones like the rest of the world that gazes at that man."

"That's right, now stop stalling."

I shake my head in humor at her comment and wonder how much I'm going to need to censor the rest of my story.

Chapter 11

"Turn if off," I mumble, irritated at the annoying sound that wakes me. Rolling over, snuggling my face down into my pillow, I try to fall back under sleep's spell. It's not happening and I finally realize the persistent noises are coming from my cell phone. Eyes too heavy to open all the way, I squint at the table next to the bed allowing my mind to wake a bit more. Groaning softly at how fatigued and achy I feel, I stretch my legs and flex my calves, the sheets sliding over my skin like satin. I close my eyes once more with a smile, happy that the beeping seems to have quit. It doesn't last long. The irritating noise erupts from my phone once again while another phone joins the chorus with annoying vibrations causing a deep frown to form on my tired face. Who needs to get hold of Katie and me badly?

I grudgingly decide to give in. Opening one eye, I reach blindly toward the sound and snatch the phone from the table. Squinting at the screen to determine who the hell is bothering me, it takes a moment for the words I'm seeing on the screen to penetrate my mind. When they do, I sit up like a rocket, feeling as if I've been launched into an alternate universe. Surely, I'm going crazy.

Among missed calls, multiple social media notifications and texts show up on my screen. A text from Katie somehow manages to stand out from the rest. *"Okay, so I'm going to need specific dick details, because it must be HUGE to warrant marriage. And you're not forgiven."*

Staring open mouthed at my phone one word keeps repeating in my mind over and over again like a mantra. *Marriage. Marriage. Marriage? What is she going on about?*

I'm still staring at my phone, but I'm not really seeing it because images begin flowing through my mind, touching down briefly before flitting away again. Asher coming up to me at the bar on the beach, him buying me more drinks that I continued to ingest. Dancing with him, our initial hesitant and stunted movements eventually becoming more orchestrated and increasing with desire. I remember my body pressed tightly to the front of his - our hips moving together in ways that felt amazing, sinful and dangerous all at once. Him asking if I wanted to go somewhere else with him, me readily agreeing, and moving our party of two to another bar at another resort, dancing and drinking even more.

When another memory hits me, my mouth falls open and disbelief makes me numb – tingles run through my fingers and toes. I remember the conversation first. The confession. The suggestion. The captivation. Then I remember our actions, and follow through. Shaking my head in denial at the absurdity of my thoughts, I glance down at my hand and freeze.

Oh. Fuck.

Movement beside me makes me still and I look around feeling crazed as I realize I'm not in my own room. Slapping my hand over my mouth I stifle a scream, my eyes finally registering who's been next to me all along. My eyes start at his covered legs, the sheet pressing against his form like a whisper stopping at his hips. The lines of muscle at his abdomen, his broad chest and shoulders, his strong neck, proud chin and the planes of his face are all devoured by my eyes next. His full lips are parted; dark lashes concealing an indigo gaze that has the power to make me breathless when it's concentrated on me. His arms are thrown haphazardly over his head, dark hair unruly, face almost boyish in sleep. He presents one hell of a picture.

I'm not going to lie, there's a moment when I can't decide if I want to throw up or stand up so I can dance like a football player scoring a touchdown. I'm in bed with Asher. I'm in bed with Asher Fucking Charming. I'm not just in bed with Asher Fucking Charming, I *fucked* Asher Charming if memory serves correctly. Thoroughly too. I almost giggle at the absurd thought.

Looking under the sheet at myself once more, then back at him, I shake my head in disbelief. *Oh my god, I'm naked in a bed with Asher Fucking Charming.* That's when more memories swallow me. Stumbling into his room, laughing and breathless. Clothing being removed one piece at a time, touching, exploring, tasting, but also smiling, laughing and *feeling*. God, so much feeling, even while completely intoxicated and I remember feeling…home.

Panic sets in. Turning to Asher, I begin to freak out and I'm sure as hell not going to do it alone. "Asher! Wake up!"

He groans, likely feeling the effects from last night as well, but when I say his name again, his eyes pop open. As soon as he focuses on me, he smiles. Not exactly what I was expecting. "Hello, gorgeous."

I'm momentarily speechless, as he stretches and I watch all the muscles roll under his skin. The sheet shifts lower on his hips and my breath catches in anticipation. Glancing at him, I realize he's watching me with a smirk and I flush at being caught staring. Grabbing the comforter off the end of the bed, I awkwardly wrap it around my body and stand up needing a little distance, otherwise I'm likely to straddle his hips and make him right at home. *Oh good lord.* "Asher, what did we do last night?"

A slow, wicked smile lifts the corners of his mouth and his eyes twinkle as he sits up in bed. "If you don't remember, clearly I'm going to need to refresh your memory. I know we were both wasted, but come on princess you wound me, even I remember last night."

Heat sears my face and chest at his words. Turning away I clear my throat and try to remember what I was asking him as images of us twisted together naked enter my mind. Somehow snapping out of it, I force myself to look at him once again, not that it's a chore, I mean *damn*. I almost groan when I see he's sitting against the headboard with the sheet at an indecent level. This is impossible. Shaking my head, I frown, "Stop using your sex mojo on me and pay attention."

He snorts, "Sex mojo?"

"Yeah, that's what I said. Stop distracting me."

"If I was trying to distract you I wouldn't be in this bed all alone."

Stomping my foot like a toddler, I huff out a breath in exasperation. "Will you be serious?"

"I'm always serious about sex."

I have to force myself not to give in and smile. "Alright, pause the testosterone for two seconds and answer my question. Do you have memories of everything we did last night?" He starts to smile seductively again, but I cut him off with a flick of my hand, "Do you have memories of last night *before* we got to the bedroom?"

He frowns at me, "Of course."

Frowning myself, I shake my head, "I don't think you do."

Asher's phone begins beeping and vibrating again. He glances at it briefly, but ignores it looking back at me. "We were on the beach, we drank, danced, went to a club-" he stops talking when his phone starts going off again. As if on cue, mine starts in again. Clutching it tightly in my hand, I'm momentarily distracted when I look at the screen and see another text message from Katie, *"Please tell me the reason you aren't calling me right now is because you're on his cock. Check out this picture on the front of Hollywood Today's website."* Attached is a photo of Asher and I kissing. I'm holding flowers in my hand and have another in my hair. I'm the one that posted it, as the photo shows my Facebook information. The caption I posted with the photo reads, "Just married, bitches!"

"Oh my god," I say, then look at Asher, "Oh god. I'm so sorry. So, so sorry."

"Why? What's wrong?" Asher asks sitting forward with concern lacing his voice.

My eyes widen with horror, "Oh god, this is going to be the biggest media nightmare for you. A damn circus." His phone starts going off again as if verifying my point.

Asher gets out of bed and walks toward me, and good god he's naked. And he's glorious. Once again, I'm distracted. My eyes roam all over his body and I feel breathless at the sight. He grasps my upper arms softly, "Ella?" My eyes find his and I'm lost in his gaze. "What's going on? Why are you so upset?"

Without another word, I swallow hard, then turn my phone to him in order to show him the photo Katie sent me. His brow lowers and I stare at his face for a moment, dissecting every twitch and furrow. Holding up my other hand, I show him the silver ring I'm wearing, it's glinting emphasizing the photo. I remember how after we had our brilliant idea to get married, we stopped at a vendor's booth that sold jewelry and looked for matching rings and found a pair within minutes. Reaching for his hand, I grab it and hold it up for him to see. No words needed, the picture and our rings clear enough.

He looks at his ring, and I swear I see a twitch at his lips and something flash in his eyes that I can't decipher. "I'm sorry," I whisper again not knowing what else to say, and turning my head away not wanting to see the look on his face. I don't know what else to say to him, anything else seems inadequate.

"You're upset that we got married?"

My head spins around so fast my neck aches. "You remember?" He nods and this time, he does smile. "And you aren't upset?" I ask, my voice rising at the question in disbelief and confusion.

He shrugs, "It was my idea. If anyone's to blame, it's me. Remember?"

Staring at him, at the curve of his lips, the look in his eyes, the memory comes to me easily. We were walking through the streets, looking at all the little shops and clubs. Workers of each place were trying to get us to come inside their establishment, some being pushy, some using humor, and others both. Asher's hand was in mine, steadying me as I hobbled on my feet a bit. He turned to me, his eyes full of question. "All night, you smile here," he says fingers brushing my lips, "but at times I can see pain in here," his thumb brushes the underside of each eye gently. "I see stress or sadness here," he touches the lines between my brows next. "Tell me why. Tell me how I can make it go away."

And I tell him. I tell him about my disastrous relationship, the back stabbing betrayal, my sham of an engagement, and the circus of a wedding. I tell him how Katie and I decided to run away and that in a way I feel guilty that I don't feel worse. It's like I had my cry, felt the rage, but then was able to let go. I remember him turning to me, laughter still on his face after I told him about punching Jeremy and even showed him the bruises still lacing my knuckles. His face lit up with his idea, "Well, we'll just show him. How about you and I get married? Nothing says I've moved on better, right?"

I laughed and told him it was the best idea ever. We efficiently bought rings, found a little chapel open for just such occasions and said 'I do' in no time. We took all kinds of selfies, bought a picture package if I recall and came back here and had wild monkey sex. We didn't waste any time consummating the marriage that's for sure. Over and over, if memory serves. I could be embarrassed about that, but hell, who would blame me?

"It may have been your idea as a joke, but clearly I'm the one that posted pictures and told the world and oh god, that is totally your publicist or agent calling isn't it? I bet they're going to be so pissed. No doubt they are calling with ideas and instructions on how to get rid of me and the evidence of this insanity." Okay yeah. I'm pretty sure I've just entered hysterical territory.

And Asher? Well he shocks me, because he *laughs*. "Princess, calm down. I remember every detail about last night. Every detail."

He says enunciating the last two words with such emphasis while looking me up and down lustfully. Chills break out over my body and I pull the comforter tighter around me as if that will help fight them off. "I could care less what my publicist or anyone else has to say about this, they don't own me." I stare at him open-mouthed not able to form words in the slightest. "They can keep calling all they want," he grabs his phone and just as it starts vibrating again in his hand, he powers it off.

"You aren't mad? How are you not mad?"

He shrugs, "I'm just not."

"But, I can't even imagine the kind of field day the press will have over this. It will screw up your career."

He scoffs, "Says who?" He runs the tips of his fingers down my arms making me shudder. "Look it's not a big deal. So we got drunk and decided to get married, oh well. You know what I remember about last night? I remember having fun – with you. The most fun I've had in…I don't even know how long. Getting to know someone without pressure and expectations, acting spontaneously and genuinely enjoying myself? It's been far too long."

"Getting to know someone is one thing, but we've known one another all of five minutes and we've had sex and are married. Oh god, I'm like the world's biggest whore."

Humor fades from his face and his jaw tightens, "Stop that. No matter what happens, I won't have you talking about yourself in that way. Not ever. Look," his thumb traces my jaw and I get the feeling he likes touching me. "How much longer are you here again? Another week right?"

"Yes. Katie leaves tomorrow night. I'd like to spend some time with her before she goes, but I'm still here another week. Alone."

He smiles, "Perfect. This week, let's have fun together. I want to have more moments with you like we enjoyed last night. I want to know more about you, I want to do things with you like swim, snorkel, eat amazing food and get suntans, walk on the beach, and if I'm a lucky bastard make love to you again." How I remain standing after that comment, I have no idea. "When this week is over, we'll worry about the marriage thing, but for now, let's just be Asher and Ella. Be mine for this week. Let's just have fun together, please? Will you do that, Ella?"

He's serious. The set of his jaw, the look in his eyes, and determination on his face tell me that much. But there's more to it than that. From our talks last night and the earnestness with his question today, there's something more. It's the way he talks about last night, it's almost wistful, and his words are full of longing and maybe a hint of desperation. I get the feeling if I say no, he'll plead with me to change my mind. He says he wants to have fun, no pressure, but I think he's also lonely. And I find myself amazed that someone with a life like his, a movie star, surrounded by people that cater to his every whim, money coming out his ears, could experience something such as loneliness. But isn't that the thing? Sometimes it's when you're surrounded that you feel the most lost, the most alone. Especially when you're surrounded with falseness and insincerity. I know what that's like.

Last night, I had fun too. I never once thought about Jeremy until Asher asked about why I seem to be carrying stress. I never felt sad or ashamed or guilty like I shouldn't be enjoying my time with him. And yes, I made one hell of a mistake in getting married, but that can be fixed. How many chances like this happen in a lifetime? None. Yeah, he may be Asher Charming, and I'd be lying if I didn't say that the thought of being with him doesn't make me halfway delirious, but it's more than that. It's the chance to have fun, to forget. It's the chance to let myself simply live and enjoy life with a gorgeous man by my side for a week. A week where our experiences will make memories, and gain me a friend, that will hopefully last a lifetime. We can just have fun, no pressure, no strings.

He runs his fingertips up and down my arms as he's waiting for my answer. My phone is continuing to chime and I give it a glance and throw it on the bed. With a nod, I look into his eyes, "Can I ask one question first?"

"Of course."

"Why? Why spend a week together?"

"I can read you, and I know that you feel whatever this is between us, just like I do. I also know that you had fun last night, just like me. More than fun. We have a connection, a real connection, and as if that's not enough, you're different. You treat me, like me. I'm a guy, incredibly attracted and intrigued by a girl and I'm not ready to let go of this feeling. Yeah, so we skipped a few steps," I roll my eyes at his flippancy and he laughs. "Like I said, we can handle that later, if necessary, until then, let's make the most of it. You're real, and genuine, and it's been one hell of a long time since I've gotten to spend time in the company of a woman with those attributes. And I find that I like it. I like you."

"I like you too," I reply honestly.

He smiles and it lights up his face. "So you agree? Let's not worry about our uh, event last night, and just enjoy each other, okay?"

Nodding, I return his smile, "You know what? That sounds perfect." Though I can't help but think, even momentarily, of the 'if necessary' phrase he included in his passionate plea for us to just resume where we left off.

"Yeah?"

"Yeah," I nod.

With a smile, he leans forward, puts his arms around me, and kisses me, and with that, all traces of worry fade away.

Chapter 12

"Spill it. Spill it now." The door flies open the second I insert my key in the lock. Katie's clearly been lying in wait ready to pounce the moment I return.

With a small smile, I plead, "I promise I will tell you everything, but let's get ready first and go to the pool. I want some sunshine."

She agrees but evidences extreme effort as she keeps opening her mouth then shutting it again when she catches herself. We hastily get ready, change clothes, and gather our beach supplies. At times when I turn and catch Katie's eye, I see she's staring at me. I know she's dying for information, an explanation. I, on the other hand, am thinking about Asher. When we parted ways, we agreed to meet up at the pool. I awkwardly gathered my clothes from around the room and went to the bathroom to dress and splashed water on my face. With a smile, wave and promise to see him soon, I ran off to my room. I'm already feeling eager to see him again.

On the walk to the pool, several workers on the property smile and greet us with an, "Hola," as we pass. I swear a few of them wear knowing smirks, but no doubt I'm paranoid. This whole thing is crazy, so of course I feel like everyone and anyone knows about it. Well, actually, I guess anyone could thanks to my informative Facebook post. I'm such an idiot.

Katie and I grab chairs and push them close together. After applying sunblock we lay on our stomachs, heads turned toward one another, enjoying the sunshine on our skin while I divulge everything. Once finished, Katie stares at me with her mouth wide open. What a unique expression for her. It's been her nearly permanent expression since I returned to the room this morning. I'm starting to worry that she's going to wear a shocked look on her face forever.

Finally she speaks. "Holy shit."

"Wow, that's it? I think I was expecting something… I don't know… more profound."

"Holy *fucking* shit?"

"Mhm, a little better."

"Ha. Ha. I just can't believe you got married. It's awesome and insane at the same time. I mean, not only did you get married, but you posted a picture that's already had over a million shares and been picked up by who knows how many gossip websites and trashy magazines."

"Oh god. I think I'm going to be sick," I roll over to my back and place a hand on my stomach suddenly feeling queasy. "Obviously, I wasn't thinking clearly."

"Or, maybe you were. Maybe you do your best thinking when you're drinking because hell girlfriend, good job. You married Asher Charming. Or should I call him Jack Danger? Do you think he'll want you to call him Jack Danger in bed?"

"Oh my god, will you shut up? Jack Danger is just the character he plays in all those movies, not his name. You know that. Besides, we're going to hang out for the week and then we'll no doubt win some record for the shortest marriage ever."

"No, I think you're wrong," she replies as she unscrews the lid on her bottle of water, "I'm pretty sure that reality star with the fake tits and ass that looks like her face is melting when she cries, was married for like forty-eight hours one time. So don't worry, she's got you beat."

"Oh great, thanks," I reply, my voice dripping with sarcasm. "Because that's who I want to emulate."

"Hey, if the shoe fits."

"Bitch," I call her, but she only laughs out loud and it makes me smile even though I pretend to be angry. "It sucks that I have to leave tomorrow. You are going to spend the week with Jack Danger, right? Man, I would love to stay here so I can watch."

"Will you stop calling him that? It's not funny and he's just a guy who happens to have a job that a lot of people get to see. It's not a big deal." I'm not sure if I'm trying to convince her or myself. "And yes, like I told you, he asked me to spend time with him this week and I agreed. Afterwards, he'll take care of everything regarding our…um… our…"

"Marriage?"

"Yeah," I clear my throat uncomfortably, "that."

She lifts her brows and laughs at me, "You can't even say it."

"No, I sure as hell can't, and can you blame me? None of this even seems real."

"Ella Charming. Mrs. Ella Charming. It has a nice ring to it. I wonder if it's his real last name of if he changed it for his celeb name?"

"Shut up." She laughs, but I'm totally not smiling this time. The sound of that name is ringing in my ears and I'm starting to panic. "Oh my god, this is nuts. I can't believe I did something so… so…."

"Awesome?"

"Not the word I'm looking for. More like stupid, spontaneous, thoughtless, dumb…"

"Oh, please. Get over yourself." Katie starts to giggle.

"What's so funny?"

She smiles wide, "Remember last night when you told me not to worry about you and to go have my own fun because, and I quote, 'what's the worst that can happen'?"

Groaning, I rub my head feeling like my hangover headache is returning, "Oh, God, I'm such a mess, but that reminds me, how was your night anyway?"

"Oh no, we aren't changing the subject. Besides, trust me when I say your night was much more interesting. The guy I was with passed out on me before we got to the good stuff. I spent the evening worried about you and wondering where you were until I saw the picture you posted. And for the record, you aren't a mess. I'm only teasing you. I honestly think this is a really good thing."

"How in the hell is this a good thing? I'm fighting the urge to vomit because the butterflies in my stomach are making me sick, and you're over there smiling like you just won a year supply of shoes from your favorite store."

"I'm smiling because this is just what you need."

Sitting up, I give her my best stink eye, "How can you say that?" I begin twisting my hands in my lap, "What the hell was I thinking agreeing to be with him this week? Why did I not insist that we take care of things immediately? I'm completely out of my mind. You know, I should call the airline, see if I can get a flight out tomorrow too."

"You sure as hell are not!"

Ignoring her, I continue, "And then when we get back, you can drive me to the nearest mental institution and check me the hell in because I've lost my fucking mind, Katie."

"Over my dead body."

"I'm serious."

"Calm down," Katie says sitting up too and leaning toward me so she can rub my back soothingly. Speaking in a low, calm voice she directs, "Take a deep breath." I do as she says. "Come on, Ella, don't you think you deserve some fun? Just like Asher said?"

"God yes, I do. But-"

"No. No 'but' – I don't want to hear it. Your life has been full of shit that happens to you. One big massive avalanche of shit that smacks you with one thing after another. The death of your mother, your father getting remarried to a demon from hell, her daughter being a hell spawn too, then the sudden and unexpected death of your father. Don't even get me started on the choices you had to make for his company, how hard you have worked and the sacrifices you have made, how angry Angelica was over the whole thing, and on top of that agreeing to marry Jeremy even though you knew better. Then you have a relationship with him that goes nowhere, you try to force it anyway then have that blow up in your face. My god Ella, for once, something is happening in your life that's exciting and full of possibility. You have a chance to let go and fucking take a gigantic leap into fun. And hell, you deserve that. And lots more. You have more than earned the right to it all and to let go and not worry about consequences for once in your life."

"You make me sound pathetic."

"No, I'm just stating the truth. And the fact is, it's one week. One week that could end up being one of the best weeks of your life. For god sakes, you should be jumping up and down at the chance, not panicking. Let your inner party girl out to play, she's suffocating to death in there."

"You act like I haven't made any of my own decisions throughout my life. That's not the case – I'm not some victim. I *chose* to take the CEO position at dad's company, I *chose* to get in a relationship with Jeremy, I'm the one who said yes to his proposal and went through planning a wedding when I knew I didn't really love him in the way that would result in the marriage I wanted. They may have been shitty decisions, but they were still mine."

"That's not what I'm saying, and I sure as hell don't see you as a victim. You are one of the strongest and toughest women I know. I do think, however, that your decisions would have been different if your life circumstances weren't what they are."

"Well, whatever. It is what it is."

"Yes, that's true, but only over my creepy shredded nasty zombie body will you not take Asher up on his offer. I know you already did, but clearly you're questioning yourself. Well, I won't let you back out of your agreement, so knock it the hell off. You are going to have a fantastic week, full of new experiences and incredible sex. Then you will report in to me and tell me all of the details. Anything less is unacceptable."

"Fine. I'll do it. I've got nothing to lose. I will not, however give you any details about the sex."

"What? That's a best friend party foul. There's a commandment - best friends shall tell their best friends about the amazing sex they're having. Especially when said best friend is having no amazing sex of her own."

"I've said it before and I will say it again, you have a commandment for everything."

"Only when it suits my needs."

"Yeah, I've noticed," I laugh and then it turns into a sigh as I eye my friend and my heart warms and I feel grateful once again for her friendship. "God, I wish you weren't leaving in the morning."

"I know, me too, especially now. But I have to get back to work. Plus, you need to enjoy paradise with your new hubby without me in tow."

"Will you stop saying that? You act like this is a real marriage. It isn't."

"You have a piece of paper that says otherwise. And a ring, I see."

No sooner does she utter those words, than I feel a tingle at the back of my neck and I know instinctively that Asher has arrived at the pool. Feeling a magnetic pull, I turn and find him walking toward me with a large smile on his gorgeous face. I let my eyes enjoy the journey from the top of his head to his feet and they want to weep with joy at the sight. The man is insanely good looking. A flash of him naked runs through my mind and I bite my lip.

"Hello, Katie," he greets her first and she returns it in a high-pitched breathless voice. I just barely resist rolling my eyes, and stand to say hello. I'm surprised when Asher takes me in his arms, and gives me a loud smacking kiss on the lips. "Hi wifey." My mouth drops open in surprise and Katie laughs along with two people that followed Asher over. They must be a couple of his friends.

"Well hello to you too," I finally compose myself enough to say, but almost swoon at the smile he's giving me. I can't see his eyes given the mirrored aviator sunglasses he's sporting, but I swear I can feel them burning into my skin as he eyes me up and down and checks me out in my white bikini. In seconds a lust filled haze surrounds us and I run my tongue along my lower lip as I check him out brazenly in return. I may have been drunk last night, but the longer I've been awake, I've increasingly remembered our night together – maybe not as clearly as I'd like, but it's definitely enough. Looking at him now, I realize how game I am for a repeat. Like now. *Yeah. Now would be good.*

I'm wondering if he can read my mind because he begins moving closer to me once more and everything else seems to disappear. It's just him and me and all my focus is on his mouth as it comes closer to mine. My eyes close in preparation, but a throat clearing breaks the spell and my eyes open and Asher pulls back looking both annoyed and chagrined, but he doesn't let go of me. Turning to his friends, I see them standing there looking at us and my cheeks flush and I hear Katie laugh softly.

"Dude, are you going to introduce us or what?" One of them says with a smile. The other is standing there with his arms crossed and I can't decipher the look on his face. There's a touch of amusement, but wariness there as well.

"Ella, these are my friends, although right now I'm forgetting why." He points at the one smiling first, "That's Andy, and the other guy is Hunter."

Clearing my throat I try to push away the slight embarrassment, "Hi, nice to meet you."

Andy reaches his hand out, his smile growing, "Hi Ella, it's nice to meet you." His smile is wide and his blonde hair stands up straight on his head. He's got a total surfer boy look going on. "I hope you don't mind me saying that you're absolutely gorgeous."

"Oh, um, thank you," I respond feeling awkward and glance at Asher to see a look on his face resembling pride as he nods his agreement.

"Hi, Ella," Hunter says. "Asher and I have been friends since grade school, so I know him well. Considering that, mind telling me why you married him? I mean, I guess you could say he's good looking, and he's got the whole celebrity thing going for him, but I also happen to know that he has some really annoying habits too. For example-"

"Seriously, Hunter? Shut the hell up," Asher laughs and pushes Hunter who then pushes him back and then they start mock wrestling each other until Asher's phone starts ringing. He plucks it out of his shorts pocket and glances at the screen. "Excuse me, I'll be right back." He steps away to take the phone call.

Turning to Katie, I see her putting on her swimsuit cover up. "I'm going to go get all of us a bucket of beer from the bar. That cool with everyone?"

"Sure," I shrug.

"I'll come with you," Andy says to Katie. "I think I want some food."

"Dude, you're always hungry," Hunter says and Andy shrugs walking off with Katie, leaving Hunter and me alone.

Awkwardly, I turn to him, trying to think of something to say. "So, you said you and Asher have been friends a long time, how did you meet?"

His smile falls from his face and he stares into my eyes, "Cut the shit. I want to know what it is you're after?"

My mouth falls open in shock at his complete about face, "Excuse me?"

"You heard me. Asher is more than my friend; he's like a brother. You may think he's some stereotypical actor that lives fast and hard, but Asher isn't like that. I'm not about to let you try and take him for some ride because you're hoping to take advantage of his position and kindness."

Completely struck speechless I'm not sure how long I stare at him before I shake off his words and start to get angry. Glancing over at Asher, I see his back is turned to us. Looking back at Hunter, I let the anger inside of me show on my face. "Excuse me? You have some nerve making an assumption like that. You don't know shit about me."

"Yeah well and you don't know shit about Asher."

"You're right, I don't, and this thing between us is exactly what I'm sure he's already told you – a drunken suggestion that we clearly took too far. And we'll handle it." His face gives away nothing, but I keep going. "What *you* don't know is that I'm a financially independent successful CEO of my own lucrative company. Not that it's any of your goddamn business, but a relationship with Asher, in any shape or form, does not benefit me materialistically whatsoever. So fuck you. And fuck your assumptions, asshole."

"Look, I'm sorry." Hunter runs a hand through his hair in what appears to be embarrassment, but I'm past caring. "I'm just looking out for my friend, and I'm not going to lie to you, I don't like this. He told me that you're spending the week together," he looks at me as if he wants confirmation, but I stare at him, giving him nothing. "I'm going to be keeping an eye on you. I don't trust you, and I'll do anything to protect him. He's a good guy and I won't let you ruin everything he's worked so hard for."

Before I can respond, Asher has returned, oblivious to what has transpired in his absence. "Sorry about that. It was my agent. I've been blowing her off so I needed to take her call."

Looking away from Hunter, I smile into Asher's face, "Everything okay?"

He returns my smile, "It's fine." He looks between Hunter and me, "You guys getting to know one another?"

Hunter smiles at Asher revealing nothing, "Yep. We sure are."

Before I can even think about saying a word, Katie returns with a bucket of beer, "Alright, who's drinking?" We all reach for a beer, Hunter and I plaster smiles on our faces and act like our conversation never took place, but I keep an eye on him out of the corner of my eye, and every time I look his way, our eyes meet making it clear he's doing the same.

"What do you want to do tomorrow?" Asher asks me, sitting beside me on my chair, taking a sip of his beer.

"I'm not sure. What do you want to do?" Everyone around us is staring at our interaction and I feel uncomfortable. I don't like being on display like a science project.

Likely seeing my discomfort, Asher stands and holds a hand out to me, "Come on, let's cool off."

Without a word, I place my hand in his and carrying our beer with us, we walk to the pool and enter it never letting go of our hands. The water is cool, but not cold, and feels great. The water isn't deep – only four feet – and we walk to an empty corner, setting our beers on the concrete. I place my arms on the concrete and rest my head in them facing Asher. He does the same, facing me. "That's better," he smiles and I know he did this for my benefit. Gave us privacy. "So, I want to talk about this week."

"Okay."

"Is there anything you want to do that you haven't done yet?"

"Katie and I have basically hung around the resort and did some shopping, so I'm open to anything. I liked the suggestions you made this morning."

"Yeah?"

"Yeah, they sound fun. Oh, how about renting some wave runners? I saw that in the information they gave us when we checked in. Their other property rents them ocean side. We can call and reserve them."

"Done," Asher says. "What else?"

"What do you want to do?" I ask him not wanting to make all the decisions for us.

"I want to spend time with you," he says automatically.

"I'd like that too," I tell him.

He reaches toward me and pulls me into his arms, and I go happily. Feeling his body against mine in the water feels erotic. The thin material of our swimsuits the only thing that separates us and I can feel the firmness of his stomach and chest against my own. It feels amazing, and I boldly wrap my legs around his waist and put my arms around his shoulders. Asher sucks a breath in at my actions and he places my back against the pool wall. "There's one other thing I want to talk about," he says pressing against me, and this time it's me that sucks in a breath at the contact.

"What's that?"

"Am I moving into your room, or you mine?"

My eyes widen and my mouth falls open, "What? Are you serious?"

He places his sunglasses to the top of his head and looks at me directly in the eyes, "I'm completely serious."

"Well... I... well I guess..."

"How about since mine is bigger, you come to mine?"

"Are you sure about this? I mean, I have a lot of stuff, and I'll get my makeup and all my hair crap all over your counter, and I'm a mess sometimes."

"I will love every second of it," he says sincerely. "I want you there."

"But-"

Before I can utter another word his mouth is on mine. One of his hands moves to my hair and he tugs it gently as his tongue licks the seam of my lips waiting for me to open. When I do, he plunges his tongue inside, tasting me fiercely. It's the sexiest kiss I've ever had in my life. Hot, wet, and insistent, I moan softly into his mouth eliciting a groan from him in return. I can feel from more than his kiss, just how much he wants me.

When he pulls away, he looks into my eyes without a word. Waiting. I succumb. "I'll move my stuff over after Katie leaves."

He smiles and laughs, "Please tell me it will always be that easy to convince you to do things my way."

"You wish." I tell him but secretly, I think he could probably do much less and I'd give him whatever he wants. I'm completely captivated by him.

Looking over his shoulder, our friends are all looking our way, but I could care less. Asher is talking about other ideas he has for us this week and I find that I really can't wait for each and every moment. I do deserve this. And I'm going to make the most of it.

This time, when our lips meet again, it's me that initiates, and I can feel the doubt fade from my mind, eagerness to live in the moment overcoming everything else.

Chapter 13

When Katie left to go back to New York my room felt empty and stagnant. It's amazing how much life she brings to everything she touches. We enjoyed the rest of the day yesterday at the pool. When Asher and I emerged from the water, she wouldn't stop smiling at us. She even snuck me a thumbs up when he wasn't looking. We chatted off and on, light-hearted, easy talk, staying as long as we could until Katie and I left to spend some one-on-one time together before she left the next day. Asher gave me a lingering kiss goodbye and then took off with Hunter and Andy.

After a morning of sleeping in, Katie and I enjoyed lunch the next afternoon, took a walk on the beach, and then went back to the room so we could finish her packing. Receiving several hugs before she caught her shuttle to the airport that evening she made me promise to check in whenever I could. She also quoted me some commandment she made up about spending a week 'sexing it up' with Asher – I don't even remember what it was exactly. She basically said anything and everything she could think of to get me to abandon any reservations I have about the week.

The thing is, there's no convincing needed. I don't have many reservations, I've already decided to give into the week and let go, but that doesn't mean my nerves are obeying my internal instructions to calm down. It's all a bit overwhelming. Sitting on the bed, I'm unsure of how to proceed. Asher asked me to move into his room, and I will, but putting my stuff together and walking over there feels extremely bold. Taking several deep breaths, I do my best to brush off the doubt and begin gathering my things. The whole time I'm mechanically packing, I'm psyching myself up to go over there and knock on the door like it's no big deal.

A knock at the door interrupts my packing. I told the front desk I was moving into another room, partly to force me to push past my nerves, but also for their convenience. Expecting a housekeeper anxious to get inside my room to begin cleaning, I'm surprised when I open the door and find Asher standing before me with a wide grin.

"Hi."

"Hi, yourself." It's hard not to look at his lips and remember our shared kisses.

"Are you all packed and ready?"

"Just about. I need to grab a few more things, then I'm ready."

"Do you need help packing anything? I'm great at folding lingerie just so you know."

"Is that right?"

"Mhm," he murmurs as he wraps his arms around me and places a kiss on my lips. "Come on, let's get you over there."

Suddenly anxious, I finish shoving things in my bag and zip it up. Asher takes my large suitcase while I grab my purse and a small tote bag and we begin the walk over to his room. It isn't too far, but Asher holds my hand the whole way and keeps looking at me with a smile.

"How was it when Katie left?"

"It was okay, I guess. I'm sad she can't stay longer, but I'm also looking forward to spending some time with you," I admit with a shrug and shy smile.

His own smile widens and his eyes shine, "Me too." When we reach his room, he holds out a hand, "Wait here." He places my bag inside the door and takes the things from my hands and walks into the room. The door closes behind him automatically so I'm unable to see what he's doing and I stand there awkwardly. He returns only moments later and before I can say a word he lifts me into his arms. "I need to carry you over the threshold like a proper husband." My hands go around his neck and I laugh at the excited look on his face.

He sets me down and gives my rump a pat. "Alright, do you want to unpack anything or can it wait for a bit."

"No rush. It can wait."

"Great, I took the liberty of ordering us dinner and it arrived just before I went over to get you. I thought we could enjoy a quiet dinner in and maybe order a movie. Is that alright with you?"

Jitters flutter in my tummy, but I cover them with a nod, "Sounds perfect."

He takes my hands and leads me further into his suite. The layout is like a small apartment. A full kitchen, small dining area, larger living room, two bedrooms and two bathrooms full of beach décor make up the space. It's more than he needs not that that surprises me, but I'm still surprised he's staying here instead of one of the homes on the mountain at the resort above ours or at a home on the new golf course that can be rented instead. They are sister resorts, the one above family friendly as opposed to this one. Rumor has it the private homes are amazing with their own private infinity pool, lavish interiors and generous space.

Leading me to the dining room table, I smile when I see not only covered dishes of food, but wine cooling in an ice bucket. He's also somehow managed to get fresh aromatic flowers arranged at the center of the table. Lit taper candles also catch my attention. "I hope you like chicken codon bleu." He starts removing the tops of several covered dishes. "I asked Katie and she said you aren't a vegetarian so I figured chicken was safe. We also have salad and baby red potatoes."

"It looks and smells great." And it does. I didn't realize how hungry I was until the aroma of the food started permeating the air as he revealed the dishes to me. My stomach rumbles in appreciation and Asher smiles having heard.

He holds out my chair for me and then moves to his own. Placing my napkin on my lap, I grab the wine and fill my glass then his. "Thank you," he murmurs. I nod and we dig into our food. We're quiet at first as we taste everything. It's delicious.

"What other kinds of food do you like?" Asher asks me watching me with amusement, as I'm not shy about eating my fill.

"All kinds of things really. Mexican food, Italian food, Chinese, I'll pretty much try anything. I like to cook too."

"You do?"

"Yes, it's one of my favorite things to do when I have the time. And I don't just mean bake, like cookies and stuff. I mean dinner. Katie thinks it's great and a lot of times will buy ingredients for certain dishes and then beg me to cook for her."

"Wow, you must be good."

I shrug modestly, "I'm not bad. I like it. It relaxes me after a long day at work. If I'm working through an issue with work, cooking can be one of my favorite ways to figure it out."

"How so?"

"I think that when I open up my mind to the creativity needed for making certain dishes – like when I concoct my own recipes for things – it opens other creative avenues. I've solved many marketing mysteries while preparing dishes."

"Marketing mysteries?" he asks puzzled.

"Oh. That's what I do for a living. I'm CEO of a marketing firm in New York."

"CEO? Wow."

"My father left me the company when he died," I admit not wanting to suggest I worked my way up. It's never felt right suggesting that I've done so. Not that I haven't worked my ass off, but would I be CEO of the company if it wasn't for my father?

Doubtful. "Reveal Design and Marketing. I love it. I love my job. Taking someone's dream and help give it life through marketing or web design or branding, is an honor and privilege. Plus, I'm really good at it," I admit with a laugh.

"That's amazing."

Shrugging, "It's silly, but it's always something I wanted to do. I remember holding up random items as a child and making up a jingle for it. My dad used to say I could convince anyone that they needed whatever it was I was selling. I came by it honestly though. I always loved going to the office with him and watching him work. When it came time to go to college, a degree in marketing and design was a no-brainer."

"I bet your father loved that you followed in his footsteps."

"He did, definitely, but you know what? He wouldn't have cared if I decided not to. He always just wanted me to be happy. Still, I wish he had been there to see me graduate."

"He sounds like he loved you very much."

"I loved *him* very much and I miss him every single day."

"What about your mother? Does she miss him too?"

"My mother passed away from cancer when I was young. I have a few memories of her – I remember her laugh, and her long golden hair. She would let me brush it sometimes." I smile at the memory. "My father and I both were lost after she passed. I remember crying out for her in my sleep, confused about why she wasn't there." I gaze off, seeing her beautiful face in my mind, remembering how happy she and my dad were together. "It was just the two of us for a long time, so it wasn't exactly easy when he remarried."

"You don't like your stepmother?"

"That's an understatement." I shake my head, "I'm sorry, I'm just going on and on. Tell me about your family."

"I will, but first tell me why it's an understatement."

Wiping my mouth with my napkin, I set it next to my empty plate and sit back. "I'm not sure I know how to define it exactly. I think if

I had to guess I would say she never cared for the relationship I had with my father. Almost as if seeking his affection was a competition. It wasn't, but I always felt that she thought so – as odd as it sounds. I was kind to her and did my best to get along with her, for my father's sake if nothing else, but there was always coldness surrounding her; a distance that I could never penetrate no matter how hard I tried. Eventually, I just gave up."

"Did your father and her seem to get along well?"

"My father got along with everyone. But-"

"But?"

"I guess I've never really voiced this before, but I'm not sure if he truly loved her, or if it was more about companionship for him and a mother figure for me. I know that I never saw them behave together the way I saw my parent's love for one another. And that makes me sad. He deserved better." Sighing, I look away from him, "And now, if she didn't hate me before, she certainly does now."

"What do you mean?"

"My father died of a heart attack while away on a business trip. It was a shock to say the least. Equally shocking was when we found out he left nearly everything to me, including his company, upon my graduation. He only provided her with the minimum required under the law. And his will was created after he married, so it isn't like it was an old copy or something. Angelica, my stepmother, well I've never seen her so furious, so hateful. She gathered the board of directors and tried to convince them all I was too young, incapable and inexperienced to take over when I graduated, but she underestimated me. The company has done very well under me for the last few years."

"That doesn't surprise me one bit." He stands and removes our plates from the table, "And your stepsister? I'm assuming given her actions with your ex that there's no love lost between the two of you either?"

Knowing he remembers the story about my stepsister from when I told him about my broken engagement, I expect to feel embarrassment, but I don't. "No. We never hit it off. She wasn't interested in a relationship with my father or me. I think she missed her own father and didn't want a replacement. All I know is that her father had a stroke and passed away a few years before her mother met my father."

He returns to the table, "I hope you saved room for dessert." He sets down another covered dish and unveils sopapilla's with chocolate sauce.

"Wow," I say in delight looking at the divine pastry, mouth already watering. "Dessert is my favorite," I say and he laughs no doubt at the look on my face. Pushing the dish toward me indicating I should grab some, I don't hesitate. Taking a sopapilla I break it in half dipping one end into the warm chocolate sauce. It's divine and I moan in pleasure from the taste. "Oh my god," I murmur.

"Good?" he asks, his voice husky making my eyes crash into his.

"So good," I nod and watch transfixed as he dips his own pastry into the chocolate and takes a bite. His firm jaw moves slowly as if he's savoring each bite. When his tongue flashes across his lower lip, my thighs clench at the sight.

Not one to be outdone, whether his actions were contrived or not, I dip the other half of my dessert into the chocolate and begin licking it off instead of putting it into my mouth. When I dare a look at Asher, his eyes are following every move my mouth makes, his own mouth parted. "Yum," I murmur.

I'm not sure who moves first, but his mouth is on mine. His tongue lashing with my own and he kisses me like I'm the only dessert he ever cares to taste. Returning his intensity with my own, when he pulls away we're both breathless. He licks his lips, "You're right. Yum." And with that, I'm pretty sure my panties catch on fire.

He gives me a light kiss on the forehead and moves the last of the dishes onto the room service cart and pushes it into the hall. When he returns, he holds a hand out to me, "How about you unpack, change into something comfortable and we can order a movie?"

"Sounds good." He carries my suitcase into the bedroom and places it on the bed with a smile.

Grabbing the remote, he searches for the movie channels. "What movie do you want to watch?"

"You're asking me?"

"Yeah, why?"

"Oh, I don't know. I guess there's just something weird about the movie star asking for my opinion on a movie."

He laughs, "Can't handle the pressure?"

"Hell no. What if I pick something you hate?"

"Not possible."

"If you say so, but I still think you should choose."

"Okay, well at least tell me what you're in the mood for," he laughs.

We settle on a comedy and while he picks one from the list available for purchase, I hang up clothes and place them in the dresser, my things alongside his feeling surprisingly intimate. There's a double sink in the bathroom and I put my items on the clear side. When I'm finished I grab my pajamas after a bit of hesitation and go to the bathroom to change.

I wasn't sure what to wear. I mean, did I want to be sexy? It's not like I brought lingerie thinking I was going to hook up while on vacation, I removed it all from my suitcase before I left, so my options were limited aside from walking out naked and there was no way I was going to do that. I settled for pink sleep shorts that say 'dream' on the butt and a white camisole. Washing my face, I pull my hair up into a top knot and walk out into the bedroom, feeling vulnerable with a clean face and casual clothes and hair.

Asher turns toward me and his gaze glides over me from head to toe. I do the same to him, seeing he's changed into sleep pants and nothing else. He walks across the room to me and I unabashedly watch his muscles flex with his movements. Asher reaches me and kisses me on the nose. "You're beautiful," he whispers. All my trepidation melts with two words.

Taking my hand, he leads me to the bed and waits for me to climb in. Following me, he starts the movie then reaches for me, pulling me against his chest and wrapping his arms around me. Pulling back for a moment, I look at him, "Wait a minute."

"What's wrong?"

"Well, I just realized all we did is talk about my family. I want to find out more about you and your family."

He smiles, "You will. We've got time for that tomorrow."

"Okay," I tell him promising myself I will keep my mouth shut and let him talk tomorrow. I feel guilty for only talking about myself. He pulls me toward him once more and sighing deeply, I rest my head against his chest. We watch the movie together, me wrapped in his arms the whole time. Occasionally, I feel his lips in my hair pressing kisses to the top of my head. I feel comfortable, relaxed, adored, and safe. I love the way his chest feels when it rumbles in laughter under my cheek when he finds something on the screen funny. I smile and laugh too, each and every time, until eventually, the sound of his heartbeat lulls me to sleep.

Chapter 14

The next morning, Asher wakes me and instructs me to dress in my swimsuit. I quickly put one on, throw on a cute matching cover up, slip on my flip-flops and we're out the door. He insists I don't need anything else. With a backpack thrown over his shoulder, he takes my hand and leads me outside to where a golf cart is waiting to take us to the lobby so we can catch a shuttle.

"Are you going to tell me what we're doing today?" I ask feeling almost giddy about spending more time with him. Plus a surprise doesn't hurt. I like surprises – the happy kind anyway.

He places a hand on my thigh squeezing, "You'll see."

His touch ignites my skin. I can feel every impression of his fingers against my leg and the heat from them moves straight up to the center of my legs. Last night, I woke up at one point to find our limbs entwined with my head still resting comfortably on his chest. I snuggled in closer and felt momentarily strange that we hadn't done more than kiss before falling asleep together. I'm not naïve. I know that when he asked me to move into his room with him that his intentions are to share more than a few kisses with me here and there. Hell, I'm looking forward to it. I'm not sure if I feel grateful that we spent time getting more comfortable with one another last night, or disappointed we didn't do more.

Pushing the thoughts away, I decide to enjoy the ride through the city as the shuttle takes us to my mystery destination. I can't help but be fascinated by the town. Before arriving, I read a little about Cabo. While well-known by its tourists, including many in the entertainment industry, for its expanse of lovely resorts and spas and famous for its beaches, surfing, sport fishing, championship golf courses, and active night life, the rides into and through the area offers a study in contrast. In fact, the clash of pop culture and American influence with Mexican tradition provides intrigue and an interesting study. The people, whether within the resort or elsewhere are pleasant, warm, welcoming and helpful, while exuding strong Mexican culture and values. Life appears simpler; people appear unhurried, easy going, more carefree. Yet, traffic is busy and more congested than one might expect enabling candid visuals.

Outside of the mainly touristy areas are closely cluttered, often wood shuttered, pastel to the occasional brightly colored adobe or cement block homes, sometimes roofless, capture my attention. What appears to be towels or similar laundry are often hanging over wood banisters. Similarly, laundry adorns clothes lines in backyards. As we get close to the tourist areas, what seems like unusual numbers of local people, stand on street corners or in front of local shops. Flea markets peer out between shops and on street corners. Occasional street vendors selling jewelry and handmade art can be seen. Enmeshed between traditional establishments and local art galleries are places like Senior Frogs, Cabo Wabo and Hard Rock Café. Tourists, distinguishable in both dress and hurried walk, carry their purchases in simple plastic bags. The view provides quite a visual experience.

It isn't long before the shuttle pulls into a resort called the Rosé. Asher tells me that this resort is a sister to the one we are staying as he helps me step down from the van and ushers me through the resort lobby. We walk with intention and move directly through the open doors in the back of the vast lobby and emerge looking at a huge swimming pool. It's then obvious that the hotel is shaped in a large U. The lobby area takes up the small vertical curve at the bottom of the U while the horizontal lines are comprised of rooms along both sides. The swimming pool is smack in the middle of it all, and runs the entire length of the resort – it's huge. A restaurant sits astride one side. Steps both from the restaurant and the end of the pool lead to the beachfront.

The pool is already crowded though it's barely mid-morning, several people already occupying lounge chairs. Sporadically positioned around the pool are wooden huts - some expose various merchandise, others contain art activities. We pass several, most with different items for purchase - jewelry, suntan blocks and oils, snack food, towels, even snorkels and goggles; two contained various shaped and types of ceramics to paint. No one actually entreats us to make a purchase, but smiles of encouragement abound.

The main attraction is a stone statue of the very naked God of the sea himself, Neptune. He must be at least eight feet tall and is looking out at the pool before him while holding his trident at his side. People wait in lines to take photos with him although I have no idea how they are getting all of him in the photo. No matter where you're standing, it seems as if Neptune is watching you – rather creepy really. I briefly think of Katie and smile knowing she would have something sarcastic to say about Neptune's very large member.

Stopping at another wagon that looks like a mini office, Asher hands me a sunblock canister from his backpack, "Here, why don't you start putting this on while I take care of something really quick."

"Okay," I nod and smile taking the can from him. Walking to an empty chair, I remove my cover up and start spraying every reachable spot on my body with the sunblock. The sun can be fierce and while I want my fair share, I certainly don't want a sunburn to interfere with other shall I say, opportunities. When I'm finished, I look to Asher to find that the man he's talking to is writing something down, but Asher's eyes are completely on me. Sunglasses perched on top of his head he's got his arms crossed over his chest, which makes his biceps bulge. His intense eyes rake my body, making me feel as if I'm naked. Chills run over me from the heat in his gaze, and I like it. He clearly finds me attractive, and it feels good. Suddenly, Asher's intense look turns into a frown. Before I can wonder about it too long someone speaking distracts me.

"Excuse me, miss?"

Breaking eye contact with Asher, I turn to find a man smiling coyly at me. He's shirtless, wearing navy swim trunks, and his blonde hair sticks up in spikes all over his head. He's muscular, and certainly attractive, but has nothing on Asher. "Yes?"

"I saw you spraying sunblock on yourself and thought it wouldn't be right if I didn't offer to help you."

"Help me?" I ask confused.

"I thought I'd spray your back for you since you can't reach it, if you'd like. I'd hate for you to get sunburnt because you miss the middle. My name is Brandon by the way, and you are?"

"She's my wife," Asher answers to my surprise before I have a chance to respond. His eyes are intensely focused on Brandon. "And I'll be taking care of her sunblock, and anything else she needs, thanks."

Brandon looks immediately to Asher and holds up his hands in retreat, "Sorry man, my bad."

"Yes, it is," Asher replies, possessiveness clear in his tone and the look on his face. It excites me and I'm not ashamed to admit my core clenches with desire.

"Sorry again," Brandon says as Asher takes the sunblock can from me and wraps an arm around my waist. Brandon starts to walk away but not before looking at Asher again and doing a double take. "Hey. Are you… yes it is… dude, you're Asher Charming. Oh my god, I'm a big fan. I've seen all your Jack Danger movies."

Asher flashes a brief smile, "Thanks. Sorry to run, but my wife and I have somewhere to be."

"Yeah, no problem man. Wow. Asher Charming. Sorry for hitting on your wife."

Asher nods and waits for me to grab my cover up off the chair before we begin walking toward the stairs that lead to the beach. "Sorry," he mumbles looking embarrassed, "not that I should be surprised. But I'm still sorry."

"Why?"

"I didn't much care for sunblock boy back there wanting to give you a hand. Not that I should be surprised. Do you have any idea how amazing you look in that bikini?"

Looking down at the pink, orange and white paisley and floral halter suit I'm wearing, I feel pleasure wash over me at his words. "Thank you, and don't apologize. A second more and I think Brandon would have been spraying me down whether I wanted him to or not. I probably would have passed out from the fumes."

Chuckling, Asher nods and finishes applying sunblock on my back. Then I return the favor before we begin walking down the beach, to where, I have no idea. I walk beside him, barefooted, thankful the sand isn't hot yet, and absorb the view of the ocean. We pass lounge chair after chair of sunbathers. Many others stand individually or in small groups; others play games of Frisbee, four square, or beach volleyball on the sandy ocean front. Looking down the beach, I see a few flying kites while others sit, making sand castles. Women, men and even some children of all ages walk up to us and entreat us to purchase various types of merchandise. I'm blown away by how much they can carry at one time. Blankets, jewelry, toys for children that fly into the air, beach towels. One woman even has hanger after hanger on her arms of dresses and sarongs.

We politely decline each person until a little girl no more than the age of six walks up to us and places a bracelet against Asher's wrist. She doesn't say a word; it's a silent plea to purchase something from her. Asher immediately halts in his tracks and drops to his knees.

"How much, sweetheart?" She stares at him and he asks her again, this time in Spanish. "¿Cuanto, amor?"

She smiles and replies, "Tres dòlares."

He looks at me, "Which one would you like, princess?"

Smiling, I lean down to the little girl and quickly browse through her treasures. I wonder if she made them, and ask Asher, "You can speak Spanish?"

"Just enough to get by."

"Can you ask her if she made these?" I ask running my finger along the tightly braided and wrapped bracelets imagining the hours she and her family put into the task.

Asher points at the bracelets and says, "¿Tú las hiciste?" The little girl nods and Asher and I both smile. This time I know enough to say, "Muy hermoso." Very beautiful.

She smiles shyly, "Gracias."

Because it reminds me of the ocean, I pick out a teal and royal blue bracelet and hold it to my wrist. "I love this one." Asher selects two others and then digs his wallet out of his backpack, handing the little girl a twenty-dollar bill. When she tries to give him change in pesos he shakes his head no. Smiling widely, she tells us thank you and scampers off, likely to go brag to someone about her profit.

"You just made her day, I think." Asher smiles and shrugs, placing the other two bracelets in his backpack along with his wallet before zipping it up once more. "Will you tie this on me?" I ask holding the bracelet to my wrist again, and he complies. When it's on tight, I shake my wrist around smiling at how it looks. "Thank you, for the bracelet."

"It's not a big deal, but you're welcome," he says kissing me on the nose and I wrinkle it in response. He shakes his head at a couple other people that approach us to see if he's interested in purchasing from them too, likely after seeing him pay the little girl.

We continue our walk and before long we finally arrive at a large tent on the beach. There are men standing around underneath holding clipboards, there's a few tables and chairs, life vests hanging from the top of the tent and a half dozen personal water craft – Wave Runners, Ski Doos, Sea Doos, Jet Skis and the like, just waiting for riders. Realizing what we're about to do, I look at Asher and smile widely jumping up and down while clapping my hands. "Are we going out?" I ask while pointing at the watercrafts.

He rolls his eyes at me in humor likely because it's pretty obvious that's what we're doing. I just keep clapping and he laughs, then turns to talk to one of the workers. While he's doing that, a young man comes up to me, smiling shyly and shows me where I can stash my cover up, then fits me for a life vest. After I'm vested I'm given a list of rules and a waiver to sign. Asher's already signed his and he's got a vest on too. Looking into my eyes, his lips half curled in a smile, he leans toward my ear slowly and whispers, "Damn. You're even hot in a life vest. Maybe they'll let us take it with me when we leave." Feeling pleasure at his words I playfully push him away, but he grabs my hand and kisses it. I continue to feel his lips even after they're gone. Ready?"

"Yes!" I reply exuberantly, which makes him laugh. I don't even care, I've always wanted to ride one of these but never had an opportunity so I can barely contain my excitement. I listen closely as a worker tells us how the wave runner works. He points out where the speedometer is, how to speed up and go slower, tells us what to do if either of us should fall off, and reminds us that we aren't allowed to go near the rocks and points to the perimeter area once more. Finished with the instructions, we climb on and two men come to each of our crafts and push us out into the water. We're supposed to glide until we're individually given a go ahead to start the engine, press on the gas, and then head on out.

As soon as I'm given the go ahead, I immediately take off, standing in my urgency, as if it will make me go faster. I'm anxious to feel the wind in my hair and the cool water splash my face. Keeping my runner facing straight, I easily glide over the water further and further away from the shore and other watercraft activity. I'm exhilarated by the speed as my runner skims the surf faster and faster and find myself laughing out loud over and over as I soar over the water like it's not even there. Occasionally, I catch the front or backside of a wave and the front of my runner hits it making a large splash into my face. I squeal with laughter every time.

Finally remembering Asher, I slow down, turn my runner around and look for him. I grin as I quickly locate him, not too far behind me wearing a wide smile of his own. I slowly release the throttle, idle, and wait for him to reach me.

"Hell woman," he laughs as he slows and circles me. "One minute I'm looking back at the guy to watch for his signal to go, the next I turn around and look only to stare at your cute ass as it flies away!" He cracks up and makes me laugh too.

"I'm sorry, I was so excited I didn't even think. I've always wanted to do this! Thank you so much! This is the best surprise."

"We're just getting started, princess. Come on, let's go!"

Without another word he takes off and I follow his lead, leaving space for the worst of his wake, laughing as we pick up speed. There are a number of other people on watercrafts as well and as we pass each other they create various sizes of wakes. Depending on their size and proximity to us, at times we're splashed in the face with salt water and I blink my eyes quickly to clear them. With each splash I can hear Asher's laughter drifting on the breeze and it makes me smile so hard my cheeks hurt. I realize he can probably hear my enjoyment as well, depending on the direction of the wind.

He's heading toward The Arch, or El Arco, a landmark here in Cabo San Lucas. It's a distinctive natural taffy-colored lofty rock formation that rises out of the water and is itself the extreme southern end of Mexico's Baja California peninsula, where the Sea of Cortez flows into the Pacific Ocean. It's also knows as "Land's End" and is a popular tourist attraction. When I won the vacation and did some research on Cabo, I read that The Arch is called Land's End because as a crow flies if you were to follow its line south from Cabo, you would not touch land again until you reach the South Pole. In fact, it is the focal point of many souvenir pictures. Moreover, when Katie and I went shopping together there were several paintings, statues, and other trinkets depicting the landmark making it clear the residents are proud of their Arch.

Getting as close to it as we can, it's very impressive and I feel very small and almost insignificant in its presence. "Ella, look!" Asher calls to me and I follow the direction he's pointing.

"Are those...? Oh my gosh!" There are gray seals on the rocks at the bottom of the arch. Some are sunbathing, a few repeatedly diving into the water and resurfacing. They are keeping a happy distance from people, but seem to be undaunted by our presence. Asher and I move as close as we dare. "I wish I had a camera so I could take a picture." I can see their dark eyes and whiskers from here. Asher's floating so close to me our runners bump into each other, but we just glance at each other and smile before looking back at the seals. A few barks from them make me smile wider, "They are amazing."

"They are." With a final look at them, Asher gives me a sly look. "I've got a proposition for you."

"Another one? I don't know if I can handle more."

"Don't worry, princess, I'll do all the handling. You just hang on for the ride."

"Clever," I tell him with a lift of my brows.

He simply smiles mischievously, "Come on! Race you!" Before I can reply he takes off spraying me in the process and I scream from the cold water. Pushing the hair out of my face, I race after him. I even get to my feet again, feeling more in control and instinctively aware that it will assist me with turns even if it doesn't really make me go faster. He looks back for me a few times, and I can see he's laughing. We continue on like this for a while – he shows off and does zigzags, and goes so fast I don't even try to catch up. Eventually, we slow down and drift next to each other once more.

"I can't believe you didn't let me win!" I teased.

He grimaces but I can see his mouth twitch with humor, "Oh shit. Does this mean I totally won't get to have my way with you now?"

I gasp in mock protest, "How dare you sir! I am a lady."

"A lady, huh? Funny, I don't remember you being very ladylike the other night."

Gasping louder this time, I feign anger, "You offend me! See if you get a repeat now."

"I can be persuasive," he says with so much heat in his gaze that it ignites a fire in my belly. Without a doubt, those words are a promise.

"This is so much fun," I tell him needing to switch topics - for now.

He gives me a long look before accepting the change in subject. "I have a couple of these in California, but I don't take them out nearly as much as I would like."

"Too busy?"

"Yeah, I have been lately. I forgot how much fun they are."

"I can tell you've done this before. I'm too afraid to crank it as high as you are. You were flying."

"What? How fast have you gone?"

"I've gotten it up to thirty five miles per hour."

"Aw, come on. I bet you can get it up to at least forty, forty-five."

I wrinkle my nose unsure, but shrug, "I can try."

"Come on," he says. Off we go again, racing in the opposite direction, being sure to stay within the several miles long perimeter we have to work with. I accelerate even more and push past my fear and get it to forty, but immediately back off the throttle and let it fall back down again. Such speeds make me feel as if I'm going to fly off. I have a vision of my body flying airborne above the craft as I do my best to hang onto the handles. Yikes, no thank you. I'd prefer to not fall into the ocean. Especially so far out here. With my luck… well best not to push it.

"How'd you do?" Asher asks when we slow down once more.

"I got to forty that time."

"That's my girl!" he laughs and pumps the air making me laugh.

"Oh! Asher! Look!" I saw a disturbance in the water and thought it was a fish jumping at first. I'd seen a few do that while riding, but realize it wasn't a fish at all, they're turtles. The water is clear enough that we can see them moving under the surface.

"Cool. I see three?"

"Four!" I say pointing at another.

We watch until we can't see them any longer. "We need to start heading back," Asher tells me and I nod. We only had an hour and the time flew by so quickly. As we turn and face the shore, it's crazy how tiny everything looks from this distance. When you're having fun and just going with the flow, you don't realize how far out you really are. As we make our way back, I'm not sure how Asher's able to tell which direction we're supposed to go, but I follow him as he brings us immediately perpendicular to the tent where we need to return. As we get closer, workers come forward and help push us onto the shore and then help me get off.

"Fun, senorita?" The man helping me asks.

"Yes! It was a blast! Thank you so much!" I tell him wobbling a little as I make my way across the sand. He smiles and nods at my exuberance, kindly grasping onto my elbow, but then Asher comes and takes my hand. Under the tent we remove our life vests, get our things, and head back down the beach toward the Rosé. This time we aren't in a hurry and we walk along the shore, dragging our feet in the water. Asher holds my hand the whole time and doesn't let go. It feels right, my hand fitting perfectly in his.

At one point the water suddenly pushes to the shore roughly and before we know it we're up to our knees. Laughing, I squeal at how cool the water is now that I'm underneath it. Having stood still for a moment when the water came in, my feet are instantly buried in the sand. "I'm stuck!" I tell Asher and with a laugh, he comes and pulls me out.

We make our way back up the steps when we reach the Rosé and stop at their showers to wash the sand off our bodies before venturing forward. He holds my cover up as I wash and then I hold his backpack while he does. "There's a restaurant here," Asher points at a place attached to the hotel with a large patio that sits on the beach. "We can eat there, or we can sit by the pool and order food from one of the waiters. Do you have a preference?"

"Hmm, I vote for laying in the sun and eating by the pool. Is that okay with you?"

"Absolutely," he smiles. He pulls his hat out of his bag again and I wonder briefly if he's worried about being recognized, but the thought passes when he grabs my hand once more and leads me to a couple lounge chairs after we grab some fresh towels from a wagon supplying them for guests. While I get myself situated, Asher flags down a waiter and gets menus for us. "What looks good?" he asks looking over at me from his chair.

"Everything," I answer honestly, laughing at how hungry I am.

We decide to order all kinds of appetizers to share - a cheese quesadilla, chips and salsa with guacamole, and mini chimichangas with all kinds of sauces to dip them in. Sounds good to me. Asher also orders us margaritas and waters and my stomach growls again in anticipation.

"Thanks again for taking me to ride the wave runner." I tell him for probably the twentieth time, but I can't help it. I still can't believe how much fun that was.

"I'm glad you enjoyed it," he smiles at me and leans toward me with anticipation. I smile and kiss him gently on the lips. He sighs deeply when I pull away, "That's all the thank you I need." Kissing him is amazing and just a simple brush of his lips against mine makes me crave so much more. I think I could kiss him all day.

He tugs on his hat again before taking my hand in his once more. This time, I have to ask, "Are you worried about being recognized?" I ask him keeping my voice low.

"No, not really. Why?"

I point at his hat, "You keep tugging on your hat, pushing it down and I thought maybe that was why. I'm sorry, I didn't think. If you would have preferred going back to our resort or eating in the restaurant in a private booth or something, we can see if we can get the food to go."

"No, no, no. I don't want to do that. I'm happy right where we are. And for the record, I love that you didn't think about that."

"What do you mean?"

"I mean, spending time with someone that isn't demanding of my time, wanting to know what project I'm going to do next and if I want to endorse this item or that. Getting called about presenting at award shows, getting invitations for event after event that I'm expected to go to, having to act perfect in public and constantly make sure I say and do the appropriate things so the press doesn't take and twist shit all around is exhausting. It's so fucking exhausting, and I know you're probably thinking 'oh, poor baby' so I'll just stop talking now."

"No, I wasn't thinking that at all. I was thinking that all those things sound like work, not pleasure, and that it must be tiring having to put on a perfect face all the time."

"It can be. I just want to be me. And I'm certainly a long way from perfect. And being with you, I feel like I can just be. You don't appear to be caught up in all the celebrity shit other than just basic curiosity."

"That's because I don't really care about it. I mean, don't get me wrong, when I found out whom you were, I kind of freaked out. But, that's because I've enjoyed your movies and I've never met a celebrity before. But, for the record, I would have wanted to talk to you whether you were an actor or if you were a...a.... mime." He lifts a brow at my occupational choice and I shrug. "Okay, well maybe not a mime, they're kind of creepy, but you know what I mean. I don't care if you're famous or not."

He chuckles softly and the sound makes me shiver. It's the sound I heard at the pool and at the fire pit. I love that sound. "Well back to your original question, the only concern I have is not wanting anyone to interrupt our time together." He opens his mouth to say more, but closes it instead.

"If that happens, we'll just leave." He nods and squeezes my hand, and I find myself staring at him. His eyes are covered with his aviators but I can tell he's looking around the pool. He's taking in the people around us, and I don't blame him, there's a lot to see. Not only the people, but the architecture of the hotel itself is eye catching. The resort is a Greco-Roman design and actually a pale pink color, thus the name I suppose. Gleaming domes, several marble busts, and rows of palm trees provide visual stimulation. Not to mention all the room patios with people hanging out. Some just relaxing, others sunbathing. "Can I ask you a question?"

"Of course."

"Why aren't you all private and holed up somewhere in some ridiculous beach house that's way too huge for only you and staying away from everyone?"

He laughs, "Well, if I did that, I never would have met you."

"That's true."

"Not my style. Never has been. My friends and family give me a hard time sometimes because they think I should live it up, but even though I could do that if I wanted to, I'm not interested. If it can be helped anyway."

"Helped?"

"Well, sometimes I call in a favor or two. Like dinner last night, that meal wasn't completely on the menu. If I want tickets to a sporting event, I confess I've cashed in on that. And my assistant calls the places I travel ahead of time to make my reservations for me. He tells the managers that I'll be visiting, making sure my accommodations are arranged and to give the managing staff a heads up. That way if an incident presented itself they would be able to hustle me out or handle it appropriately."

"Has that ever happened to you? A situation that needed handling?"

"A couple times," he shrugs. "Sometimes I get recognized and people get a little excited." He says this so casually that he gives the impression it isn't a big deal at all, but I can tell by the tightening of his jaw that he feels otherwise.

"Wow, I can't even imagine what that must be like."

"It can be scary if it gets really out of hand, but mostly it's just strange. I would rather do what everyone else is doing, be where everyone else is. It can get lonely otherwise. I fly under the radar whenever possible – I don't want to be treated differently, but at the same time, the status has come in handy a few times."

With that, our food is delivered and Asher pushes his chair over until it's touching mine. We eagerly remove the silver metal lids from the plates and dive in. We make sounds of contentment, laughing at one another in the process.

After chomping on a chip with guacamole so good I could eat a vat of it, I ask Asher another question. "How did you get into acting?"

His face immediately flushes and he grimaces. "You're full of questions."

"Uh oh, is this a bad one? You don't look too happy that I asked it, but I'm sure it's something you get asked a lot."

"It's not a bad question, it's just that the answer is embarrassing."

"I really can't imagine you have anything to be embarrassed about. You are Jack freaking Danger, action actor extraordinaire." I pop another bite into my mouth and chew happily.

"Oh, is that what I am?"

"Isn't it?" I ask taking a sip of my margarita.

"No," he shakes his head. "No it isn't. I'm just me. I like to read when I'm not working. Love football season, and have my own fantasy football league I run with my friends. I'm a fan of the band One Republic, am a big fan of Robert Redford, and would like to train for a marathon some day. My family and friends mean a lot to me. They keep me grounded, which trust me princess is a good thing because Hollywood is fucking weird. And yeah, I've got a good looking face and I fill out a suit well, and hell, I love my job, but it's just something I do. Not who I am."

"I know that, Asher. I didn't mean to suggest otherwise with my comment before."

"I know and you didn't."

"Well, so far, I'm liking who you are. A lot," I tell him emphasizing my words. He leans over and presses his lips to mine. This time, I part my lips for him and his tongue meets mine. He tastes like the salt from his margarita. The kiss isn't long, but it definitely brings home my words to him before – I like him. When he pulls away, I can't help but smile.

"Why are you smiling?" he asks, lips curved up in the corner.

"Because I'm excited to hear the story about how you got into acting." He groans and the small smile drops from his face. "I can tell by the way you blush that it must be a good one."

"I don't blush."

"Yes, you do."

"No, I don't."

"Stop trying to distract me and answer the question."

"Did you know you're sexy when you're bossy?"

"Asher! If you don't tell me I'm just going to look it up later. I'm sure there's all kinds of information readily available on the Internet. And then I'd only have someone else's version."

He groans again, louder this time. While he may be doing it because he doesn't want to tell me something, it's sexy as hell. Even a couple women next to us glance over toward him, their eyes not leaving him once they find the source. "Okay, I'll tell you but you can't laugh."

"Okay, I won't laugh," I tell him automatically hoping I'm being honest.

"Um, well, see, there was this commercial I was in."

"Wait, wait, how did you get the commercial?"

"I was in college and just needed some extra money. A buddy of mine told me that commercials or modeling gigs pay a lot of money, so on a whim I went to an audition. Believe it or not, I was cast in the commercial and when a casting director saw it air, he contacted the director and asked for my phone number."

"I bet that was a crazy phone call."

"Yes, I didn't believe them at first and thought it was one of my buddies pranking me. Anyway, he asked me to come in and read for a part in a movie. It wasn't a big role, but I guess I had the look they were searching for. Seems silly now, but I swear it's the truth. When they offered me the part, I had to rush to find an agent because I needed help with the contract and all that. Next thing I know, I'm in a movie called Strain. Which is kind of ironic, really."

"Why is that ironic?"

"Because the commercial was for a constipation solution." He blurts the sentence out fast and it happens to come while I'm drinking a sip of my water. That water, flies out of my mouth in a spray a sprinkler would envy. Asher looks at me in surprise, and then I begin to laugh. "Hey! You said you wouldn't laugh at me!"

"It's your fault," I tell him in between gasps for air. "You're the one that made the joke about strain and constipation." He shakes his head, but his eyes are twinkling with mirth. "Who would have thought that a constipation cream commercial would have brought you such a stream of good luck?" I snort in laughter. "See what I did there?"

We laugh and while looking at the crinkles in the corners of his eyes, his beautiful smile and the husky sound of his laugh that I love so much, suddenly this moment is surreal. If anyone had told me that someday I would be sitting in Cabo San Lucas with Asher Charming laughing over constipation I would never have believed it. It's gross and yet incredibly funny.

"That was a really bad joke," he says when we stop laughing.

"It was. And also, full disclosure, Ash?" His smile widens likely from my shortening of his name. "I'm totally looking up that commercial on the internet. I bet you anything it's out there."

"You better not!" he exclaims.

"If I had my phone I would totally be looking right now. Roaming charges be damned."

"Not cool, princess. Not cool."

We smile at each other and I find myself wishing the day would never end.

Chapter 15

We hang out at the pool for a few hours talking about some of our favorite movies, actors and actresses. He finds my love of chick flicks amusing and swears to star in one just for me. On the way back to the resort, I rest my head on his shoulder. It seems silly, but both of us are exhausted. The sun's rays have sucked up all of our energy and we're left feeling drained. When we arrive back to the room, I look longingly at the bed.

As if reading my mind, Asher says with a yawn, "I'm thinking a nap before dinner would be nice. What do you think?"

I can't agree fast enough as his yawn makes me yawn too, "Sounds like a perfect idea."

We don't take time to disrobe or shower, we just kick off our shoes and crash on the freshly made bed. He pulls me into his arms and I smile at the feeling and think about maybe letting my hands wander a bit. That's the last thing I remember until I wake up a little while later. For a few minutes I enjoy the feeling of being in his arms again. Twilight is upon us casting the room in shades of deep gold and amber, the effect soothing and I could probably go back to sleep if I just shut my eyes, but knowing I won't sleep a wink tonight, I restrain. Otherwise I could be tired and cranky tomorrow, not what I want. Since Asher is still resting, I slide out of bed as quietly as possible to use the restroom and take a shower before I get changed for the dinner reservations Asher told me we have.

Charming

Shutting myself in the bathroom, I relieve my bladder then start the shower water. While waiting patiently for it to warm, I disrobe and then check myself out in the large mirror above the double sinks. Looking at the front of my body, then the back, it appears my sunblock job and reapplication was a good one. I'm a little pink on my shoulders, but I'm turning a nice tan everywhere else. The freckles on my face, shoulders and back are out in droves; the ultra violet rays I've been catching have brought them out of hiding.

Moving my eyes down my body once more, this time I view myself with a critical eye. I run my hands over my full breasts, thankful they sit high and proud. Holding my arms out at my sides, I view the toned lines and my jutting collarbone. My tummy is slightly rounded and my hips are curvier than I'd prefer, and my thighs will never have a gap between them, but there isn't much I can do about that now. Besides, men love curves, right? And Asher and I have already been intimate, not to mention I've been prancing around in a bikini, so where the hell are these nervous feelings of inadequacy coming from? My body has never bothered me before.

With a sigh of disgust at myself for my feelings of insecurity, I turn away from my reflection and open the door to the shower and step inside. The resort supplies bottles of shampoo, conditioner, and body wash but I brought my small travel bottles with me too. I am however intrigued by the sight of Asher's products and can't help but pick them up and smell them. Instantly, his musky delicious scent wafts from the bottles and I consider rubbing it all over my body, but not wanting it to seem strange if I walk out smelling just like him, I refrain.

Quickly washing my hair and body, I turn the shower off and begin the process of drying my hair and applying makeup. I've got getting ready down to thirty minutes, which includes getting dressed, not bad if you ask me. While I'm finishing up my makeup, my phone which I brought into the bathroom with me, rings flashing

Katie's face. With a smile already on my lips I answer the phone knowing she can hear it in my voice.

"You're calling me already?" I tease.

"Sorry, Mrs. Charming, I just can't stay away. How are you doing?"

"I'm doing fine, and don't call me that."

"Whatever, I'm totally going to call you that while I can. Soooo, whatcha' doing? Have any sex stories to report to your bestie yet?"

"Oh my god, Katie. Is that why you're calling me? You just left yesterday!"

"Yeah, exactly. What the hell good is a rebound if it doesn't include sex? Besides, my leaving was almost a whole twenty-four hours ago. Do you know how much sex can be had in that time? All the sex, Ella. All the sex."

"You're insane."

"That sounds like it's coming from a woman that needs to get laid. What the hell is going on there? Don't tell me you bailed. Oh my god, did you? I'll fly back and wring your neck myself if you did. What other reason would you have for not sexing up that hot piece of ass?"

"We just cuddled last night. And we've been gone all day today." I tell her about our day and she listens intently. Then, I finally confess, "I just had an insecure moment and was inspecting my body in the mirror. Is my stomach too round? It is isn't it? And aren't thigh gaps the thing right now? I don't have one, you know. Why didn't you say something? I spent all day long in a bikini with him. Now you're telling me to get naked?" I feel like I can't breath; panic is making me light headed.

"Oh my god, who are you and what have you done to my best friend Ella? You're being insane. Inhale and exhale a few times will you? You're hot and you know it. You're just nervous, now tell me why. I mean, you already boned him, so he's already seen you naked."

"Boned, Katie, seriously?" She just laughs and I roll my eyes. "He saw me naked when we were both drunk. He probably had no idea what he was seeing."

"Oh please, girl, that's ridiculous. Knock this shit off. You were unhappy and basically just friends with Jeremy for three years, you're single now. Live it up, will you? You are a sexy and confident woman and Asher goddamn Charming asked you to spend the week with him. It sure as hell isn't because you're the only girl that would have been available or hell, willing to do so."

"Oh, that makes me feel so much better," I grumble.

"It should. Of all the people he could have approached at the beach that night, he walked up to you. Right?"

"Right," I tell her slowly starting to feel more confident and silly over the fact I was being so insecure. But then it hits me. This isn't because I'm nervous to be with Asher. The chemistry between us is off the charts and just thinking about being with him again makes my thighs clench together. This is because of all the shit with Jeremy. It's not because I'm still hanging on to feelings for him or feeling like I'm not ready to move on, this is because his affair has made me doubt myself. Why the hell am I letting him have that control over me? He doesn't deserve to have any impact on me whatsoever. I'm being so stupid. I tell Katie my realization and add, "Part of me thinks that if I wasn't enough for a loser like Jeremy, then how am I enough for Asher?"

"Babe, you can't compare them. That's not fair to you or Asher. What happened with Jeremy was because of something inside of *him*. It didn't have anything to do with you. He was unable to handle an independent woman and wanted someone that would hang onto his every word and be completely reliant on him. You aren't that kind of woman, thank god. He's pathetic and you should count your lucky stars that you saw the light with him."

"Yes," I tell her more emphatically, "you're right. And I am *so* going to get my sex on." My voice is confident, but not too loud because I would die if Asher heard me.

"Hell yes you are. My job here is done. I knew I felt a need to call you for a reason."

"I'm glad you did."

"Me too. Now don't overthink it again. Go with the flow. If it happens, it happens, if it doesn't, okay. But take a deep breath, enjoy the attraction between the two of you and go be a unicorn."

"Did you say a *unicorn*?"

"Yes. A unicorn. Go get your horn on. Get it?"

"Oh my god."

"I know, right? I'm amazing. In fact, I think I'm going to put that on a t-shirt. No wait, maybe a necklace. Or a mug!"

"Alright, Katie. I'm going to hang up so you can go get started on your merchandise store."

"You laugh, but you just wait and see. You'll totally want a necklace too."

"Bye, Katie," I say while she continues to talk to herself, mumbling something about tote bags and pens and who knows what else.

"Okay, bye!" she says and I giggle.

Wrapping a towel tight around my body, I finally leave the bathroom wishing I had thought to bring clothes in with me. Stepping into the room, I find that Asher is awake and propped against the headboard flipping through the TV channels. "You're awake?"

He nods, "Have a nice shower?"

"Yes," I reply.

He finally turns to look at me and does a double take when he sees I'm only wrapped in a towel. For one crazy heart stopping moment, I think about dropping it, but I don't. He stands up and moves in front of me, his eyes devouring every exposed inch. Tracing a finger along the top of the towel, he smiles, "How likely are you to let me take a picture of you right now?"

My eyes narrow, "Not very."

He sighs regretfully, "It was worth a try." He grins and then places a soft kiss on my lips. "But seriously, it should be a sin to look this good in only a towel, princess." He runs his fingertips down the side of my arm and it leaves goose bumps in its wake. "Did I hear you talking to someone?" he asks glancing at the phone tucked in my hand.

"What?" I ask still looking at his fingers on my skin.

"Were you on the phone?"

"Oh. Yes, Katie called me."

"She okay?" he questions and I love that he even asks.

"She's great. Just checking in."

"Ah, okay. Well, I'm going to get in the shower myself and when I'm out, let's go to dinner. Sound good? You're hungry, right?"

"I am," I nod.

"Okay, I'll hurry," he leans over and gives me a lingering kiss on the lips and I can't help but feel like it's a prelude to later.

After he grabs some clothes and goes into the bathroom closing the door behind him, I rifle through my own clothes trying to decide what to wear. Selecting a coral sundress I hold it in front of me and look at myself in the full-length mirror located inside the closet door. The neckline cuts into a low v and tapers in at the waist before it falls to the tops of my feet. The right side has a slit all the up to my upper thigh – it's perfect and will definitely look amazing against my tan skin. After I'm dressed I add simple gold earrings and a bangle bracelet before sliding my feet into gold strappy sandals. I briefly think about pulling my hair up, but decide against it and swipe coral lip gloss across my lips to complete the look.

The water in the bathroom has stopped running, so I know Asher will be ready to go in no time. Walking to the window, I open the curtain a little and take in the view. The sun is setting and it's casting the sky in gorgeous orange and pink tones, I can't get enough of the sunsets here. Sighing at the sight, I'm so caught up in the vision it creates that I don't hear Asher come up behind me until his arms are wrapping around me. "It's beautiful isn't it?" I ask him.

"Yes, you are." Turning to him, I find him looking at me with a sexy smile, the look in his eyes heated.

"Thank you," I murmur then appreciate the view of him in a white dress shirt rolled up his forearms with a few buttons open at his chest. He's paired it with tan pants and sandals. The white shirt against his sun kissed skin makes his skin glow and his dark hair is styled to perfection. I watch transfixed as a random bead of water still clinging to his chest drops and disappears under the fabric. Swallowing hard, my eyes meet his. "You look very handsome." We hold gazes for a few beats before he kisses me on the forehead, then takes my hand.

"Ready? I've got dinner reservations all set."

"You think of everything."

He shrugs, "Only when it matters, and I believe great food is on our agenda this week, remember?"

"Yes, I do."

We walk to one of several alcoves on the property where a phone to call for a golf cart resides. We wait quietly on the nearby bench. When we're dropped off at our destination, Asher takes my hand. He instructed the driver to bring us to the resort above ours on the bluff, The Sunset Beach. We walk through the lobby and follow the signs to a restaurant called La Nao. A chalkboard at the entrance declares tonight seafood night, and as soon as Asher gives his name, we're led to a table in the corner on a large patio and the ocean is alongside us. We've arrived just in time to get an even more astonishing view than we had in our room of the sun's disappearing act.

After we order, I look at Asher with a smile, "So, you came here with a group of friends for a bachelor party and a wedding. I'm surprised we haven't run into anyone. Do you know what they're all up to?"

"No, not really. I'd imagine a lot of drinking, partying and whatever trouble they can find."

"Are they upset you aren't hanging out with them? I kind of feel bad for monopolizing all of your time."

"No, don't. Some of the guys have left already, and a few are still here. The bachelor party was the weekend we arrived, the wedding the day before ours," he says with a grin and I roll my eyes. "A few of us planned to stay a little longer, but it's cool, the truth is I don't care what they think. And they're likely too busy making fools of themselves to even miss me."

"Making fools of themselves, how?"

"Oh, I'm sure they're trying to one up each other in their attempts to score with random chicks."

"Ah, so hitting on girls is usually the thing you guys do together?" It's a justified question after his comment, but I almost wince. I sound slightly irritated or perhaps jealous. Am I jealous? Irritated? I don't think so. Maybe. Ugh.

He's no fool. His grin turns wicked, "Jealous, princess?"

"No," I tell him but considering my denial sounded more like a question than fact, I don't think he believes me.

"Don't worry, baby. I didn't marry any of them."

"Hmm, is that for lack of trying?" *Dammit, Ella, you still sound jealous. It's not like this marriage is even real. What is wrong with you?*

"Nope. You're the one and only. Besides, none of them had your super power."

"Super power?"

"Yep. One time between your thighs wasn't enough. I had to marry you immediately."

I gasp and giggle, "If I remember correctly, we got married before that transpired."

He laughs, "Yes we did. Good point. But it's still your fault."

"My fault? It was your idea!"

"It was, that's true, but that's only because of your eyes."

"My eyes?" I ask in confusion.

"Yes. The first time I looked into your eyes at the pool they called to me like a siren. Something in them seemed to contain the other part of my soul. I looked at you and saw my most important role yet." I'm not sure if he's serious or not, but regardless I find it hard to breathe. "Plus they also screamed fun and great sex."

Somehow I find my voice, "Oh, is that right?"

"It's true. Plus of course there was the fact that I distinctly heard you say that you'd give up your butt for me. I mean, who could pass on an invitation like that?"

My water glass practically falls from my hand and of course at that moment the waiter comes up to take our order. I choke and begin coughing. The waiter and other diners look over to make sure I'm okay. Asher gets out of his chair and rubs my back. Eventually, I calm down and somehow manage to order but I'm so embarrassed I'm shaking. An egg could be fried on my hot face it's so heated. When the waiter leaves, I wipe the tears from my eyes and try to find words, "I am so embarrassed." I put my face in my hands. "I can't believe you heard that."

His hands pull mine away from my face, "Don't be embarrassed, it was funny and I know you and Katie were drinking. Besides, don't worry, I won't hold you to it." He winks at me and I know my face must redden further because he laughs outright. "Don't be mad or embarrassed, seriously. I couldn't resist teasing you."

"Totally too late for that," I mumble still unable to look him in the face once more. He chuckles again and I simply shake my head not knowing what else to do. Somehow, and I have no idea how, I manage to change the subject, "I told you about my family. Please rescue me from my slow death from embarrassment and tell me more about yours."

A look of pure love and devotion crosses his face and if he never said another thing I would already know exactly how he feels toward them. "My mom and I are really close. I mean, how could we not be? She raised my sister and I on her own after my dad bailed when we were kids."

"Bailed? That's awful."

"It was, but my mom protected us from it as much as she could." He takes a drink of his water and clears his throat. "I only ever saw her cry over him one time, and it was the day she finally told us that he wasn't coming back. When I was walking to my room I heard a sound in hers. The door was ajar and I looked through the crack to find her sitting in a corner, knees pulled up against her chest and tears falling down her face." He looks lost in the memory for a while, his eyes unfocused.

"He just left you all? Do you know where he went?"

"No idea. He told my mom he was going to get some cigarettes and beer at the store and never came back. When he first left we asked her where he had gone and she told us he went to go visit some family. A few days later, I think when it was clear to her he wasn't returning, she sat us down and told us the truth. We never really talked about him after that and we haven't seen him since. If my mom knows where he is or what happened to him, she isn't saying, and I don't care to know."

"I don't even know what to say, Asher, I'm so sorry that happened to you."

"There's nothing to say. It's his loss, no use in being angry over it. Besides, my mom more than made up for my shitty father."

"She must be amazing that you would say such a thing."

"She is," he smiles.

Horror washes over me, "Oh god, she must be so mad at you right now."

His smile falls and I know immediately I'm correct. "There may have been a phone call with some yelling."

"Oh no," I whisper and stop myself from apologizing because it isn't my fault. It isn't his either. We both did this and it is what it is but I still feel bad. Though, I was the one who posted the wedding announcement on Facebook.

Before I can analyze it further he states fairly indignantly, "She'll get over it."

"And your sister? Did she yell at you too?"

He laughs and it surprises me. Our food is brought to the table and as soon as our waiter leaves he picks up where he left off, "Allie? No, not at all," he laughs again. "She called me and thanked me for eloping because it saved her from having to deal with attending a long drawn out wedding with my nieces."

"Did you tell them that it's just for a week? Or would that make things worse?"

"No. I didn't tell them that."

"No doubt that would only upset them further."

"I'm an adult and while I love them, my decisions are my own."

Nodding my understanding I smile and ask, "How old are your nieces?"

"Isabella is three and Francesca is five. The other two bracelets I bought today? They're for them."

"Aw, beautiful names. I bet they love their uncle very much."

"As long as I supply them with lollipops and ice cream they think I'm the best uncle ever, of course." His grin makes me laugh because it's pure cockiness.

"Of course," I laugh agreeing. "And no doubt you supply them with plenty of both."

"Absolutely. Especially since I get to give them back to my sister afterwards." He laughs, takes another bite of his food and then asks me, "Do you like kids?"

"I do. I used to wish for a little brother or sister."

"Do you want children of your own some day?"

"Definitely," I reply immediately.

"Well that's good to know, given our marriage. These are things I need to know," he says with a lift of a brow. Neat trick – my brows can't do that.

"Most people learn these things about each other *before* they get married," I joke back.

"True. But I think I prefer our unconventional way of going about this."

Rolling my eyes, I don't respond and we continue to make idle conversation. He tells me stories about the trouble he and Allie got into as children, and I tell him some of my favorite memories about my parents. It's a nice dinner and the food we eat is fresh and delicious.

When we leave the restaurant Asher takes my hand. He does that every time we walk somewhere, the gesture becoming familiar. When we walk back up to the lobby we pass a gift shop, but I stop and turn back, "Can we look for a minute? Do you mind?"

"No, not at all."

We walk inside and I take my time looking through the merchandise. Given the shop is here at the resort they have all kinds of self-promotional items with the resort name on them like shirts and hats. They also have tons of swimsuits, towels, sunglasses, and even shoes. Of course there's a ton of souvenir trinkets like magnets, key chains, and other kitschy things. What catches my eyes are the sarong wraps they have for women in many different colors and designs. Sorting through them, I select one that would look great over a few swimsuits I have. Walking over to where Asher's checking out the sunglasses we try them on and make duck faces at each other and he even snaps a few photos with his phone. Walking up to the register to pay for my swimsuit wrap, Asher takes it from my hand and pays for it, and a couple pairs of sunglasses we tried on, which elicits a protest from me. "You don't need to do that. I can pay for it myself."

"I know you can, but you're not going to."

"Um, excuse me?"

"There's nothing to excuse, princess." He pays the clerk and thanks them with a large smile before turning to me and holding the bag out for me to take. Standing with my hands on my hips I glare at him making my annoyance clear. He leans toward me and kisses my head. "Don't be mad. I wanted to buy it for you."

"It's not necessary. I don't expect you to buy me anything."

"That's exactly why I did."

With a soft sigh, I smile and give in, "Thank you."

He leans forward and kisses me softly on the lips, "You're welcome, princess." He takes my hand once more and as if on cue the golf cart arrives to take us back to our building.

We walk slowly down the walkway toward our room, but no words are exchanged between us. The tension between us feels charged – thick and laced with lust and anticipation. I wonder if tonight is the night, will he make a move? Asher unlocks the door and holds it open for me, his hand on my lower back as he guides me inside. After taking a few steps, I stop and stand still, listening to the door close behind us. The room is silent, except for the rapid sound of our breathing, and my own heartbeat pounding in my ears.

Asher approaches me, the sound of his steps on the carpet give that away, but it's the heat of his body behind me that I feel all the way to my bones. My breath hitches in anticipation, and I'm not sure what comes over me, maybe it's pushing myself past the insecurities I feel about him not wanting me, maybe it's not being able to take anymore of the sexual tension that's been between us for hours. No scratch that, it's been every second since I've met him, at the pool, at the fire pit, at the beach and since. Maybe it's just that I simply want fiery sex and passion to take me away, make me feel nothing and everything at the same time.

Spinning around, I barely catch Asher's lowered brows and a question of - concern? permission? - on his lips before I drop my purse and the bag from the store on the floor, and push Asher against the door we just walked through. It's rougher than I intend and his head hits the door and his eyes widen. Before I can doubt myself I put my mouth on his. As soon as our lips meet it's like kindle igniting. I feel the burn of his lips all the way to my toes. He stiffens and hesitates for a breath, maybe two, and then he's kissing me back. Our mouths move together in a rhythm that's solely ours and when his tongue touches mine, we both groan together, the sound music to my ears.

My hands latch themselves into his hair and I tug as I press my body forward touching it to his. His hands glide down from my waist and cup my bottom. Leaning down he lifts me up and my legs immediately wrap around his waist. Quickly he whirls around and now it's my back against the door, my heels locked around his waist, his thickness pressed against my core. Voicing my pleasure, I'm almost embarrassed by the fact that I could orgasm from this alone. When his lips leave mine, I cry in protest, but release a shuddering breath when he buries his face in my neck then kisses and nibbles his way down to my collarbone.

"I want you," I tell him.

Pulling back enough so that he can look into my eyes, he stares at me intently before turning without a word and taking us into the bedroom. Placing me gently on the bed, he removes my shoes, and then watches intently as I slide the zipper down at my side. "Wait," he says and my heart stumbles in my chest. *Oh god, what if he doesn't want this and I've just made a complete fool of myself.* "No, princess, get that look off of your face." He leans down and cups my face in his hand. "I want you probably more than you want me, but tonight, this is about you. Only you."

"What? Why? I want to be with you. I want us to be together."

"I want that too, believe me, but not yet."

I'm confused and start to zip my dress back up, but his hand stops me. His mouth meets mine again and he kisses me in a way that leaves no doubt to his words. He does want me too, so why is he waiting? I want this. He moves back enough to help me remove my dress over my head, and when his eyes burn intensely as his gaze rakes over my exposed skin I say a silent prayer of thanks for my appreciation of sexy bras and panties. The sheer and lace bra and panties that match look tantalizing against my golden skin, and from the breath he hisses out slowly, I know he appreciates the view.

He lowers his head and when his tongue licks across the line of my bra over my breast, I suck in a breath. He does the same to the other and with a noise of impatience yanks the cup of my bra down on one side exposing me and latches his mouth onto a nipple making me moan. He teases, sucks and bites gently, his tongue twirling around in whirls.

Pulling away, he quickly removes his clothes but keeps his black boxer briefs on. My eyes devour the sight and I appreciate the body he clearly works hard to have. He crawls on top of me like a tiger and I'm grinning in anticipation. "I like you in lace, princess," Asher says. "But I like you even more naked."

His hands move behind my back and he unsnaps my bra. Sliding it down one shoulder he presses kisses trailing the fabric's retreat. When he pulls it away from my skin entirely, he murmurs a curse at the sight and then his lips are licking and sucking at my breasts once more and this time it's me that hisses in response. My back arches off the bed, and my hands roam through his hair.

Pulling away, he moves to my panties next and slides them down my legs, tortuously slow, his eyes on mine the whole time. He throws them over his shoulder and a wicked smile graces his lips as he grabs hold of my legs and yanks me over to the edge of the bed making me cry out in surprise. Bending forward he places a soft kiss between my breasts. Then another at my navel before moving to my hips and placing one there. Dragging his lips across my skin, he moves to my other hip and kisses there as well. Grabbing my ankle, he begins kissing up the inside of my leg dangerously slow. Anticipation is burning in my core and I'm wet between my thighs, eager and desperate for him to take me. Instead, after he places a kiss on the crease where my leg meets my groin which leaves me breathless, he starts with my other leg. "Asher!" I admonish, but he just chuckles softly, "What, princess?"

"I…I want…I want you to kiss me."

His eyes burn into mine, "Kiss you, where?"

I hesitate before answering and then press trembling fingers between my legs, "Here."

Without removing his eyes from mine, he places his hands on my hips and pulls me a little closer to the edge of the bed before he lowers himself to his knees on the floor. His head moves toward my center, and I close my eyes in expectation, but nothing happens. Opening them once more, I find him still looking at me. He waits for a beat, his message clear, then lowers his lips to my slippery folds. At the first pass of his tongue, the sound that leaves me is almost animalistic. When he sucks, my hips buck sharply off the bed. When he nibbles, I lose any and all of my inhibitions, spreading my legs wider, silently begging him to give me more.

Asher moans and the vibration runs all the way through my body making my toes curl. My hands find his hair and I move my hips against his mouth desperately searching for release. Every stroke rockets through my body and I'm lost. I'm lost in a lust filled haze and this time when my eyes roll back in my head, Asher doesn't quit his ministration.

I'm panting, keening, and mumbling words and curses without thought. "God, yes." The feeling inside of me is building and each time I get close, Asher eases the intensity and starts all over again. My last groan of complaint makes him laugh wickedly against me and I curse at him in frustration. "Here you go, princess," he says just before two fingers enter me and curve.

Stars. I see stars. I'm so high, I can see them, touch them, pluck them right from the sky and hold onto the light I'm seeing forever. "Asher!" I yell his name, mindless with passion. He's there with me every step of the way, riding it out, making sure I feel every last drop of pleasure he pulls from me.

When he rises above my body and looks down at me, his eyes are the darkest blue I've ever seen them. Full of desire, I've never seen anything so beautiful and I know I'll desperately try to find a shade of something, anything, that will match it so I can remember it when I'm gone.

Working to catch my breath, I smile lazily at him, "That was…"

"Amazing? The best ever? Astonishing? Exciting? Brilliant?"

"Okay, okay," I cut him off with a laugh, "You're right. It was all of those things."

"For me too," he says and leans down to place a light kiss against my nose. His hardness is pressed against my thigh and my brow furrows. Running my hands down his chest and to his stomach, I intend to brush the front of his briefs and ask to return the favor, but before I can do so, he shakes his head. "Not tonight."

"But, why?"

"I wanted tonight to be all about you. We'll talk more tomorrow. For now, I just want to hold you in my arms until we fall asleep. Okay?"

"Okay." We move onto the pillows and his arms wrap around me. I've never ever had an experience with a man where all they cared about was taking care of me. It seems I'm experiencing some firsts with this man, and it feels amazing. I feel, safe, happy and content in his arms.

I feel beautiful.

Chapter 16

When I wake the next morning, it's to find Asher already dressed and sitting on the side of the bed. "Hey."

"Hey," he smiles and he's looking at me in a way I can't decipher, but I like it.

"Why didn't you wake me up?"

"I was going to in another half hour or so if you didn't wake on your own. There was no need to get you up before I had to."

"Why are you up already?"

"I couldn't sleep, had some business to deal with, and I needed to arrange our day."

"Yeah? What are we going to do?" In response he simply shrugs and gives me a mischievous look. "You're not telling me again?" I push my lower lip out and pout but he's unfazed and only reaches out and grabs my lip.

"Nope. I like surprising you."

"Well, I was thinking-"

"Uh-oh, that sounds ominous."

His cheesy retort deserves one of my own so I stick my tongue out at him and he tries to grab that too. I smack his hand away playfully. "Very funny. But seriously, I was thinking that maybe we should do something with your friends this week too. I know you said they probably don't even notice that you're gone, but we both know that's not true." His expression gives no inkling to his thoughts yet, so I press on, "I don't want them to be angry that I'm taking up all of your time. We can meet them for dinner maybe, or by the pool again, or go into town, whatever you want. It's up to you. But I don't think you should alienate them for some chick you've only known a short time and will only be with for one week."

His nostrils flare and his jaw tightens and he looks rather annoyed. He gets control of his emotions quickly, but not before it's clear how he feels and I think I've made a mistake bringing it up. I wasn't trying to suggest he's a bad friend or something, but when I'm not here, they will be. And who knows what they had planned for the week; plans that I interrupted. I don't want to create any kind of dissension, so it's the right thing to do. Or at least to offer. "We can do that I guess, although I don't enjoy the thought of sharing you with anyone."

"Oh, it won't be that bad. What's an hour or two of our time?"

"No, don't say that. Time," he begins, but stops and pulls me from bed standing me before him. Running his hands up and down my arms he's looking to the side and I can almost see the thoughts trying to form in his mind. "Time is everything. Some people take it for granted, and some would give anything for more of it. For some their time is only beginning and others, it's ending forever. Time is probably one of the most significant things we can own in our entire lives."

"I never thought about it that way."

"I didn't either until I started feeling like I didn't have a whole lot of time to myself. I've learned to appreciate it in a way I never had. Two hours of time we give to my friends matters. That's one hundred and twenty minutes. It takes what…a moment for things to happen? An event to occur, a word to be said, an action you didn't want to miss. Just one single moment in time could create a memory that lasts a life time, and I want to share all of those minutes and moments this week with you."

There's an ache in my chest at his words and if I could melt into a puddle on the floor, I would. Pressing my lips to his, I try to pour every emotion I'm feeling into our kiss. Everything I'm feeling and everything I'm not sure how to define. I kiss him gently on the lips, then the cheek, his chin, then back on his mouth once more. Pulling back I smile softly, "There, I gave myself a moment with you that I will always remember. Sweet kisses on the day I began to appreciate time in a way I never had before. Thank you for that. And, to be clear, I want to share every possible minute with you too," I tell him honestly, not even realizing how much until that moment. "But I just want you to know that if you change your mind, I would be more than happy to share a little bit of our time with your friends. But only a little," I smile.

"I'll think about it."

"Okay," I nod, then change the subject. "Alright, so tell me. What the heck should I wear for whatever we're going to do today?"

"What else? A swimsuit."

Nodding, I go off to get ready. The whole time I can't help but think about how I'm enjoying time with Asher. It's jarring how close I feel to someone I've technically only met, even though it feels like we've known each other a while. It's strange. We're so compatible. And genuinely enjoy being together. If I had to leave tomorrow I'd be devastated. I'm glad we still have some precious time together because I'm not ready to even think about going home.

Once I've got my black suit on, I throw the sarong around my waist that Asher bought me and take a look in the mirror, admiring how it looks. How I look. After I slip on some silver flip-flops, Asher walks into the bathroom. I smile at him and he returns it, then checks his hair out in the mirror. Turning his head side to side, he begins styling it to perfection and I find myself momentarily staring, cognitive of how genuinely handsome he is.

Snapping out of it, I turn to do my own hair and pull it back into a sleek ponytail. When I'm satisfied, I grab the toothpaste and my toothbrush and run it over my teeth. I smile around the brush when Asher's reflection in the mirror shows that he's brushing his teeth too. There's something intimate in the motions of getting ready together, side by side. We continue to embrace each other's reflection, unable to stop smiling. I'm not even embarrassed when I have to spit.

As soon as we finish brushing our teeth Asher pulls me into his arms and kisses me with his minty mouth. "Are you sure you want to go out and not just stay here?" I ask him with a flirty smile.

Groaning he runs his hands over my back and grabs my bottom. "Don't tempt me."

Laughing, he takes my hand, "You look great. You ready to go?"

"Yes, do I need anything?"

"Nope. I've got everything taken care of."

Asher leads me from the room and it isn't long before our taxi pulls up at a marina. Boats are parked at a wooden pier as far as the eye can see. The ocean is to our right and to the left are quaint looking restaurants and shops, clearly a touristy area. Asher takes me to a restaurant called Tico's which he claims has an excellent brunch. We're seated at the window and given menus. One glance and my mouth waters while my stomach quietly emits a hungry growl. Given my love for cooking, I don't eat out too often and I've already eaten out more on this vacation than I have in months. I'm loving it, although part of me is itching to get in the kitchen and create something.

After we order, Asher takes my hand and smiles. He opens his mouth to say something, but before he can I finally give voice to something on my mind. "Why didn't you want to have sex last night?" I'm almost embarrassed for the way I blurt it out, but I'm so curious I hardly care what he thinks about my inquisition. I can't wrap my brain around the fact that he didn't want to get something in return for the pleasure he showed me – it's an anomaly.

"Did you not enjoy last night?"

"You know that I did," I smile shyly. "It's just, I was ready and certainly willing to do more, and I guess I was surprised that you didn't feel the same way."

"You're wrong, I do feel the same way, but I don't want to push you into something you aren't ready for."

"Wait, are you not hearing me? I was more than ready. I *am* ready. I'm ready *right now.* We can forget eating and go back to our room if you want." I know I'm sounding nuts but I can't help it. Thankfully he laughs at my enthusiasm.

"Look, other than the night we were married, we haven't spoken at all about what happened to you. And well… alcohol was involved that night, so we didn't delve into the subject too deeply."

"What happened to me? What are you talking about?"

"I'm referring to your ex."

I don't know why but of all the things he could say, that's not at all what I was expecting. "What does he have to do with you and me?"

"Look, Ella," he lets go of my hand to run it through his hair. "I know that you were hurt. And the fact is, it happened very recently. I would feel like the world's biggest douchebag if I took advantage of that. I'm worried that you could sleep with me...again," he adds with the flash of a smirk, "and regret it. I would hate that. For you and for me. It's a risk I wasn't willing to take last night, but it wasn't the moment to talk about it."

Seriously, who the hell is this guy? He's the complete package - considerate, fun, intriguing, charming, and hot as hell. I'm completely taken back by his words and certainly not in a bad way. I'm bowled over that he's even given thought to this, let alone that he would even care. I mean this is a summer fling - a rebound. I guess I never really took into account that he would be worried about my feelings. It takes me a few beats before I'm able to put coherent words together. When I do, I reach forward and take his hands. Blinking rapidly to keep the tears burning behind my eyes at bay, I shake my head in wonder, "I can't even believe that you were worried about this."

Frowning he squeezes my hands, "Why?"

"I don't know, I guess I've never had a guy really consider my feelings before."

"Never? Seriously?"

"No," I shake my head as if it emphasizes my response. "Never." I hesitate only briefly before I decide to dive in and lay it all out there. "You are only the third person that I've ever been with...intimately. And I don't mean only as if that's a bad thing, it's just... well... I guess I'm trying to say that it isn't as if I'm really experienced and the experience I've had isn't the best."

"What do you mean?"

"Well, I had a high school boyfriend and it wasn't anything other than adolescent lust at its worst. We hooked up at a party. All of my friends had had sex already and I guess I gave into the pressure of thinking I should be having sex too. One night I was making out with a guy at a party and, I'll spare you the details, but losing my virginity was an awkward moment of inept limbs, sloppy kisses, and inappropriate giggles. Definitely not an experience I cared to repeat."

Laughing a little I look at Asher and see that he's not laughing, he just looks, contemplative. Taking a deep breath I push on – discussing Jeremy with Asher was never even a thought in my mind, but I know that it needs to be done so that Asher understands. The fact that it's something I need to do speaks to Asher's character because this matters to him, so I find that it also matters to me. "Jeremy, my ex, was my college boyfriend, but we met through our fathers, ironically, even though mine was gone by that time. You see, his father worked with mine, and when my father died and left me the company, while I didn't take it over immediately, I was still involved on a small scale until I graduated college. At a work function I attended, Jeremy was also there with his father; we started talking that night, and then began dating. His family loved my father, and I knew my dad valued Jeremy's father – his was a name I'd heard before. So, a relationship with Jeremy was something that just… happened. But the truth is, it shouldn't have. I realize that now. And I guess I knew it most of the time, but thought it might eventually evolve to something that my dad would have liked or wanted. It's amazing how a little distance and well, finding out your ex got another woman pregnant, gives you validation." I laugh bitterly, but Asher's jaw only tightens in response.

I tuck my hair behind my ear in a nervous gesture and look into his eyes, "I didn't love Jeremy. Not in the way a woman should love a man she's about to marry. I'm ashamed to admit it, but I realized my unhappiness and knew I was simply going through the motions long before I finally ended things. I regret that when I finally realized what I was doing that it happened to coincide with his betrayal, but it is what it is."

"What made you realize the truth?"

"You mean, besides the fact that on my wedding day, the day that's supposed to be the happiest day of a woman's life, I was anything but? There was also the fact that I drug my feet every step of the way, and barely had a hand in planning my own wedding. I was less than engaged in the entire process. And when I reflected on what my parents had, and what I wanted, there was a great disparity. Or, how about the fact that I had already decided to walk out before the ceremony began?" Asher's eyes widen and I nod my head. "I had just decided to get the hell out when my stepsister walked in and dropped the bomb in my lap. But that only reinforced the rightness of my decision. Before she uttered a word, I had already realized that I didn't love Jeremy at all and couldn't go through with a loveless marriage. I didn't want a life with him or even a friendship. I just wanted the connection that he had to my father." Tears fill my eyes and I don't try to stop them this time. "I loved my father so much, Asher. And he would be so ashamed of me."

"What do you mean? Because of us? Because you married me?"

"No, not at all," I smile at him, "he would like you a lot actually. And I know you would have liked him too. Although, he would give me hell for our wedding he would say, 'Are you loving life, Ella? Because as long as you're happy I'm happy to let you figure out your journey, whatever that entails.'"

"He sounds amazing."

"He was. But, I think he would be ashamed of me because the marriage that he had with my mother was beautiful. It was full of light and love and respect and passion. The way he looked at my mother, and she looked at him… that's burned into my memory. It doesn't matter how young I was during that time, I remember. I couldn't forget it if I tried. He would be ashamed that I thought for one second that Jeremy was good enough for me. I can guarantee he wouldn't have chalked that up to my life's journey because anyone could see that we were so wrong for each other."

He hands me a napkin and I wipe the tears that I didn't even realize had fallen down my cheeks. "So please, do not make one more decision or question anything between us because of what happened with Jeremy. He has no place here. I've been happier with you over two days than I've been with Jeremy… well since I can remember. Yes, I felt betrayed. Yes, I was hurt. But it was more about letting go of that tie to my dad, and making him proud of me, than anything else."

Asher stands from his chair and comes to sit next to me instead of across from me. Taking my face in his hands in an act that's become familiar, he places a gentle kiss on my lips. "I just didn't want to hurt you too."

Looking into his eyes for a moment, I smile then lean forward and press my mouth to his again. He opens for me and I sweep my tongue into his mouth, eager to show him without words just how fine I am and to erase any doubt from his mind. When I pull away, he has a soft smile on his lips and nods his head before he returns to his chair once more.

Our food was delivered while I was talking and Asher gave them a nod of thanks but I had never stopped talking or acknowledged it. Now I feel ravenous and dig into the food I've ordered. "Tell me more about your dad," Asher says.

"What do you want to know?"

"Tell me something that not many people know about him. Something that makes you happy."

Immediately I grin, "I know just what to tell you." I laugh as many memories flow through my mind, but one stands out from the rest.

"Well don't keep me waiting."

"My dad knew how to play the harmonica. He always had his, a silver one, tucked into his blazer pocket or the front pocket of his shirt. No one knew. It's not something he would play in public and he never put on a show, but he would play for my mom and me. I remember dancing around the kitchen as he played; he would stomp his foot in time to the music and my dancing. My mom would laugh at his enthusiasm and sometimes when I close my eyes, I swear I can still hear her."

"Did he still play it even after she passed away?"

"Yes, but not as much. I mean, as I grew up I quit dancing when he played, but he would still pull it out when he was trying to cheer me up, or sometimes he would simply hold it in his hand rubbing his thumb over it as if doing so brought back the same memories of my mother for him as they do for me. Late at night sometimes, as I would fall asleep in my room, he would play in his office and the music would drift down the hallway. I have his harmonica. It's one of my most valued treasures."

"Thank you for sharing with me."

"Thank you for asking."

Asher opens his mouth to say something else but before he can an individual sitting down at our table interrupts us. "Excuse me, but aren't you Asher Charming?"

Surprise clear on Asher's face, he takes in the woman seated to his right smiling cheerfully at him. She's scantily clad – wearing a bikini so small her double d's are barely contained. She's wearing a cover up over the top, but given the fact it's white and sheer, she may as well not have bothered. She must be cold, because I'm pretty sure her nipples could cut through steak and while she's practically devouring my husband, yes that's right, my husband, with her eyes, she's twirling her hair. Her eyes are hungry and the look on her face clearly says, "fuck me." I don't like it. Not one bit. My eyes move back to Asher's face and bless him his aren't looking anywhere but at her face. It lowers my hackles a little. But only a little.

"Yes, I'm Asher."

"Oh my god, I knew it. I'm such a big fan."

My mouth falls open in shock when she leans closer to Asher and presses her boobs against the side of his arm. Annoyance and possessiveness flash through my body making it heat up in a sick wave that makes me almost rise from my chair. A quick day dream of me grabbing her by the hair and flinging her away from Asher like she's as light as a feather and where I'm apparently wonder woman flashes through my mind and makes me grin. Asher looks shocked and is barely disguising the grimace on his face. "Um thank you. I appreciate your saying hello. I hope you enjoy your day," he says to her kindly but clearly in a dismissive tone. However, it's clear she doesn't get the point. At all.

"Oh my god, what are the chances that I would run into you in Cabo San Lucas? Why are you here? Are you filming a movie?

I totally saw in the tabloids that you got married. Is this her?" She jerks a thumb in my direction, but her eyes don't leave his face. And if I'm not mistaken her tone became a bit irritated when she asked that particular question.

"I'm sorry…"

"Tabatha."

"Tabatha," Asher says, "But I'm having breakfast with my wife." And there go the chills at that description. "We're in the middle of an important conversation so I'm not really able to answer all of your questions right now. Thanks again though for stopping by."

"Can I get a picture with you first?" And I'm convinced it's going to take brutal force to get her the hell away from my man. *Wait, my man? Where did that come from?* Anyway, she's not leaving.

"Um-" Asher hesitates and looks at me then back at her. Looking at Tabatha I see that she's sticking her lower lip out in a pout silently pleading with him to give in. "Okay, sure."

She cheers when he agrees and jumps up and down in her seat making things… jiggle… god help me. Looking away from her so that it keeps me from attacking, I see a couple girls by the door watching every move their friend makes with avid eyes. I suppose I should be thankful that they didn't all mob our table.

With regret and apology in his eyes, Asher pulls his hand from mine and I give him a smile, knowing this just goes with the territory of what he does for a living.

Tabatha holds up her phone and puts her face close to Asher's. Without warning, Tabatha turns her face and tries to plant her lips right on his. Somehow he manages to see her coming and turns his face so she misses his lips, but they still land near the corner of his mouth. Asher jerks away, and this time, I do partially lift from my seat, because she crossed a line, but she yells thanks over her shoulder and jets out of the restaurant as fast as she can. My eyes follow her as she jogs away with her friends and they are all giggling and looking at her phone. When I look back at Asher, I see he's dragging a napkin over his face trying his best to get the bright pink lipstick off but it's just smearing even more.

Dipping my napkin into my water glass, I move to his side of the table, place my hand on the side of his face and gently nudge it to look at me. "Ugh, I'm sorry," he says.

"Why are you apologizing?" I ask him as I dab my napkin on his face and try to remove the lipstick he hasn't already removed himself.

"Because, she kissed me, right in front of you."

"Does that happen a lot?"

He lifts his shirt up at his stomach and uses the inside of it to scrub at his mouth. "Some people are definitely more aggressive than others, but for the most part people are respectful. They just want a chance to say hi, shake my hand, exchange a few words and take a photo. There's always someone that pushes too far though, like our new, uh, friend Tabatha."

"You've been kissed more than once then, huh?"

"Kissed. Groped. Pinched. I've gotten gifts of lingerie sent to my hotel room, and have also received phone numbers and room keys. I've even had bras and underwear thrown at me before so I guess the answer to that question would be yeah, definitely."

Instantly I feel bad for him, "That must suck... I mean... I'm assuming that must suck?"

He smiles, "Yes, it does. I'm not a fan of people that cross the line. That's why I've been enjoying my time here so much. I mean, being an actor is my job and it wouldn't be an easy thing to give up. I love it. And in some ways the fans and their quirks and actions come with the territory in great part, but I don't care for being violated like that. I don't care how famous someone is, or isn't, no one no matter what deserves that kind of behavior. I'm sorry it had to happen when we were together."

"Please stop apologizing. It's not your fault."

"No, but that doesn't mean it's something that's easy to see or be around."

"I'm not the kind of person that would let someone else change my mind about another. Certainly not someone that doesn't know anything more about you other than your name, movies, and maybe a few random facts they read in a magazine. Shame on her for doing that. Now, let's talk about something else."

With a smile, we do just that. We talk about his family some more and some of his favorite childhood memories. We talk about some of the things he did with his friends in Cabo before we met up and we talk about some of his movies.

"So you're telling me you don't actually do any of the car chasing stunts in your movies? Oh my god, I just don't think I can be with you now."

He laughs and chases me down the street.

Asher takes me to a structure that looks like a small outhouse. He gives his name to the man working inside and the man points toward a boat. With a smile, he takes my hand once more and nods and thanks him. "Come on," he says to me. "Look for boat number thirty-five."

When we find it, Asher smiles and says hello to the men on the boat and hands them a piece of paper. They take a look at it and help us climb on board. As soon as we are seated comfortably, and offered life jackets, which we do not put on, but place at our sides, the men start moving around the boat. I've not been on a boat before so am unsure what they're doing exactly, but a couple of them unwrap ropes around an anchor secured to the dock and curl them up on board the boat. Another man starts the boat and before long, we're taking off moving rapidly away from the shore.

The wind is in my hair and the scent of salt water in my nose. The sun is warming our skin and I look at Asher with a big smile. I think I could get used to doing these firsts with him. "We're going for a ride?" I ask him.

"Yes, but they're taking us to a spot where we can go snorkeling. I rented the boat for a private snorkel session, just the two of us. Well and them," he gestures with his head toward the guys manning the boat.

Grabbing sunscreen out of his bag he tells me to remove my cover up so he can protect me from the sun's harmful rays, to which I giggle a little and then I do the same for him. Once thoroughly protected, we sit back and enjoy the ride to our snorkeling destination. Putting his arm around me, he holds me tightly as I snuggle up to his side, content to enjoy this with him.

Once we reach an alcove where we are promised the best snorkeling in Cabo, we suit up in our snorkeling gear. Life vests, fins, mask and snorkel in place, we're shown where to go in order to see the most fish and are given safety instructions on what to do should we feel unsafe or see a shark. Nervous flutters occur at the mention of a shark, but I calm when we're told that seeing one would be rare, they aren't generally around this area.

When we carefully move to the side of the boat to jump, I look down into the water before looking back at Asher. I smile around the snorkel already in my mouth at how silly he looks in his snorkel gear. And then realize I likely look just as silly. He reaches out to grab my hand and removes his snorkel from his mouth, "Together?"

Nodding, he holds up his hand and says, "On three." He puts the snorkel back in his mouth and counts with his fingers. On three, we jump. Our hands separate in the fall, and I squeal at how chilly the water feels. It takes a few minutes to get acclimated, but once we start swimming around, it's hardly noticeable. Sticking our heads in the water is strange, and I keep forcing myself to breathe through the tube in my mouth. The sound of my breaths is distracting yet comforting at the same time. Asher reaches out and takes my hand again, and we explore the water together.

I have no idea how long we spend in the water swimming and exploring but it feels like ages. The volume, variety, and color of fish we see are astounding - some are normal looking and some are so crazy, I never could have imagined they exist. The most amazing part is how beautiful they are: from the lightest shades of yellow to brightest blues, and oranges and red – both the coral and fish are simply breathtaking. We definitely see every color in the rainbow. Some of the fish are as small as a pebble and others are so large they nearly cause me to panic, concerned about how they would respond to our being in the same vicinity. But they merely swam on toward their intended destination. Which made we wonder where they were all going. We continually pointed out our sightings to each other, eager to share. It was incredibly fun.

We agree to head back to the boat and finish up, keeping our faces in the water the whole time. Suddenly, Asher yanks on my hand and points. Far below us, making wide zigzags in the water, is a shark. Granted, it's small, but I don't give a crap and I take off like the shark is already biting my ass. Complete panic engulfs me and I start swimming like Michael Phelps.

Once I get to the boat, I'm out of the water, being helped back inside by the men there. Ripping my gear off, I turn around just in time to find Asher climbing into the boat behind me. He's laughing so hard he falls to his knees trying to catch his breath. "Oh my god," he pants.

Placing my hands on my hips, I glare at him knowing automatically he's laughing at me. "What's so funny?"

"You! That shark was probably the size of your arm. And it wasn't one you needed to worry about."

"Whatever. Speak for yourself. It may have been small but I betcha it still would have enjoyed chewing on your dangly bits."

His face turns serious immediately, "Don't even joke about that." His hand automatically covers his crotch and I don't think he even realizes he's doing it.

"That's what I thought. Not so funny now, is it?"

"Well… at least now I know that if we're ever in a life or death situation, your thoughts are every man for himself."

"Uhh, oops?" I reply at a loss for words to defend my actions.

We stare at each other then simultaneously start laughing until tears fall down our faces.

Chapter 17

Present Time

"It sounds like the two of you really hit if off," Faye says as we both laugh at how much fun Asher and I had together.

"We did. I know that I will never forget my time with Asher," I smile but inside I would swear my heart just broke a little more.

"You're really hurting. Is talking about this making it worse for you?"

Considering her question, I pause, "Talking about our time together gives me mixed feelings. It's so fresh that sometimes the pain feels so potent that I can't breathe. But at the same time, talking about it confirms my feelings and I know that I have reason to feel the way that I do. Leaving Asher is the hardest thing I've ever had to do. Somehow, it's harder than when my mother passed away – I was so young when that happened, the pain then was on a different level than it is now. It hurts as much and feels as crippling as when my father died, but again, it's not comparable as they are both unique in their own right. It hurts deeper than Jeremy's betrayal and I was with Jeremy much longer than Asher. Even though I didn't love Jeremy, that still seems odd." Looking at Faye in wonder, I ask rhetorically, "How can that be? We only spent a short time together yet the loss of him is something profound; I know it will take me a long time to get over."

"But, did you really lose him? I mean he's not gone in the way your parents are."

"No, he's not, but being with him would hurt him. And I can't do that to him. I…I love him too much."

"You love him?" A soft smile is upon her lips and her eyes twinkle. "After only a week?" While she asks that question, it's not with disbelief in her tone or on her face. Instead she almost seems… amused, unsurprised. I feel like she's asking me not in judgment, but rather because she wants me to say it again.

"Yes. I love him. And I have learned that love is limitless. There's no time, boundary, rhyme or reason to love. It just simply is."

Her smile widens, "Why are you so sad then?"

"Because I think with love also comes sacrifice sometimes."

"And your leaving is a sacrifice?"

"Absolutely. I'm sacrificing my happiness for Asher. Because it's the right thing to do."

"And does he agree with that?"

"I don't know." Her brows raise and I cringe. "I'll explain."

"I'm listening."

And so I begin telling her the rest of my story.

Chapter 18

When Asher and I get back to the room after our boating excursion, I suggest that Asher jump in the shower first and tonight, I'll order us dinner. With a smile, he agrees and saunters off to the bathroom losing his clothes along the way. I raise an eyebrow pretending it doesn't affect me as much as it does, and he laughs. Moving to the phone, I grab the various menus of all the restaurants on both resort properties to make my decision. I want to take care of Asher tonight. He's been surprising me every day so far and it's a small thing I know, and doesn't come close to what he's done for me, but I want to take control for the evening.

I'm glad to see that while Mexican food is definitely a consistent theme, there are many other cuisines to choose from. I consider Japanese for a moment, but then decide pasta is a safer choice. I select baked ziti, and a garden salad, dressing on the side knowing it's likely to be good – who can mess up pasta sauce. I forego the garlic bread, despite that it is likely to be tasty and elect Italian bread instead. For obvious reasons. I grin as I add strawberries, whipped cream and champagne to the order.

I've barely hung up the phone and I hear Asher shut the shower water off. Moments later, he emerges wearing nothing but a towel. Sporting a mischievous grin, he walks toward me and my mouth waters watching his muscles shift with each step. Random drops of water trail down his body and I lick my lips. Immediately a scene from one of his movies flashes through my mind, and I remember women in the theatre sighing at the sight. I wonder if I should tell them that the real thing doesn't even do the image on the screen justice.

With every step Asher takes toward me, I take one back. His grin turns downright wicked when my back meets resistance from the wall. Placing a hand on either side of my head, boxing me in, he moves close to me. Oh god, he smells mouth watering.

"Princess?"

"Hmm?" I ask my gaze moving to and settling on his lips.

"The shower is available for you now."

"Yeah…ummm…" I giggle. God, I giggle! I sound ridiculous but somehow I can't shut it off. "I kind of got that given the fact you're standing in front of me." I giggle again. *Oh, god, I'm eighteen again. I should just start popping gum and twirling my hair too.*

His mouth moves infinitesimally closer to mine making me unable to focus on anything other than what that mouth can do to me. How it can make me feel. How it can make me moan and shudder. His mouth is on mine and he's kissing me thoroughly, as if he wants to make his thoughts and intentions for the night clear. I'm right there with him, every movement of our lips against one another, every slide of our tongues, every taste, every whimper. His fingers trail down my arms and then wrap around my waist, mine wrap around his neck, pulling him closer to me, kissing him harder. He presses his body against mine and I can feel every inch and curve intimately. When he pulls away, his stare is so intense; I swear he can see into my mind, my heart and my soul. I'm breathless, my chest heaving with need, want and desire. He matches me breath for breath. He moves toward me again and I know if I let him take my lips once more, I'll be a goner. Ducking under his arm, he yells a surprised, "Hey! I wasn't done yet."

Quickly grabbing my clothes, I make a dash for the bathroom, but look over my shoulder at him and laugh at the look of astonishment on his face. Laughing was a mistake. In retaliation, as I reach the bathroom entrance, he drops his towel from around his waist. Gasping, I almost smack right into the wall instead of going through the door. He winks at me seductively and starts walking to me again, but somehow I manage to come to my senses and dart through the door and shut it quickly. *I must be absolutely crazy.*

Leaning my back against the door, and squeezing my eyes closed, I try to catch my breath. Holy hell is that one fine specimen of a man. I don't know how I got so lucky to get his attention, but hell the man is the complete package. Jumping in the shower, I wonder if a cold shower does the same thing for women as it does for men. I elect to try. Quickly washing, I tell myself to remember that I have a plan. Shower, eat and then operation seduce Asher. Not that it's going to be a very hard thing to do. We are both beyond ready, but the anticipation is making the blood in my veins even fierier with need.

Finishing, my deduction is that the cool water did nothing to simmer the passion running in my veins, but that's okay. Drying my hair and applying a touch of makeup, I turn to the clothes I've elected to wear.

A knock comes at the door startling me, "Princess? Dinner's here."

"Okay. Go ahead and sit at the table, I'm coming!"

"No, sadly, you aren't. Not yet anyway."

Stifling a laugh, I call, "Be there in a minute."

Hurrying, I dress in the most seductive thing I brought on vacation, quite by accident. A lace tank top, with matching lace boy shorts that have a cute ruffle on the butt. I usually wear them under my jean shorts with a top so you can't make out the ruffle through my clothes. They're surprisingly comfortable and I always feel kind of naughty in them. Like I have a sexy secret. Alone, they are definitely sexy. They're a pale pink color that leaves nothing to the imagination. I'm saying a prayer of thanks that I impulsively left them in my bag when I took other lingerie items out.

Turning back to the mirror, I give myself a once over, fluff my hair, spritz on some body spray, do a quick turn checking out my ass and give myself a nod of approval. With a deep breath, I open the door and peek out into the bedroom. Asher is nowhere to be found, so I surmise he's sitting at the table like I asked.

One barefooted step at a time, I make my way to the dining area, and when I reach the entryway, I lean against it waiting for him to notice me. He doesn't at first; he's busy arranging our table and the food. I grin when I see he's had a similar idea to mine; he's wearing nothing but black boxer briefs. I admire his strong broad back and suppress a shudder when I imagine scratching my nails down it. I'm glad that's all he's wearing- less to rip off that way.

When he sits in his chair, he picks up his silverware that's rolled into his napkin and happens to glance at the doorway. When his eyes meet mine, he freezes, and his silverware clatters to his plate. His eyes rake my body, stopping momentarily at the junction of my thighs, and again when he reaches my breasts. When his heated gaze returns to mine, he licks his lips and I barely keep myself from running right into his arms.

Slowly, purposefully, taking one step at a time, I ease myself into my chair. Usually he pulls my seat out for me, so I know I've really rattled him. It makes me bite my bottom lip so I don't smile. "Does it look good?"

"What?" His voice is husky with lust and he swallows hard, his eyes appearing slightly unfocused.

"The food. Does it look good?"

"God, it looks so fucking good," he says eyes still on me and I know he's not talking about the food at all.

Forcing myself to lift the metal dome off of my plate, I glance at the pasta dish sitting there. "It does look good." I grab my own silverware and unroll it. Taking a small forkful of my ziti, I place it in my mouth and groan with pleasure at the taste. It's for show of course, but it actually does taste quite delicious. Flitting my eyes up to his, I swallow my bite. I moan just a bit for emphasis. "Oh god, it's so good. Aren't you going to eat it?"

He chokes, and it takes effort not to laugh. "Excuse me?"

"The pasta," I clarify, "are you going to eat it?" His eyes are still on my lips and I swear he's practically sweating; his brow is glistening just a little.

Reaching across the table, he whispers, "Come here." I lean toward him and watch wide-eyed as his thumb grazes the corner of my mouth and then he brings it to his own, tongue flicking out to lick the sauce from it. "You're right. It's delicious."

Sweet baby cupid in a diaper, I've been struck stupid by this man.

Finally, he lifts the dome from his own plate and mechanically begins eating his food. His eyes volley between his plate and my face the whole time. I make a show of eating my food. Licking when necessary, moaning occasionally, chewing slowly, all the while trying to make idle conversation about our excursion and the fish we saw today, about how fun the boat ride was and how beautiful Cabo is in general. If the constant shifting in his seat is any indication, Asher's not really interested in the conversation at all. Sure he's responding but it's all robotic, his eyes watching every move I make. I don't think he's going to tolerate much more.

When a drop of sauce falls from my fork onto the inside of my other thumb, I lick it off without thought. I'm startled when Asher suddenly stands. "What's wrong?"

His chest is heaving, his eyes on mine. Before I can utter another word, his hand swipes the table and each and every item crashes to the floor. My mouth falls open; my fork falls to the ground. Before I can even think about uttering one word, he's around the table and is pulling me out of my chair. Yanking me against his body, he kisses me hard, long, and with so much passion, it's hard to breathe.

Pulling his lips from mine, he lifts me up and sets me right onto the freaking table. "Sorry, princess, but this isn't going to be slow. I can't wait. I need you now."

A sharp exhale of need escapes me, "God, yes," I agree without any hesitation. I'm on board for this plan. Completely.

He pulls his briefs down his legs quickly and a condom appears from god knows where. He rips it open with his teeth before putting it in place. Not taking time to remove my clothes, he pushes my tank up over my breasts and simply yanks my panties to the side. Touching me intimately, he hisses out a breath when he feels that I'm more than ready for him. Dinner was certainly foreplay, he's ready and I'm more than willing. Placing himself at my entrance, we become one with a quick deep thrust, both of us exhaling with a sense of relief at finally being joined.

Every push and withdraw is the most intimate communication and expression of feelings. With each push I feel his desire, with each withdrawal I feel his need for more. There's sweat on his upper lip, fire in his eyes, and the devil in his movements because they're insanely wicked. His hands are all over my body - touching, stroking, massaging, igniting.

"So good," I tell him. Grinding my hips into his, I desperately seek release and encourage him to keep going, desperate for him to never stop.

"I won't," he says and I realize I must have told him not to stop out loud. Reveling in the feeling of him inside of me, together as one, I marvel at how right it feels, how complete I am.

He pulls me to the edge of the table, his hands find the tops of my shoulders and he hangs on as his tempo increases. One of his hands travels down my body and begins slow, steady circles exactly where I need him most. His eyes are desperate for me to feel what he's feeling, to find completion with and because of him. Lifting up on my elbows, I gaze at the sight of our lovemaking, the sight of our joining pushing me right off the edge of the cliff I was barely balancing on. Asher immediately follows, then his body collapses onto mine. Wrapping my arms around him, I can't stop running my hands over his back extending his pleasure in any and every way.

Eventually, he pulls from me and I exhale at the loss. He helps me off the table, and excuses himself to the restroom. I pull my clothes into place and start cleaning up the mess on the floor.

When Asher returns he immediately joins me, and when I look at him, I see color has flooded his cheeks. "Um, sorry about this," he apologizes.

"Really? You're sorry? Because I'm not, and you certainly didn't seem sorry a few minutes ago."

He grins widely, drops the plate from his hand and cups my face. "You're right. I'm not sorry," he leans forward and presses his lips to mine before pulling back. "I'm not sorry at all. But, I suppose I could have shown a bit more patience."

I shrug, "I thought it was hot," I confess. "Besides, I pushed you too far and on purpose."

"You are a cruel, cruel woman."

I roll my eyes, "Oh please."

"Evil," he adds.

"You wound me."

"Horrible."

"You loved it."

He smiles again, "You're right. I did."

With laughter, we each clean up the mess and then I grab the dessert tray that was thankfully still sitting on the cart, completely intact.

"Interested in some dessert?"

His eyebrows lift and he licks his lips. "Princess, what do you think that just was?" he waves his hand over the table.

Showing him the strawberries and cream under the tray, I suggest, "Okay, well how about dessert part two?"

"I like this plan, but how about we take part two into the bedroom?"

"I too like this plan." With a wink, I turn and saunter into the room knowing I'm giving him a perfect view of my pert ruffled bottom. When I hear a groan behind me, I smile to myself. He follows behind with two glasses and the bottle of champagne, otherwise I have a feeling his hands would be roaming. Pouring each of us a glass, he hands me mine. "A toast," he says, "To whatever the hell those underwear are doing to your ass and sex on tables."

I laugh out loud and clink my glass with his, "I'll drink to that. Cheers!"

We each sit in the middle of the bed, the tray of strawberries between us. Asher grabs a berry and dips it in whipped cream. I expect him to take a bite, but instead he holds it up to my mouth with a lift of his brows. Opening my mouth, I take a bite and moan in pleasure as the flavor bursts on my tongue. Chasing it with champagne, I murmur, "Delicious."

Asher smiles and leans forward; the tip of his tongue darts out and touches the top of my lip. "You seem to have a little trouble leaving remnants of food behind."

"Thank goodness I have you to take care of it for me."

"Yes, thank goodness," he murmurs huskily.

This time, I take a strawberry and dip it and then hold it to his mouth. Before I place it to his lips, I purposefully drag it over his lip, leaving whipped cream behind. He takes a generous bite, and I smile. "Oh no. You have a little bit on your mouth now." Before he can say a word, I happily clean off his mouth with a lick of my own.

With a devilish grin, he dips his finger into the whipped cream, foregoing the strawberry this time, and swipes it across my mouth. "Oh no, not again!" He kisses me, making me moan deeply. I want him again – I can't imagine ever not wanting him. I feel sadness briefly knowing the time I have of his being mine is short, too short.

Surprised by my thoughts and not wanting to deal with the feelings they evoke, I push them away.

When he pulls away, I down my champagne in three gulps, seeing Asher do the same. Taking our glasses he sets them on the bedside table, and removes the strawberries as well. When he comes back on the bed, this time, it's me that pounces.

Pushing him onto his back, I trail a finger back and forth over the waistband of his briefs while he watches me. Tucking my fingers under the band, I slide them down his legs then throw them over my shoulder making him laugh. Stretching my body out on top of his, I revel in the erotic feel of him being naked, while I'm still clothed in lace.

With a happy sigh, I place a kiss to his lips and pull away, feeling eager to explore every glorious inch of him. Placing a kiss to his jaw, loving the feel of his stubble I drag my lips across his jaw nibbling and kissing along the way. When I place a kiss behind his ear, he sucks in a breath and groans, making me smile that I found a sensitive spot. Storing that information away for later, I keep moving, down his chest. I swirl my tongue around his nipples and enjoy each time his breath hitches in pleasure.

Moving my way south I nuzzle the trail of hair that runs to his groin, kiss his navel, playfully bite his abs, and suck on one of his hipbones making him groan. Then when I take him in my hand and lower my mouth to him, I revel in the sounds he makes as I try to show him how good he makes me feel. I want to make him feel the way I do when he pleasures me.

Before I can bring him to completion he yanks me up his body and flips us over in one swift move. He removes my clothes and this time, our movements are slower. He not only pleasures me with his body, but with his words too. He whispers my name. Tells me how good he feels. Asks if I feel the same. He brings me to the edge of desire and just when I think I'm going to lose myself to the fall, he stops then starts all over again.

We worship each other, kissing and touching each part of our bodies. This time when we become one, no words are exchanged between us. We let our bodies, eyes and our sighs do all the talking for us.

Never has sex been this intimate for me. It's always felt like a duty, something I knew I had to do to make my partner satisfied, but always somehow leaving me unfulfilled. As we find completion now, then again hours later as we turn to each other in the night, I feel an ache in my heart. Instinctively I know that this feeling, whatever it is, it will change me forever.

Chapter 19

"I guess we can do that," Asher says into the phone pressed against his ear. He looks at me and rolls his eyes and I know whatever he's agreeing to isn't something he really wants to do. "Yeah, I know she will because she's brought it up a couple times. It's me that hasn't been interested." He sighs now, "Alright, fine, enough. I'll go, I mean *we'll* go. Just text me when and where after you guys figure it out, okay? No, it doesn't matter to me, we'll just meet you there. Okay, bye."

When he hangs up, he throws his phone onto a chair. Before he can move a muscle it starts ringing again. With a frown he picks it back up, glances at the screen, then I assume he must press ignore because he throws it back down again and the ringer stops as he dives into bed. He rubs his temples and I brush his hands away and begin rubbing them for him. "Headache?" I ask.

"A small one," he says and releases a deep breath as he enjoys my mini massage. We've stayed in bed all day long, only coming up for air when we've wanted sustenance. Then, we just ordered room service and went back to bed again. I should probably feel guilty for being so lazy, but I'm not. It's been a great day. And I'm not sure all of our time in bed could be classified as lazy.

"What was that all about?" I ask while I trace figure eights on his stomach.

"That was Hunter. He, Andy, and a few others are going to a club tonight and want to know if we'd like to go along."

"And it sounded like you agreed. Very reluctantly."

He sighs again, "I did. In all honesty, Hunter kind of made me feel guilty so I agreed. Plus, you brought up doing something with them a couple times so I knew you wouldn't mind."

"I don't," I tell him.

"I know, but I do."

"Well, how about we go, make an appearance, stay for a brief time, and if we aren't having fun or lose interest or merely want to be together, we leave?"

"Cool. Plan on being there five minutes and then we'll take off."

"Asher!" I admonish with a laugh but he just grins that drop dead gorgeous smile of his and kisses me.

Hours later I walk out of the bathroom ready to go. When Asher's mouth drops open at the sight of me, I twirl for him. "Holy shit."

My outfit is two pieces. A navy blue halter that almost looks like a twisted scarf. Two pieces of fabric cover my breasts, and a string runs across at my collarbone holding the pieces together but the deep v showcases my breasts. The fabric then crisscrosses under my breasts before they tie in the back in a bow. The navy blue skirt is form fitting and reaches my ankles, with a deep slit up one leg. It certainly showcases my curves in a big way. I was hesitant to buy it, but Katie insisted I rocked it. Given the look on Asher's face, I need to thank her a thousand times over. "You like?"

He points to the bathroom, "Go change."

"What?" I ask stuttering over the word, shock clear in my voice.

"No way I am taking you out in front of my horny friends looking like that."

Rolling my eyes, I walk to him and place my hands on his chest before lifting my head up, offering my lips. He lifts a brow, but kisses me, his lips soft on mine. "I could care less what any of them think. I dressed up for you."

"All I'm going to be thinking about is undressing you."

"Even better," I wag my eyebrows at him making him laugh.

"Alright, let's get this over with."

"You sound *so* excited."

"The only thing that makes me excited is you," he kisses me again, but this time, it's a deep kiss, his tongue stroking against mine. My arms wrap around him and I press my body closer to his. He breaks from my lips and kisses his way down my neck, groaning, "You smell amazing," he rumbles in my ear before biting my earlobe in a way that generates responses all the way down to my toes.

Reluctantly I pull away, "Come on, we need to go or we're never going to leave this room."

"Fine with me," he murmurs not removing his lips from my neck.

"Asher," I say with a slight admonishment to my tone.

He pulls away with a sigh, "Okay, fine. But I'm warning you, my patience isn't going to be long. I'll be counting down the minutes until I can get you underneath me again."

With that we head out of our resort to go to another. Half hour later we're walking through the doors of Infusion, my hand in Asher's, his eyes roaming the club looking for his friends. He must locate them, because he raises his hand in a wave. With a kiss on my cheek, he begins leading me through the throngs of people. When we arrive at a table, eight others surround it and greet Asher with varying comments.

"Wow, so you weren't kidding he is still in Cabo," a blonde woman says rolling her eyes at a man that's wrapped around her. He smiles and kisses her on the nose. Before he turns to Asher, "Good to see you, man."

Asher nods and says, "How is the honeymoon, you two?"

They each smile and kiss one another, making the others around them groan in response. "Well that answers that," Asher comments pulling me up next to him. I didn't realize I was a little behind him.

"Well I don't believe my eyes, is that Asher Charming?" Andy says with a lopsided smile and a drink in his hand.

"About time you join us, man," a dark haired guy says with a smile and Asher fist bumps him.

"I told you he said he was coming," Hunter says to a brunette that looks at Asher with clear desire in her eyes that immediately makes me uncomfortable. The girl standing next to her eyes Asher too, but with less intensity.

"Looks like the sunshine and sand agree with you, Asher. Looking good." The brunette says and I want to pull her hair. Hard.

"I don't think it's the sun and sand, Spring." Asher says with a smile at me and I grin back shyly. *Ha, take that, Spring.*

"Everyone, this is my wife, Gabriella. Ella, this is everyone." I wave and then Asher points at each one, "You remember Hunter and Andy," I nod.

"Hi, Ella." Andy says with a smile, "You look amazing," he says with starry eyes.

"Gabriella." Asher says sternly to him in response to him using my nickname. I jab him in the side, but he just lifts a brow at me. Rolling my eyes I say, "Hi Andy." Hunter gives me a tight smile, but I don't expect anything more.

"That's Rob," he says pointing at the dark haired guy that is now grinning at me.

"Well, well, well, it sure is nice to meet you," he says and Asher points at him. "No."

Rob just grins at Asher making Asher narrow his eyes at him before he moves on.

"The newlywed's that can't keep their tongues out of each other's mouths are Joe and Carolyn." They pull away from each other and both grin at me. "Hi," they chime and then Carolyn says, "We're glad you are joining us tonight."

"Thank you, and congratulations on your marriage."

"Thank you," they say at the same time and I grin. They're clearly in love and it's sweet to see.

"Then, you probably heard me say that's Spring." Asher nods her way and she gives me a wiggle of her fingers and a strained smile in a weak hello. So of course I smile widely hoping I can annoy her more. "And that's Monica," he says pointing at the woman standing next to Spring. She gives me a closed mouth smile and turns away quickly to talk to Carolyn and Joe.

"What would you like to drink?" Asher asks me and takes my order before moving away to get the attention of a waiter. While he does that I look around the club. It's eclectic, with random art all over the walls – everything from street signs to huge plastic fish hanging on the walls. The dance floor is in the middle of the place, tables all around and a bar on the opposite end of the entrance. Waiter and waitresses walk all around taking orders. A second floor is visible from where we are standing. It appears another bar and more tables and chairs are up there.

Music is pumping from the speakers and many dancers are already moving together on the floor. The energy is high and I think of Katie knowing she would be in heaven. The people watching here is crazy awesome, not to mention the girl loves to get her dance on. I grin when I think about the text I sent her earlier. All I said was 'operation unicorn a success'. Her response was immediate and demanding of details. It made me laugh, but I told her it would have to be later because I was 'otherwise engaged'. She called me a 'lucky bitch', before I powered if off.

"So, Gabriella, what have you and *our* Asher been up to?" Spring asks me and I don't miss the pointed remark. And of course Monica at her side has now zeroed in on me as well, her eyes going back and forth between Spring and I.

"All kinds of things. We went out on wave runners, visited the Rosé and hung out at their pool. Asher rented a boat for the day and we went for a ride and snorkeled. We saw some amazing fish and coral."

"That's cool," Andy says with enthusiasm. "I'd like to do that before we leave."

"You should, it's totally worth it. We've also eaten so much food, it's insane. I'm not used to eating out so much, but everything we've had has been so good. I've definitely indulged."

"Oh, that explains it," Spring says.

"I'm sorry?" I ask not understanding.

She leans toward me and mockingly whispers, "Feeling a little bloated?" and gestures toward my stomach. Monica next to her flashes a smile before trying to wipe it off of her face, but it's too late, I already saw it. Women are such bitches – but that's okay, I can handle them.

"Spring!" Carolyn says in shock having heard her. A glance around the table shows Andy and Rob glaring at her, Joe looking at Carolyn and Hunter pretending he didn't hear anything by swirling his drink and looking around the room.

Resisting the urge to give her satisfaction by looking down at myself, I shake my head. "No, Summer, those are called curves."

"It's Spring," she says in anger while Andy and Rob bark out a laugh.

"Sorry, Fall," I reply again just as Asher walks up and hands me my drink. Taking a few large gulps, I set it on the table before turning to him, "Want to dance?"

"Absolutely," he says and swallows a few gulps of his own drink before taking my hand and leading me to the dance floor. "You okay?" he asks me concern lining his brow.

"I'm fine, why?"

"I know that Spring and Monica are bitches. It's part of the reason I didn't want to come out with them. If they say anything stupid, tell me right away, okay?"

"I can handle a couple of bitchy girls, don't worry."

"I'm sure you can, but you shouldn't have to."

Without another word, he pulls me to him and starts moving his hips in a way that's so decadent I'm about to overdose on pleasure right there in the middle of the dance floor. "Where did you learn to move like that?" I ask.

He throws his head back and laughs at the look on my face, pulls me closer to him and puts his hands on my hips. Placing my hands loosely around his neck, I'm immediately lost in him. I feel nothing but his body against mine. The sound of the crowd is lost because all I hear is the rhythmic noise of his breath in my ears. Sneaking kisses here and there, I taste his sweat-slicked skin. I inhale his musky scent, as my eyes trail over his body, seeing nothing else. All my senses are poetry in motion, each ode a sonnet just for him.

His eyes are burning into mine and I couldn't look away if I tried. This time, when his lips meet mine, it isn't in a sweet chaste kiss, rather it is the kind of kiss novels are written about. It's a spine tingling, toe curling, stomach fluttering kind of kiss. His lips are hard on mine, his tongue demanding, his fingers are digging into my hips and there isn't a whisper of space between our bodies. When we pull apart we're both breathless and I almost laugh because this keeps happening to us. "Asher." I say and he nods. "Yeah. We're leaving."

"Okay, I just have to go to the bathroom first."

"Alright, but I don't want you to go alone."

"I'll be fine."

"Please, Ella."

Not wanting to argue, especially when I see the concern in his eyes, I nod, "Okay."

He pulls me back to the table and everyone is staring at us, so I'm sure they were watching us on the dance floor. Maybe I should care, but I don't. Andy and Rob look amused, Hunter annoyed, Spring and Monica are spewing daggers of hate from their eyeballs and the newlyweds are oblivious to everyone. As it should be. "Carolyn, Ella has to use the restroom but I don't want her to go alone. Do you mind going with her?"

"Jesus, Asher, I could have asked her," I tell him feeling a little embarrassed he asked someone to hold my hand to the bathroom.

"I'm sorry. I'm just being protective."

"I'll go with her," Spring says and my eyes widen in surprise, as do Asher's and Monica's.

"Okay, thanks," I say and we both head off.

We don't have to wait long, thank goodness, and we do our thing quickly. As we're walking back, I'm honestly not surprised when I feel Spring's claws digging into my arm as she pulls me to a stop. "Look, I don't know what game you're playing here, and God knows what the hell Asher sees in you, but when this week is over and you run away back to your little life, stay the hell away from him."

"Excuse me?"

"Maybe he just needs to get you out of his system, maybe he's just lost his damn mind, I don't fucking know. But I do know, that long after you're gone, I'm still going to be here. You're interesting to him right now, the flavor of the week, but that's all you are. Don't think it's more than that for one second."

"Listen up, Winter. I'm not scared or intimidated by women like you. So you can take your advice and shove it up your ass. Whatever Asher and I do or don't do, or feel or don't feel, or decide to do, has nothing to do with you. You're just a jealous bitch trying to make herself feel better by trying to bring me down, but it isn't going to work." Leaning forward I lower my voice so she has to ease in closer to me, "And just so you know, he's even better in bed than whatever little scenario your sad mind has tried to conjure up to keep you warm at night." Her eyes widen and I feel satisfaction run through my veins. "Now if you'll excuse me, my husband is waiting."

Spinning on my heel, I walk back to the table. He's in a conversation with Hunter, but as if he senses I'm near, he looks up and into my eyes, so I walk straight into his arms. Kissing him, I smile, "Are you ready?"

"More than ready." Looking at everyone, he gives a salute, "Alright gang, thanks for inviting us out. We had a good time, but we are out of here."

Hunter holds up a hand, "Asher, wait, we weren't done talking."

"Yes, we are. I don't have anything else to say about it right now."

"Because it doesn't matter now, right? I mean, who cares how hard you've worked." Hunter's tone is angry and I look from him to Asher. Everyone at the table is quiet and it's clear I've missed something here. Asher looks irritated, but when he sees me watching, the tension in his shoulders falls.

"We'll talk later, man. It's all going to be fine."

"It was great to meet you, Gabriella," Carolyn says which begins a round of goodbyes. Spring of course hangs on to Asher a little too long which makes him look uncomfortable, his eyes meeting mine in apology. I smirk and wink at him, "Bye, Winter. Enjoy the rest of your time in Cabo," I add making Asher, Rob and Andy all laugh out loud.

With a wave, to everyone, Asher guides me out of the club with a hand on my back. We hail a taxi and tell him to take us back to the resort.

Asher is quiet on the way back, his arms wrapped around me. I'm feeling annoyed by the interaction between Asher and Hunter. It's clear that Hunter hasn't gotten over his doubts about me. "You okay?" I ask Asher.

"I'm perfect," he says kissing my forehead and pulling me closer to him.

We remain in separate worlds of thought the rest of the way to the resort, but all worries or insecurities I've created get shed one at a time with each piece of clothing Asher strips from me when we get back to our room. As he pulls me into his arms, presses his body to mine, and places me on the bed, everything else is forgotten, my only thoughts once again lost in him.

Chapter 20

My time with Asher is almost over. It's the first thought that enters my mind as soon as my eyes open this morning. How has it gone so fast? I'm not ready. The time with him has been better and meant more than I ever thought possible. A week at work feels a hell of a lot longer than a week on vacation, that's for damn sure. Whenever I think about leaving, about saying goodbye, I get an ache that leaves me pained in my chest and my stomach hurts so much I want to throw up. I feel ridiculous, so I do my best to push it aside and not think about it.

"A penny for your thoughts," Asher says startling me.

Lifting my face to his, I'm surprised to find he's not only awake, but that his sparkling blue eyes are focused intently on mine. Smiling automatically, my gaze falls to his exposed chest then I look back at his face again, before my eyes drop to his lips. "You're awake?"

"I haven't been for long. I've just been enjoying the view in my bed. Then your eyes opened and I watched more emotions fly across your face than I could count. More importantly though is that I can't interpret them. So tell me what you're thinking about."

Hopping out of bed, not at all embarrassed by my nakedness I round the bed and head to the bathroom. "I'm thinking I need to brush my teeth so I can kiss you."

Maybe it's my imagination but I swear he looks disappointed. Not in my wanting to kiss him, but that I'm clearly avoiding the question. I almost ask him why he's bothered, but my thought fades away when he smiles, "You know I don't care about that. Get over here and let me give you a proper good morning."

"I care," I tell him. "I don't want to gross you out."

"Not possible," he calls behind me. I quickly relieve my bladder and then brush my teeth only to be joined at the counter as he retrieves and brushes his own teeth. I can't contain my smile behind my toothbrush.

Beating him back to the bed, I watch his body as he emerges from the bathroom and makes his way back to me. I could never get tired of looking at him. It's a thought I have frequently, but it can't be helped. "Enjoying the view?" he asks me with cockiness.

"Are you?" I retort saucily because his eyes are devouring me just as much as mine are him.

"Hell yes I am."

"Me too." I say as I watch him lay back down. "But I'm game for a hands on viewing if you are."

Before he can respond I shift quickly to straddle him. Looking down into his smiling face, I move my hips suggestively making him growl, "I like this idea."

Lifting up just enough to position myself, his hands squeeze my hips, causing me look at his face instead of our bodies. "Just a second." He reaches in the table and grabs a condom with an expression of regret likely due to the interrupted activity, but it's a necessary interruption and I feel silly for not thinking.

When his hands are back on my hips, I take him home watching his eyes roll back in his head. "Christ," he murmurs and I revel in the fact I have the ability to make him feel as good as he makes me. Shivers run over my body as I watch him lose control. I relish it. His face is painted in ecstasy, and it makes me more desperate, wild and uninhibited in my desire to please us both. This feeling…it's primal.

Rocking forward and backward, breaths coming faster and faster with our movements, my head drops back and moans communicate feelings. His name leaves my lips over and over, sometimes whispered sometimes in a yell, always with great feeling.

His hands find my breasts and stroke, pinch and knead. "Harder," he instructs. Placing my hands on his chest, I obey. Our eyes meet and hold, the only sound the music our bodies make together. Every thrust, every stroke, something inside of me begins to unravel. When his fingers move between my legs, I'm soaring in seconds. He follows me immediately and I collapse onto his chest.

"Now that was one hell of a good morning." His chest vibrates under my ear. A thought occurs to me and I begin laughing.

"What?" he asks amused.

"I was just thinking that here I was so adamant about brushing my teeth and I didn't even kiss you."

"I think you should rectify that immediately," he demands.

So I do.

When he pulls away, he tucks me into his side, pushing my hair behind my ear. "I have special plans for us tonight."

"You do?"

"I do," he nods. "But what we do with our day is up to you."

I contemplate the options but know exactly what I'd prefer. "I have heard that the Sky Pool at Sunset Beach is amazing. It looks out over the whole bluff and you can see the ocean for miles. How about we go up there?"

"I think that sounds perfect."

And so, after we shower, together of course, we find ourselves taking a golf cart to the resort above ours. The cart drives up and up and up until we're let out at a ramp where we have to walk even further. Once we get to the top, the jaunt we had to take to get here, we immediately affirm was well worth it. We can see the expanse of this resort and our own far down below, but what captivates us is the ocean, its craggy shoreline and white caps visible for what appears to be miles upon miles. A small number of sailboats and fishing boats bob up and down with the tide and present a beautiful picture. Far below we watch as the water crashes upon the shore. Further still large rocks jettison along the coast and the surf crashes against them making huge splashes of white water that's so picturesque I snap several pictures with my phone. When I get home I plan to blow up several of the best shots and frame them – the perfect homemade souvenir.

When we bring ourselves to walk away from the railing, we grab towels from a worker manning the small adobe hut and walk to find chairs. While walking, I investigate the pool. It has two semi-circle shaped tiers: a large pool on the bottom and another glass-side enclosed one above. Upon closer observation, I note that the one on top is actually an infinity pool and water spills over the front into the one below. People stand against its edge, some conversing, some merely observing, others appearing contemplative. Many hold beverages served by the bar positioned to the side, which also entreats others to sit on its stools that erupt from the water. Steps take one between levels. Both levels are surrounded with lounge chairs, tables and sun umbrellas and are well-populated this morning. Conversation and laughter abound. It appears that everyone is enjoying their vacation.

Following Asher as he looks for seats, his ball cap pulled low over his eyes, I can't help but laugh along with others as a guy and two girls laugh loudly and dare each other to fall over the infinity edge into the bigger pool below. They each flop gracelessly over the edge to cheers from onlookers. One woman we pass who may be in her late fifties covers her eyes with her hands and mutters, "Have kids they said. It will be great they said." Covering my mouth with my hand I suppress a giggle. Asher looks back at me and the glee in his eyes indicates he heard her too.

Simultaneously we spot an observatory looking area above the upper pool. We hasten our pace and eagerly mount the steps to its platform where the breath-taking view seen from the railing is magnified. I turn in slow circles, eyes first opened then closed, with arms extended out from my side, as the slight breeze breathes into my pores, dazed with the sheer magnificence of our surroundings. Asher looks at me, adoringly, inevitably taking me within his arms and holding me until we have ingested our fill.

Securing chairs side by side Asher spreads out our towels, we do the sunblock thing and then get comfortable. It's a beautiful day and as I feel the sun warm my skin I feel grateful for being in such a beautiful place and having met the man next to me. I know that this whole vacation will be one I never forget.

"Do you have a new project coming up soon?" I turn on my side and look at Asher, my gaze roaming over him like always. I can't help myself.

"I do. I have a few meetings with the director and my agent when I get back to LA and then a week later I have to report to the set."

"That's exciting. What is the role? Is it another Jack Danger movie?"

"No, but I am filming another one of them at the end of this year. In this one I'm playing a detective that's accused of committing the perfect murder."

"Ooh, who do you murder?"

He smiles, "Who says I murdered anyone? Why are you so quick to assume my character did it?"

Rolling my eyes, I ask, "Fine, please allow me to rephrase."

"Proceed."

"Who died that you're accused of murdering?"

"My girlfriend in the movie."

"Oh yeah? And who plays your girlfriend?"

He names an actress that's so drop dead gorgeous I'm embarrassed to admit it makes my stomach fall a little. Stupid reaction. "Wow," I reply.

But, I can't get anything past him, "Whoa, why did your face fall?"

"Did it?" I shrug, but my next comment and question totally gives me away, but I can't seem to stop myself. "She's beautiful. Have you ever dated her?"

His nose wrinkles at my question as if he tasted something bitter. "What? No. Not at all. Not interested. Besides," he rubs his hands down his body and I follow their trail, "All this is for my wife."

Laughing at the way he totally complimented himself in that sentence, I ask, "So, who have you dated in Hollywood?"

His face turns serious, "What makes you ask?"

Oh god, it must be really bad if he's asking and not answering. "Well… I'm not blind, I mean I've seen some of the press about you."

"You shouldn't believe everything you read."

"I'm not saying I do, but I can't even log into social media accounts without being blasted with entertainment headlines and whatever is trending, and you've definitely trended more than once. Which I have to say is so weird to say to you."

"Why?" he presses.

"Spending time with you has been so…"

"Yes?" His brows raise and he watches me expectantly.

"Normal."

His head falls back and he laughs, "I am normal – in every way. You know that for yourself," he says suggestively.

"Yes, it's totally normal to have starring roles in movies, have women literally throw themselves or their clothes at you, propose marriage on social media – yes I saw that headline too – and to have more money than God."

"Okay fine, so I'm not exactly normal in every way I guess, but I don't get caught up in all that Hollyweird shit. I'm not interested. I love what I do, and I'm lucky to be doing it, but I've told you, it's not what makes me who I am. I also have great friends and family that helps keep me grounded when I need them. But usually, I can do that on my own."

"So the rumors?"

"Most of them have been just that. And if the rumor is with an actress I'm starring in a movie with it's normal and pretty predictable that rumors about us dating start to circulate. A lot of times the production company doesn't do anything to contradict them either. In fact, sometimes they initiate them. All press is good press they say."

"Does that ever bother you?"

"It never has because the people that matter to me know what's what. Besides, all you have to do is look at photos from any of the award shows I've gone to."

"Why's that?"

"I always bring my mom or sister."

"Aww, that's so sweet."

I swear a blush comes to his face, "It's not that I couldn't get a date if I wanted," he says cockily.

"Nope, too late. I already think you're super sweet now. And a momma's boy. You can't change it and try to make you seem like a player. I know the truth."

He grins and I don't think he particularly cares that I know the truth. My guy is a softie. *Whoa, my guy? Where did that come from?*

"Speaking of friends," Asher says as he looks down at his phone. Holding it to his ear he gives me a brief smile, "No, we don't want to go out with you again," he says without a greeting and I shake my head at his rudeness but he just smiles and mouths, "Well we don't."

"Tomorrow morning? I don't know…" I raise my brows in silent question. "Hold on." He puts his phone down, "Hunter wants me to meet him for breakfast in the morning. We have a couple things to discuss, not sure if I mentioned that Hunter's kind of my assistant."

"What? He is? No, you never mentioned that."

"Well he's been my friend for ages, but he's one of the only people I trust so I asked if he would take the job and he did."

That explains a lot. I mean, I knew they were friends but he also has a vested interest in Asher's career so he's protective of him on more than just a personal level. "Well go meet him for breakfast. It must be important."

"I doubt it's anything that can't wait, like I've already told him, but I should quit blowing him off. You sure you don't mind?"

"Not at all."

He makes arrangements for an early breakfast and we enjoy the rest of the day at the pool, at times cooling off -or alternatively heating up- in the water, standing under the mock falls, swimming, imbibing in delightful summer drinks, or otherwise, sunning. The time could hardly have been more perfect.

We go back to our room and take a quick shower together before we get dressed for the evening. I don't ask Asher what I should wear, I know what I want to put on. Slipping on a floral sundress that's sheer but lined, I love its weightless feeling on my skin. It crosses in the front, ties at the side, and where the ruffled hem meets in the front as it wraps, it's a little shorter. The showstopper is that it's completely backless. Foregoing undergarments I search for the pink flip-flops that match the pink in my dress but I can only find one; instead I elect to go with my sparkly gold ones.

Ready, I step out from the dressing area and Asher's appreciative glance devours every inch of me. "You look beautiful."

"Thank you," I respond, in turn admiring his navy blue pants and white shirt rolled up on his forearms. "You look edible," I tell him and he smiles wickedly. I can almost hear the dirty thought running through his mind.

Taking my hand he leads me out of the room. I'm surprised to find that we aren't leaving the resort at all and when we walk past the pool and onto the beach I look at Asher in question. He just smiles and turns to the man that walks up to him. "Mr. Charming, we have everything ready for you."

"Thank you," he says as he takes my hand and leads me to one of the huge bed-like cabanas on the sand. They are out of this world amazing. Huge four-poster bed-loungers with white flowing canopies from each of the four corners that enable closure for privacy. A fluffy mattress and huge soft-looking pillows lie on a base that is suspended by ropes in all four corners, allowing it to swing gently. Next to the cabana is a table and chairs set with covered plates. Taper candles are positioned in the center of the table, ready to be lit once the sun sets.

"Wow." I don't have any other word to describe how incredible this surprise is.

Asher turns to me when he's done speaking with the staff, "Do you like it?"

"I love it."

"Good. We have this for the night."

"The entire night?"

"Yes," he nods and I smile. "Are you hungry? Do you want to eat?"

"Not just yet. Can we enjoy the sunset first?"

"Of course."

He reaches up and closes the canopy that exposes our backs to the resort. With it closed no one in their rooms or at the pool can see into the cabana. He gets on the large bed first and then helps me climb on and wraps me in his arms. We stay like that, wrapped up in each other, as we watch the sun descend. My eyes well with tears when the fact occurs to me that Asher and I have limited sunsets left to enjoy together. The thought chokes me up and I bat my eyelashes furiously trying to keep the tears from falling down my cheeks. I don't want to ruin our night.

We look on in awe as the sky ablaze with color makes the ocean appear as if it's on fire. The sun lingers on the edge of the horizon, before dipping and then disappearing, leaving behind tranquility and a feeling of awe and respect. "It's so beautiful," I whisper as the spectacular scene touches and moves the deepest part of my soul. We lay still, connected, unmoving and as the stars ascended to take their place in the night sky and moonbeams bounce from the water in the distance, I realize what I just viewed was akin to the sensations and experience of my short time with Asher. Uniqueness, a blaze of beauty and magnificence, real, stirring, moving, and I want these feeling to linger forever.

Asher's fingers are on my chin and he lifts my head to face him. "Almost as beautiful as you, Ella." I realize he had repeated these words, but in my revelry, I had not heard. But gazing in his eyes, I see an indecipherable look and in the next instant my lips are on his. He kisses me as if it's one of our last. There's desperation in the way his hands clutch my body to his, in the way his mouth moves against me furiously then slows down as if he's trying to savor every minute. When we pull away we stare into each other's eyes. Reaching up, I brush my thumb over his cheek, a thousand things going through my mind.

"Let's eat," he says hesitantly and before I can again grasp any one thought and hold onto it to investigate it further or uncover his.

We eat fresh seafood together and he keeps me laughing by telling me different pranks he's pulled on the set. He's done everything from super glue a cast member's finger to his nose, to putting nipple clamps tied to a locked collar on a passed out drunk cast member that weren't able to be removed without a key, to hand-delivering a fake certified letter to a fellow cast member that carried information of a lawsuit by another cast member causing significant mayhem and drama. I had no idea he enjoyed being a prankster and targeted his co-stars with such antics and jokes. The gossip columns did not capture this side. Note to self, stay aware and watch out.

"God, I love the sound of your laugh," he says unexpectedly as I was laughing at the story of when he had a friend dress up as a police officer and fake arrest someone on the set.

"I laugh a lot around you."

"I like it."

His eyes are heated and wordless when we finish dinner and move back to the cabana. Before reclaiming his spot, he carefully closes the side cabana drapes, leaving the one facing the ocean open. It's so dark, we can only see the twinkling stars, the white reflection of the moon off the water and the ripples of the water under the light. With the salt in the air, the ocean crashing in our ears, and Asher at my side, I don't think I could be happier.

He turns to me and smiles as he slides a hand up the side of my leg. When he reaches my naked hip, his eyes widen, and I smile seductively. "That's correct. I'm not wearing any panties," I tell him obviously. He groans and he squeezes his eyes closed. "Asher?" I whisper and wait for his eyes to meet mine. When they do I gasp at the way his indigo eyes almost look black from lust. "Make love to me."

Without a word, he removes the clothes from my body and I remove his. When we are naked he kisses down my body until he's positioned between my legs. When he kisses me intimately, my back curves off the bed and my toes curl in response. My hands move to his head and I shamelessly pull his hair, stroke his head while grinding my hips into his face desperately searching for my release. When it comes, I see more stars than the ones in the sky.

Kissing his way back up my body, he rolls on the condom and then positions himself above me. His eyes bore into my own and with each small thrust he makes as he enters me, he unknowingly peels back the protective layers I've kept over my heart until the truth is shining so bright, I'm amazed it doesn't blind both of us. When we are hip-to-hip, chest-to-chest, heart-to-heart, the realization that I am in love with this man washes over me with startling clarity.

I want more than anything to tell him. I want to scream it, moan it, whisper it, and repeat it over and over like a curse or a prayer. I want to beg and plead with him to love me too. I want to ask him to let this marriage be the real thing – to keep me forever. To let me have him. But I can't. It's pointless. It doesn't matter. I've no reason to believe he feels the same way about me, and our time together is coming to a close. He needs to get back to his life, his career, his family and friends. Exposing my feelings will only set me up for unfathomable pain and the rational part inside of me can't allow myself to break again – not now at least – not here.

So, instead, as we make love, I try to tell him with my actions. I tell him I love him with the way I clutch his body to mine, with the way my fingers dig into his skin, and with the way I kiss him - as if I can't taste enough of him. I tell him I love him in the way I take control and kiss my way down his body until I give him pleasure. Every stroke of my hand, flick and lick of my tongue, and with every kiss from my lips, I try to communicate my heart. I tell him I love him as my nails dig into his chest, I tell him I love him with the way I yell his name when I reach euphoria, and with the way I keep pace with him, thrust for thrust, groan for groan until he climaxes too. I tell him I love him with the smile I give him when he pulls away to look at me. I tell him again with the kiss of my lips on his and with the way my eyes devour every inch of his face begging him to see, to know. When he wraps me up in his arms, and his slow steady breaths reach my ears, I finally allow myself to shed the tears I can no longer contain.

Chapter 21

Sleep doesn't come for me until I see the sun peek out from the horizon. All night I refused to succumb because I wanted to enjoy every second of my time with Asher, whether he was awake or not. What he told me about time before, how it's one of the most important things we can own, he was right on target. I'd do anything to have more of it. But I had this time and it was glorious, memorable. He continued to caress and snuggle me throughout the night. At one point, the breeze increased just slightly. He awoke, momentarily and adjusted the linens and tightened his arms to ensure my warmth. Otherwise, he slept peacefully while I continued to reflect and inspect my feelings. Until finally, my mind gives way to physical demands, and I sleep.

When he wakes me with a kiss later, I'm tired but happy when I look at his rested and happy face. "I'm sorry to wake you, gorgeous, but we need to get back to the room. I need to get ready for breakfast with Hunter and the staff is here to clean up after us. I let you sleep as long as I could."

"Oh, of course." I hold the sheet to my body and look around for my dress. He hands it to me and I slip it back over my body and stand, taking my shoes in one hand and Asher's hand in the other. We're quiet as he walks me back to our room. It's as if we don't want to disturb the left over magic from the night that still lingers in the air.

While he moves to the restroom to get ready for breakfast, I collapse onto the bed, still feeling tired from my lack of sleep. I must doze off because the next thing I know, Asher's waking me again. "Wake up beautiful princess," he says making me smile before I open my eyes. "Hi," he smiles when I open them, "you're sleepy." I nod. "Well why don't you stay right here and when I get back, I'll join you. I'll bring you some food too, I'm sure you'll be hungry."

"That sounds perfect."

"Okay. I didn't want to go without giving you a kiss."

"I'm glad," I murmur and sigh with pleasure when he presses his lips to mine. I cup the side of his face and keep my hand there when he pulls back.

"I'll be back soon."

"Take your time. I'll see you when you get back." He nods, gives me one more kiss, then stands from the bed. He's almost to the door when I call, "Hey," he spins around a smile on his face. He's wearing a simple black t-shirt and jeans with his ball cap. "I was thinking I would call the concierge and get us a few groceries and I could cook for us tonight. Would that be okay with you?"

His smile widens, "You would cook for me?"

"I would love to cook for you."

"You know," he begins resting a hip on the doorway, "in some cultures that means that a woman is going to accept a man into her bed. When she offers him food."

"Does it now? Well, I guess we did this whole thing backwards then. But we already know that, don't we?" I place a finger to my chin, "I guess we could role play. Pretend I haven't already had you in my bed and I can feed you food and maybe fan you with a palm frond or something. Make my intentions clear."

His eyes narrow, "And what are your intentions?"

"To get you back in my bed of course, duh."

He smirks, "Of course it is."

"Alright stud, see you later."

"Bye, princess." But instead he runs over to the bed and gives me one more kiss before he pulls away, looks at me intently, then walks out of the room.

Falling back onto the bed I sigh at how in love with him I am. It's probably wrong that thoughts of handcuffing him to my bed and never letting him leave have crossed my mind. Laughing at myself, I'm startled when I hear a knock at the door and then laugh again. I run to the door wondering if he forgot his key, grab my robe on impulse and throw it on as I open the door, "Did you forget your key?" But it isn't Asher at the door, it's Hunter.

"Oh. Hi."

"Is Asher here?" he practically snaps at me. So much for formalities.

"No, he-"

He cuts me off, "We're supposed to meet for breakfast." He sighs as if divulging even that is painful for him.

"Yeah, I know. He just left. Maybe he went to your room?"

Without a word, he turns and starts walking down the hallway. His attitude pisses me off and before I can think twice about it, I blurt, "What the hell is your problem?"

He spins around, "Excuse me?"

"You heard me. But I'll say it again. What the hell is your problem? I told you I have no ulterior motive here, and I don't. I don't get why you hate me so much."

"I don't hate you. I just don't like you."

"Oh, well that's so much better."

"Look, I think if you gave a damn about him, you'd let him do something about all of this bad press before it effects his career. He's worked his ass off. And with the shit that hit the fan yesterday-" He stops and sighs putting the bridge of his nose in his hand as if he's getting a headache. "Maybe you don't care about the shit that's being said, but I do. And he should. It matters."

Shaking my head I stare at him, "What the hell are you talking about?"

He stares back, open-mouthed, "You don't know?"

"No."

"Your friend, the one I met before-"

"Katie."

"Yeah, her. She hasn't called you? Don't you have an assistant or something?"

"Let me grab my phone." Holding the door open, he steps into the room and I go to my purse and grab my phone. The last time I remember using it was when I took photos at the sky pool. Pulling it out, I push the home button but nothing happens, the screen remains dark. Walking back into the next room, I hold it up, "It's dead. Maybe she's tried. What the hell is going on?" Now he has the nerve to look hesitant and that infuriates me. "Oh hell no. You don't get to make accusations and assume shit about me and then back down when you realize I don't know what you're talking about."

"The press has been going nuts since the word got out that you two got married. Asher's been ignoring calls from his publicist and agent refusing to discuss it, so of course the press is having a field day."

"Well that's nothing new, right? Asher told me they are like rabid dogs with a bone."

"That's true, but word is that even the producers of his upcoming movie are asking questions and he's not dealing with any of it. Aside from that is the fact that there was a major story that came out about you yesterday."

"About me? What do you mean?"

"Your father's wife? She's stating that you're mentally unstable. She gave details to the press about how you were supposed to get married and went crazy at the altar. There's even a sad interview with your ex-fiancé. She said that marrying Asher is the cherry on top of your going crazy sundae and that you aren't within your right mind. Moreover, she says you've been unstable for a number of years. After your mom died? And I guess there's discussion by the Board of Directors at the company where you work about terminating you."

"Oh my god," I whisper, horror making me feel sick to my stomach. Hunter may not know why Angelica would be doing this, but I sure as hell do.

"Sorry to break it to you like this, I thought you would have been told and I couldn't fathom why you didn't care."

"I'm sure Katie is going crazy trying to reach me."

"I'm sorry to make this worse, but if you care at all about Asher, you will do something about this. This press is really bad for his image. He's a good guy. He doesn't get caught up in all the Hollywood hype and shit. He doesn't deserve to have the image he's worked hard to maintain dragged through the mud for some chick he met and wanted to hang out with for a week. No offense."

This isn't really about Asher – though it's impacting him – it's about me. The room is whirling around me. So many thoughts are going through my mind. Angelica is trying to take my company out from under me. I know she's trying to get the board to side with her and to push me out of my own company. I need to deal with this. And unstable? She's telling people I have been mentally unstable? And as much as I hate this, Hunter is right. Asher doesn't deserve this kind of trash attached to his name. This is all because of my family drama and he doesn't have anything to do with this, but he'll still reap the consequences all the same. One whispered word against him is too much. "I need to leave. Now." I look around the room frantically thinking about everything I need to pack but I don't really see any of it. I want to cry, scream, and throw up in response to my own words.

Looking back at Hunter, he's looking at me with pity. "I think that would be best." Each word he says hitting me between the eyes like a hammer.

Nodding absently, I try without success to keep the tears at bay, but they flow down my cheeks freely. Hunter looks at me with a mix of horror and confusion and my anger flares again. "So sorry to burden you with my tears. You can leave now."

"I just don't get it."

"Don't get what?" I snap at him.

"Why are you crying? This is just a fling for you."

"Says who? You? Why would you just assume that? You know *nothing* about me."

"Oh come on, you expect me to believe that all of this, the whole sham of a marriage and spending time with Asher all week isn't you trying to take advantage of him somehow?"

"Take advantage of him? Because of his money? Oh wait, I have my own. So, what then?"

"I don't know, you tell me."

"Fuck you. And the horse you rode in on."

"That's what I thought," he has the nerve to say. A smile of triumph on his face.

"You couldn't be more wrong. I love him. I'm in love with him. And leaving, that's going to kill me." More tears fall down my face as my voice breaks with my confession.

Hunter is frozen staring at me with a look of disbelief. "I really don't care what you think, but it's the truth. I didn't ask for him to walk up to me at that party. I wasn't even the one that suggested getting married. I didn't come here looking for anything other than to get away from my life in New York for a little while. I never expected to meet Asher. I never expected or thought it was possible to be completely charmed by a man in less than a week and fall in love. I didn't ask for any of this."

"God, I had no idea. I'm so sorry," Hunter's face falls and I believe his words, but every ounce of my emotion is tied up in my leaving Asher. I don't have enough in me to care about how Hunter feels.

Walking into the next room, I grab my suitcase and start throwing all of my stuff into it. I don't take time to fold anything, I just shove anything and everything I can grab inside. Going into the bathroom, I gather all of my things from there too. "Fuck!" I curse suddenly.

"What's wrong?" Hunter asks, and I jump a little not expecting him to be right there.

"My phone is dead. I need to make a plane reservation, and can't."

"Let me help you."

"I don't want anything from you."

"Please, let me do this. To make up for being an asshole."

"It won't make up for it. But, I will take your help because I'm out of options." He nods and removes a messenger bag from his body. He pulls a computer out of the bag and pulls up the airline once he connects to the internet. His phone begins ringing and with a look at me, I know without him saying who's on the other end. "Hello? Hey man. Yeah, I'm sorry, I'm running late. No! No, it's not cancelled, I'll be there in a few minutes. I know, but you promised because we need to deal with this whether you like it or not. Okay. Good. I'll be there soon." He hangs up and his fingers fly over the keyboard once more. "There's a flight in a couple hours."

"Okay, that works."

He turns the computer to me and I book my ticket. While I grab the rest of my things, he calls the concierge and gets me a taxi ride to the airport. All packed up, I look around the room and my heart aches at the thought of leaving, but I have to. This was never going to be something other than a week. I love him, and that's why I need to do this. Besides, maybe on some level this will make things easier. I'm not sure I could stomach a goodbye.

"For whatever it's worth, I'm sorry that this is hurting you," Hunter says and I scoff in response.

"Just promise me that you'll explain to him. I'm going to leave him a note, but take care of him okay? I don't mean now, he'll get over this, I just mean always. And stall as long as you can at breakfast. I don't think he'd come after me, but just in case, alright?"

He nods, and with one more glance at me, he's gone. Forcing myself to keep it together a little bit longer, I take out a piece of paper from a notebook in my carry on bag and a pen.

Dear Asher,

I'm sorry that I won't get to make dinner for you tonight after all. It would have been amazing. Just so you know — I really am a good cook. I'm sure you've noticed by how clean our room is that I'm gone. Maybe you're thinking, 'she's talking about cooking?' or 'thank god her clothes aren't all over the place now', I don't know, but I'm only talking about cooking first because what I want to say isn't easy. You see, the impossible happened this week. I came to Cabo not even knowing I was looking for something other than just needing to get away. It wasn't until I met you that I realized what's been missing. I never expected to meet you, let alone fall in love with you, but I guess fate had other plans. I'm sure some would think that love this fast is impossible; I think I would have thought that too, but it's true. I'm in love with you. And because I'm in love with you, I can't allow my life to come down on your head due to someone wanting revenge against me. I'm so incredibly sorry that my broken family life has bled onto you and your career. I can only hope that it didn't leave a stain. I promise I will handle it. Just know that with you I found out what it's like to feel love, to be happy, to have fun, to be carefree. I found a magic I didn't even think existed for me in you, and my life will forever be better for it. I will treasure this week and the memories we made. I'll look for you in that chick flick you promised me. I hope that somehow in some way, I also left you with a gift — anything of importance - like you've given me.

My address is on the back of this paper, so when you have the divorce papers you can send them to me for a signature.

Keep being you, Asher, because you're amazing.

Love,

Your Princess

Placing the note on his pillow, I grab my bags and walk out the door. A golf cart is waiting to bring me to the lobby so I can catch a cab and I'm sure it's Hunter's doing. He may be sorry, but he's anxious to smuggle me out of here as soon as possible. Guess I can't blame him. I'm all business until I get into the cab to ride to the airport. When the door shuts behind me, and we make our way out of the resort, I turn around and give it one last look. Down far below, I can see the cabana on the sand that was occupied by Asher and I just hours ago. My heart hitches at the sight, and I close my eyes and turn around, finally letting the tears flow uninhibited down my face, feeling as if my heart is breaking inside of my body.

Chapter 22

Present Time

When Faye hands me another tissue, I smile gratefully. Just as my story ended, our plane landed. We sit patiently waiting for the door to open and for people to start filing out. It's been a long flight and I'm eager to get home. To see Katie. To get back to my normal routine so I can put this pain behind me. To settle this with my stepmother and others.

"Oh, sweet girl. No wonder your heart is breaking." Nodding, I'm unable to form words. "And so you left without a single word to Asher?"

"Only the note."

"He hasn't blown up your phone with calls?"

Shaking my head, I smile sadly, "We never exchanged numbers. We were together all the time and it never came up. I don't even have his email. Other than my address that I gave him in the note I left, we don't have any contact information for each other."

"Oh, dear," Faye says with a shake of her head.

"It's better this way. If I had his number I would probably call him or think about calling him, or call and hang up over and over like some teenager." I laugh a little bit, but it's forced.

When it's our turn to exit the plane, it takes me a few tries to budge my suitcase from the overhead bin and I laugh a little remembering shoving it in there to begin with. Following Faye off the plane, we wait for our luggage together and then hug each other goodbye.

"Thank you for sharing your story with me," Faye says, her sweet hand holding mine.

"Thank you for listening. It helped to talk about it. I think I would have gone a little nuts all those hours on the plane just holding it all in."

"Keep your chin up, sweet girl. These things have a way of working themselves out. Believe in magic."

Shaking my head sadly, I try to smile for her, but I'm sure it looks more like a grimace. "Love is the closest thing to magic I think. The way it makes one feel, how it makes you feel things you've never expected, has the power to make sad things disappear and makes you believe in the impossible. I'm afraid that I've lost my belief in magic. At least for now."

Faye pushes the hair that escaped my ear, back behind it, "Then I'll believe enough for both of us for now."

Smiling at her, we exchange email addresses and phone numbers and hug each other again tightly. As I watch her walk away I admit that I'm thankful for whatever magic placed her in the seat next to mine.

Chapter  23

"I've got it," Katie exclaims loudly looking up at me excitedly. "I know exactly what we should do!"

Eyeing her from across the room I almost dread whatever she's about to say. I know that look on her face and it's orneriness. Really, the girl's got two expressions, ornery and not ornery.

It's been almost two very long weeks since I came home from Mexico. Each day has passed excruciatingly slow. However, I have finally stopped crying every day which is a tremendous victory. I don't even want to think about the amount of tissues I've gone through.

When I walked in the door from Cabo, Katie pounced on me immediately. She'd been frantically trying to reach me after the news story broke thanks to my lovely stepmother. My phone was still dead and I'd never had a chance to warn her that I was on my way home or to talk to her about what happened. She clearly wasn't expecting me to walk in the door two days early and even though she was full of questions, she took one look at my face and knew that whatever happened it hadn't ended well and in that moment, I just needed her.

I experienced a sick sense of déjà vu when I was on the floor in Katie's arms once more as I cried all over her shirt. Eventually I was coherent enough to give her every single detail about what happened from the moment she left Mexico. I even told her about the sex. Needless to say, she was one happy girl. Correction, she was one jealous happy girl. She also wanted to kill Hunter with her bare hands. I believe it was something along the lines of chopping off his balls and feeding them to the hungry pigeons all over New York City. Or something along those lines. I was too delirious with tears when she was going on about it, but I appreciated the sentiment.

"I don't know if I want to hear whatever it is that you came up with."

"Aw, come on," she pushes.

"Fine," I sigh. "Lay it on me."

"No really, it's a good one. We should probably even make a new commandment with it."

"I'm scared already."

"We should go on another vacation!" She declares like it's the best idea in the world. "No seriously," she says when she sees the look on my face. "It can be our thing. We can become husband collectors. We can go around to different places like London, Greece, and Italy and marry someone in each place. When a friend is broken-hearted thou best friend shall take her on vacation and get her married immediately. See? A commandment."

Sadly, if I want to go all over the place and marry people and collect husbands I can. After a week of not hearing from Asher, and because I needed to consult my attorney anyway about the shit that was thrown in my lap from Angelica, I finally gave my lawyer, an old family friend, a call. He gave me great advice for my work situation, but during our discussion I mentioned my marriage in Cabo and how I was waiting for divorce papers from Asher. I had to mention it because like it or not, my quickie marriage was relevant when dealing with my mental stability because of the accusations Angelica brought up to the press and our board of directors. I said something along the lines of not knowing how long is too long before I should worry about the fact I hadn't yet received divorce papers from Asher in the mail. I had been reluctantly checking each day. I wasn't sure if I was going to feel great sadness or relief when they arrived.

Imagine my shock when I found out my marriage to Asher was considered only a commitment ceremony in the eyes of the law. There was nothing legal about it whatsoever. In order to be considered legally married in Cabo San Lucas, they require individuals to have four witnesses present at the ceremony, to obtain a blood test a few days prior to the ceremony, for a judge to preside over the ceremony and a couple of other things. Needless to say, our little wedding inside of a church was nothing more than pomp and circumstance because there wasn't a thing about it that was legal. Therefore, divorce papers were never going to arrive because there was no need for them. We weren't really married. I didn't think my heart could hurt worse, but I was wrong. Not only did I feel like I lost my last connection to Asher, but I added feeling stupid on top of that.

Considering this information, I should probably have removed the ring on my left ring finger, but I haven't been able to bring myself to do so just yet. While it may not have meant anything legally in the eyes of Cabo or in the U.S., it meant something to me, and I'm not ready to part with it.

Shaking the thoughts from my mind, I return my focus to Katie and our conversation. She's done what she set out to accomplish, I laugh. "Only if we can go to Scotland and see if James Fraser lives there," I tell her. She's the only one who understands my *Outlander* obsession. "Maybe I can grab him for my collection."

"Deal!" she agrees.

"Come on," I tell her, "we're going to be late."

"Aw fine," she says as she applies one more layer of lip gloss.

The two of us are meeting up with a couple of other friends at a bar for drinks. Katie is dragging me out and I don't really want to go. I have one hell of a board meeting that's going to be hell tomorrow, so I'd rather be at home and gear myself up for that, but Katie won't allow it. I agreed, but told her no more than an hour or so.

When we walk inside of the wine bar, Vanessa and Riley wave to us. They're already seated at a table. We take a seat and the waitress is there in seconds. Ordering a glass of Riesling, I smile at our friends and it quickly turns into a frown when I notice the apprehension on their faces. I know that everything that happened with Asher was tabloid fodder, but Katie told me she had already communicated what's what, but clearly something is bothering them.

"We can leave if you want to," Vanessa says.

Katie gives her a strange look, "We just got here. Why would we want to leave?"

"You didn't see them?" Riley asks looking uncomfortable.

Katie and I exchange a look and Katie asks, "What the hell are you talking about?"

Vanessa leans forward, "Ella, keep your eyes on me. Katie you can look, but Jeremy and Jackie are here."

Staring at Vanessa and Riley's wide eyes, I see Katie's head swivel out of the corner of my eyes. I don't move, not because I'm surprised or shocked, but because I feel nothing. Not anger. Not sadness. Not regret. N-O-T-H-I-N-G. Where there used to be feelings for Jeremy there is now one big barren hole.

"Oh no he isn't," Katie hisses.

Looking at Katie I raise my brows in question, "What?"

"He's coming over here."

"You're kidding."

"No. He actually left Jackie sitting there, and is coming to our table."

No sooner are the words out of her mouth than I feel a tap on the back of my shoulder. Turning, after first noticing the various pissed off looks on my friends' faces, I look at Jeremy for the first time since I walked away from him on our wedding day. He gives me the lopsided smile I used to adore, but once again I marvel that I don't feel one single ounce of anything for him. It's gone. Loving Asher made me realize that I never felt love for Jeremy. My father is always alive in my heart and I don't need to hang onto a person or an item that was connected to him to keep him here. He'll always be a part of me.

"Hi, Ella." Jeremy says hesitantly, his eyes looking from me to all the women I'm with.

"What do you want?" Katie quickly asks in an interrogating voice.

"I'm not talking to you," Jeremy says.

Katie starts to get out of her chair and I almost laugh. "Hello, Jeremy. What brings you to our table? It appears you're otherwise… well whatever you are with her," I say waving to the table where Jackie sits glaring daggers at me.

"I just wanted to tell you that I'd still like for us to get together and talk. I would like the chance to explain."

"That's not needed nor is it necessary. I don't care for an explanation."

"Look, can we talk in private for a minute?"

"No, thank you. Whatever you have to say to me, you can say in front of them."

Sighing deeply, he rolls his shoulders a few times before proceeding. "I saw in the paper that you took off to Cabo and ended up marrying that actor guy and I guess I just feel bad that I drove you to do something so crazy. I didn't know that losing me would…well make you go off the deep end. And, by the way, I never intended to cheat on you, it just happened."

Staring at him in disbelief, I look at Katie as if I need her to confirm that I just heard what I think I heard. The look on her face is a clear indication that he did in fact just spout complete and utter foolishness. Looking back at Jeremy, my mouth open and feeling speechless, I begin to laugh. I laugh so hard, that tears pour down my eyes. Katie joins me too and I look at her, "You heard that, right?"

"Oh, I heard that."

"Can you believe that shit?"

"You know, the sad thing is that I do believe it," she says making me laugh harder.

It takes effort but eventually I calm down enough to respond, "Jeremy, you didn't make me crazy. And trust me, the ending of our *relationship* was the best thing that could ever have happened. I fell in love with a man and in the short time I was with him I learned what real love is and what it feels like to be unbelievably happy. You can take your apology, or your guilt, or hell, given the fact that you're with Jackie, maybe it's your regret, regardless, you can take them all and shove them up your freaking ass." Jeremy's face floods with color and I feel satisfaction at the sight. "You know the truth is, I should probably be thanking you. If you hadn't cheated on me, I never would have met Asher. And the thing is, I would endure going through that infamous and doomed wedding day of ours a thousand times over again if it meant I would always end up with those days I spent with Asher. Now, if you'll excuse me, I'm here with friends and we have some catching up to do."

Turning back around, I give him my back and never look at him again. Pride is shining in Katie's eyes and Vanessa and Riley can't stop smiling and giggling at witnessing our little interaction. Maybe I should feel bad for being so cruel, but the truth is I blame Jeremy in part for what's going on now with Angelica and all the crap in the press that was said about Asher. He gave an interview to the press about our wedding like he was some victim, never once mentioning his role in the demise of our relationship. Not to mention he undoubtedly hoped to make out in the end should the board decide I'm not in my right mind to run my company.

I enjoy the rest of the evening with my friends. I stay longer than I intended, but the longer I'm with them, the more I realize that their support is making my heart feel lighter than it has in days. We keep our conversations pretty superficial – talking about the latest fashion and the latest gossip amongst our friends.

When Katie and I walk in our front door a few hours later, I give her a hug and wish her sweet dreams before escaping to my room. Shutting the door behind me, I change into my pajamas and then get into my desk drawer pulling out a manila file I keep inside. Rifling through the contents, I select what I want, then pull a shopping bag out from under my desk and take out a wrapped package.

Peeling away the tissue paper, I take the back off of a silver picture frame. Placing the picture I just selected inside, I close the back then bring the frame to my bedside table. The photo is the beach in Cabo. It's a panoramic view of the shore and off to the side are rocks with water spraying into the sky from the impact. Looking at it makes me sigh with pleasure. If I close my eyes I can almost feel the sun on my face, wind in my hair and the sand in my toes.

It's the first time since my return I've been able to frame an image printed from the many photographs taken while away. It's also the first time I've been able to look at one and feel fondness and not heartbreak. Today was a better day.

Chapter 24

My hands are shaking and I honestly don't know if it's due to nerves or if it's because of the three cups of coffee I've already had. I woke up with the sun this morning unable to sleep. I was too wound up thinking about the meeting with the board. I actually did something I haven't done in a long time. I got out of bed, got dressed, put on my running shoes, and went for a jog.

It's something I did a lot after my father passed away. Running somehow helped relieve my stress. I'm no marathon winning runner by any means, but I can do a fast paced walk, light jog while looking pretty good in running attire, with the best of 'em. Typically, with every smack of my feet against the pavement I've been able to beat the stress or sadness from my body into the concrete. It's true that sometimes I nearly ran myself sick, not always able to stop, but I felt a need to run until I felt nothing at all.

Nothing.

That's something that I could walk away with today.

Angelica has been manipulating things behind the scenes for a while. I'm sure she and Jackie had some kind of plan when it came to my relationship with Jeremy and planned on using him to push me out of the company. I remember she intimated that when she told me about their affair, and it wouldn't surprise me at all. And when she didn't have Jeremy to use as planned, she determined to use the wedding fiasco against me. And my time with Asher and what happened between us only played nicely into her hands. It gave her the right ammunition she needed to put her little plan into action, I'm sure.

Planting the story in the news about my mental status and allowing herself to come across as the worried stepmother was brilliant really. The board of directors, while old friends of my father's whom have known me since I was in diapers, are old fashioned. They will protect the company they helped build at any cost, and if that means pushing the founder's daughter and CEO out in order to preserve its reputation and standing that's what they will do.

I get it. I do. Our company gains clients because of our unmatched reputation in this industry. It's a company built on integrity and intelligence. How can we expect to thrive and gain new business when potential clients could be worried that the CEO is out of her mind? Or that I could embarrass their company's voice or brand?

I have no idea what's going to happen today, but I know that I'm not going down without a fight. From the information I've been able to gain from gossipy board members, the rumor mill at work, and from my assistant April, they are under the impression that I completely lost my mind over the heartbreak of Jeremy's betrayal. Some of the board members were at my wedding; they saw first hand how that went down. And I'm told that Angelica told them that I was on medications for a long-term mental health condition. One that had never been exposed to protect me. I suppose I can see why they might think I'd lost my mind. I suppose a lesser woman than me could.

Then there's my marriage to Asher. They believe that it was a quickie wedding because I was reeling from the loss of Jeremy. That I was acting out. Or further evidence of my instability and irrationality. It doesn't help that there were people that came forward with stories about our time in Cabo. Asher's "friend" Spring gave an interview telling the press how worried she was about Asher because his new bride seemed "unstable."

The woman that took a picture with Asher at the restaurant and kissed him on the mouth, sold the photo to the press and gave an interview stating that I almost "lost my mind" when she kissed Asher, her friends that were nowhere near the table when it happened, backing up her story and adding details about how I yelled and screamed for them to get away from "my man."

The man that offered to help me with my sunscreen snapped photos of Asher and I together. The weird thing is that he took them not only of us at the pool but getting ready to go out into the ocean on our wave runners too. That means he had followed us which is incredibly creepy. His story stated that I flirted and came onto him, asking for help with the sunscreen, and that Asher lost his mind and almost hit him for touching me.

I mean really, I'm not sure why Hunter was so worried, if anything, it sounded like poor Asher had trouble reeling in his crazy wife. My guess is he's eliciting more sympathy than anything else.

It's a real possibility that the board is going to ask me to step down and submit my resignation or put me on a forced leave of absence until I give in and resign. The thought of losing my father's company makes me ill.

Smoothing my skirt down my thighs before I step out of the car that has taken me to the office building, I straighten my jacket and force my head high when I walk into the office like I have each day since my return. Never let them see you sweat.

When I reach my office, my assistant is there immediately with a cup of coffee like usual. I shouldn't take it from her considering the cups I've already had, but I do. "Most of them are already here and are in the boardroom," April tells me and I nod, unable to find words. "Five minutes," she reminds me.

Turning toward the large window in my office I take in the view of the city I love. Forcing myself to inhale and exhale, I remind myself that no matter what happens today, I haven't done anything wrong. And if I've learned anything over the last couple weeks it's that when things happen out of our control, there's nothing I can do. And it's senseless to worry. All I can control is myself. I can live by the morals my beloved father and mother instilled in me, I can be true to myself, I can have courage and be kind, and I can trust that while it may not make sense to me at the time, that the path we walk is all part of a greater plan - and all I can do is walk down the road and have faith that it will all work out in the end. And it will. No matter what happens inside that boardroom today.

With one final deep breath, I leave my office and go into the boardroom. Everyone is here. Including Angelica. As soon as she sees me she smirks and I look away immediately and take time to meet the eyes of every person there before I walk to the head of the table. "Hello everyone. Shall we begin?"

Why does it not surprise me that Angelica was elected to do the talking? Funny considering she holds less stock than anyone else in the room. "Let's not waste time with formalities. You know why you're here. The board and I have serious questions about your ability to run this company given your recent...behavior... indiscretions."

"My indiscretions." I repeat.

"Yes. This company is founded on honesty, hard work, and a good solid reputation that's capable of promoting businesses via new and innovative approaches that support them in achieving their goals and realizing excellence. Not only do we strive to increase their revenue, we are known for increasing their market share, extolling the excellence of their products, and helping them achieve a reputation of reliability and credibility while enhancing their stature within their industry. "

"I'm well aware of what this company does, of its mission statement, goals and values. You may recall, that I helped fashion those."

"Good, then you'll understand that when your own behavior exposes compromised moral judgment that we're concerned about our reputation and the subsequent loss of business from existing and new clients. They need to be able to trust that their business is in good and capable hands. Given your mental instability right now, I'm not sure that your position as CEO is in this company's best interest."

"Unbelievable," I mutter.

Pamela, a partner and friend of my dad's almost since the company began speaks up, "Ella, you have to understand that we are concerned. No well-respected business is going to trust our company with their future if they aren't comfortable with the CEO that runs the corporation. That's simply fact."

Henry, a sweet man that used to sneak me candy when I would wait in my father's office for him to finish up work sometimes speaks next, "We know you've been through a lot. Maybe it's a good idea to take a leave of absence until you're feeling better."

"I'm feeling fine," I say exasperated. "Anyone else? If not, then let me say a few things. Normally I would be angry that my personal life is under scrutiny. Normally, I would state that it isn't anyone's business. In fact, I'm sure that some of the conversation and discussion is violation of the law, and I'm sure HR would agree. However, given the situation, I will indulge you - for now. As you know, my marriage to Jeremy didn't exactly go to plan." I almost cringe at my description, but how else would I describe it? "Just before I was due to walk down the aisle, I was told by my stepsister and stepmother that Jeremy had been having an affair with my stepsister. I'm sure you remember that Angelica, you were there."

"See what I mean?" She says to everyone. "That never happened."

"However what you don't know is that before I found out that little tidbit, I had already elected not to go through with the wedding. I wasn't in love with Jeremy, I never was. I had the mental clarity to decide that marrying someone I didn't really love was a mistake. There is no question that I could have handled that day differently, but I handled it as well as I think reasonable given the entire situation. Then, as you all know, I decided to take my earned, and might I add, well-deserved time away, the time that had been planned for my honeymoon, as my vacation. And yes, while I was in Cabo I met a man and we were married, in a non-binding, non-legal wedding ceremony, but the supposed stories of my behavior printed in the paper are simply not true. My time with Mr. Charming, was not a slip in judgment. I did nothing that would undermine the integrity or reputation of this company – or my own. And quite honestly, I'm not sure what I can do or say that can convince you of any of this. You see, at the end of the day I know it's going to be her word against mine. What do you want me to say here? How can I convince you that none of the stories and rumors are true? That the fact that my wedding didn't occur isn't some tragedy that I've had to endure, that sent me over some figurative edge, but rather, was my choice. I would be happy to conduct an interview in the press stating the truth. I have not done so out of respect for all of you and this company. Would you like me to undergo a psychiatric evaluation? Fine. I'm appalled, infuriated, and simply amazed that you would so easily believe a rumor instead of me, someone you've known for years, someone who has been unwavering in her dedication, loyalty and passion about this company. And in truth, someone who has steered this company since my father's death to yield more revenue that has benefited each and every one of you around this table. Yes, it astounds me that I am needing to stand here and defend myself. So tell me, what is it you would have me say or do? But let one thing be clear, I will not admit to something that is untrue to meet your needs and I will not apologize for something that is not my fault, or for which I have no control. As always, I'd prefer to let my history of work do my talking for me. And one more thing. I have learned, that while I may be young, time is precious. It is sacred. And I will not waste any more of mine or yours on this topic. We will resolve this now."

Something comes over me and I realize I'm simply done playing their game. I don't owe them a damn thing. "My father," I say slowly looking around the room at all of them again, "he would be ashamed of every single one of you. He led you all to be so much better than this. And so have I."

There are gasps in the room, but I barely hear them. Pushing my seat back from the table, I stand to leave. Before I can take a step, the door bursts open and my eyes swing to the doorway.

I'm frozen.

Time stands still.

The air in my lungs leaves my body and I blink rapidly trying to clear my vision. I'm almost convinced that what they all believe is true and I *have* lost my damn mind. "I'm so sorry, Ms. Barrie, I told him you were in a meeting and could not be disturbed."

Asher is standing in my boardroom. He's here. In New York. He's in front of my entire board of directors. And oh god, he looks amazing. I don't want my eyes to leave him in case he disappears, but movement behind him makes my eyes widen. Douchebag Hunter is standing behind Asher, a small smile on his face. Swinging my gaze back to Asher, I devour him with my eyes. He looks divine. Black dress pants and a blue shirt that makes his eyes blast blue from across the room adorn him and he looks as sexy as I've ever seen him. "Asher?" I say and it sounds choked as if I'm almost afraid to believe it.

He begins walking to me and I still can't move. "I'm mad at you. No, scratch that, I'm *furious* with you."

"You're furious with me?"

"Yes. Do you have any idea how crazy I was when I got back to our room and found you were gone? All you left behind was a note."

He pulls it from his pocket and it looks worn, like it's been opened and closed several times. "A note that tells me you love me. A note that tells me you're leaving me. A note is all I had left of you." He takes another step toward me. "I lost it when you were gone. I didn't know what I had done or what had happened. I immediately felt lost, alone, and behaved abhorrently. I practically trashed our room. Hunter found me there, in the middle of self-destruction and fessed up and told me about your conversation and that he encouraged you to leave. That he believed all that shit that was being said...or certainly had believed it. I then turned on him and practically beat the hell out of my best friend."

"It's true," Hunter pipes up with a smile, and I notice that he's got a yellowing black eye.

He takes another step toward me. "I spent four of the best days of my life with you," he says and I swear right then and there my heart stalls in my chest. "I fell in love with a you at first sight, Ella." No, I'm wrong. Now my heart has stopped. "I don't give a fuck what people say about love at first sight because I know it's real. Do you know what I said to Hunter the first time I saw

you?" I shake my head no unnecessarily. Of course he knows I have no idea. "You were next to me and my friends at the pool. You and Katie were drinking and I heard your laugh, I saw your smile, I heard your hilariously inappropriate comment about your ass and I looked at Hunter and I said, 'I'm going to marry that girl'."

"It's true, he did," Hunter says again.

"When I took you out the night I approached you on the beach and we went dancing and you were drinking, you didn't notice that I had hardly drunk anything at all. We had fun together, you opened up to me about what that asshat Jeremy did to you and how your stepsister and stepmother were minions from hell."

Glancing at Angelica, I see her face flush and she stands and crosses her arms, "I think we've heard enough. You can leave now," she has the nerve to snap.

Asher looks from her to me, "Who is that?"

I almost grin at his clear annoyance that she's interrupted him. Forget the fact that he is in my boardroom, interrupted a meeting, and is surrounded by my board members. "That would be the infamous stepmother, minion of hell."

"Oh yeah? Well Ella excuse my interruption of us for a moment, because this seems to be the perfect time to mention this. Hunter?" Hunter takes a piece of paper from his messenger bag and hands it to Asher. "Imagine my surprise when this was sent to my assistant. It's a written notarized statement given by the editor of the *New York Times* stating that your stepmother paid him off to put that story about your defunct wedding and her interview as well as your exes in the paper. She also paid an investigator to dig up any and all information she could find about our time in Mexico and she told him she would pay him extra to spin the stories in the manner that would serve her purpose."

Henry stands and takes the paper from Asher and looks it over. "He's telling the truth."

"Hell yes I am. Now if you'll excuse me, I was in the middle of something," Asher says then turns back to me as if he hadn't just dropped a huge bomb in the middle of the room. "Anyway, where was I?"

"You were telling her about the night you approached her on the beach," Pamela says with…is that a helpful longing tone in her voice?

"Ah, yes. Anyway, that night, I wasn't drinking much at all Ella. When I suggested we get married, I knew exactly what I was doing. When we woke up the next morning and you were so surprised, did you not notice that I didn't share your shock or worry in the slightest? If you recall, I told you I remembered every minute of the night we were married. Now, I've since found out that our marriage was a civil ceremony and not legal and I'd like to rectify that even though it was real to me, but I'm getting ahead of myself."

My god how many times can a woman stop breathing and not pass out? Or die?

He takes another step toward me. "I kept waiting all that week, searching for an inkling that maybe you felt the same way. That you'd want more than just one week with me. I almost told you I love you so many times, but I didn't want to frighten you and scare you away. When our week was over I was going to either tell you, or ask you to keep seeing me. Either way I was never going to let you go. But then you left. And I had no way to get in touch with you other than your address. So, I flew home and I met with my directors and I did all the meetings that I had lined up and the whole time all I could think about was getting to you. I counted down the time until I could show up on your doorstep and declare my love for you. It's been the longest two weeks of my life and if I wasn't under contract to do those things or face severe repercussions I would have been here sooner, but I've died a little bit every day that we've been apart. I don't want to be apart from you anymore. I love you, Ella. I've loved you from the moment I saw you."

He's standing in front of me now, and he takes my hand, and gets down on one knee. The sight makes tears immediately come to my eyes. Hunter hands him something and to my surprise it's the pink flip-flop I couldn't find when I was getting ready for an evening with Asher in Mexico. He must have found it when he packed, "You left this behind when you left. I actually found it under the bedside table. Anyway, when I found it, I thought it was fitting, because you're my princess Ella, and I want to be your prince Charming. I know this shoe fits your foot so basically that means you have to say yes. So please, say that you'll marry me, for real this time. I never want to be without you again."

"I have missed you so much. These last two weeks have been agony. I never expected you, Asher Charming. I never saw you coming, and you have been the best surprise I've ever had in my life. Yes, Asher. I will marry you."

He rises to his feet and takes me into his arms and I'm home. His lips land on mine and he kisses me so hard and with so much passion that I feel the days that we were apart fade between us. Pulling back, he pulls the shoe out and I look down. He cut a small slit into the bottom of the shoe and stuck inside it is a gorgeous engagement ring – princess cut of course. He slides it on, and smiles when he sees my wedding band is still in place. And I look at his hand and find he's still wearing his too.

"I love you Asher. I love you so much."

"It feels amazing to hear those words in person instead of in a letter."

"I'm sorry. Please forgive me, I didn't want any of this," I gesture to everyone around us, not even caring that they're there, "to hurt your career."

"It can't. The fact is, with my job, things will always be said in the press. People will sell their souls for a buck, and that's just par for the course. Anyone with half a brain knows that's how it is, and anyone who would believe the shit these people write need to get a life. They certainly aren't the ones I would want in my life."

As if on cue, Henry stands again and says, "I think we've seen and heard enough. Angelica, you can either leave or be escorted from the property, I can guarantee that the board will be convening about your role in all of this and likely buying out your share of this business. You are the one we cannot be associated with. Ella, I want to formally apologize on behalf of all of us for bringing you here today and putting you through this. I couldn't be happier for you, and I wish you all the best. Until next time, my dear." And with that he saunters out of the room, everyone else following behind.

Angelica shoots daggers at me as she is forcibly removed but this time it is Asher who returns her looks, clearly daring her to say or do something. When she's gone, he turns back to me, "Promise me you will never run like that again. If something happens, you'll talk to me, we'll work it out, we'll take care of it together."

"I promise." He kisses me again and when we break away I see that everyone has left the room. It's just the two of us. "Ever made love on a boardroom table?"

His grin turns wicked, "Can't say that I have."

Walking to the door, I flip the lock, then turn back to the man I love, "Well, you're about to."

Epilogue

Running the box cutter along the sealed tape and pulling the top open with my other hand, I pull out the contents one by one. Smiling as I unwrap each photo, I set them aside, not yet sure where they will be hung. Realizing what I'm unpacking, a smiling Asher comes up and stands next to me reaching into the box to assist me. "I think we should hang one in every room. I want to be reminded of falling in love with you everywhere I look."

Whenever I think it isn't possible to love him more, he proves me wrong.

Looking around our new home, I take a mental picture, wanting to remember this moment forever. Asher's choice to live in New York is a big deal. A huge deal. Knowing how I feel about Katie, my roots and the company and our clients, he wanted us to establish our residence here. So he said it would be no big deal for him to travel. And since the Board has agreed that I can work remotely from anywhere, I have freedom to travel with Asher as well. It was the perfect solution. We were lucky and easily found a quaint little apartment on the Upper East Side. The movie that he started filming after Cabo, was being shot here in New York, a fact that he never had a chance to tell me. It's been wonderful having him here and over the last month that he's been filming I've visited him on set a few times. It's truly a remarkable experience and I love watching Asher in his element.

Katie was sad to lose me as a roommate, but the good news is that Vanessa's roommate relocated, so they had a perfect solution. She moved into our old place and I didn't feel so bad about leaving her after that. Of course we talk every day and get together all the time. She constantly asks Asher to hook her up with a hot friend or hot costar.

Knee deep in wedding plans, I am counting down the days until I get to begin my official marriage to the man I love. He's involved in all the wedding planning and never once seems bored or says, "whatever you want". He's gotten laid for that multiple times so far – maybe that's why he never says it. He's caught on.

Katie and I went shopping last weekend and I found the perfect dress. It was unexpected, just like everything else has been on this journey. Therefore, it was perfect. A very light shade of blue, it was the perfect reminder of that princess in blue I love so much. After Asher's proposal it made perfect sense – I knew it was the one. And when I tried it on and looked at myself in the mirror, I could see *the look*. The one I had searched for before. The one Cinderella wore the day she married her Prince Charming. It was there in my eyes, I could see it. And I knew it always would be.

"I'm going to unpack that last box in our bedroom really quick," Asher says. "The pizza will be here any second. Do you mind getting the door?"

"Of course not."

He kisses me on the cheek and starts to walk away, but I grab him by the arm and pull him back. Giving him a much more thorough kiss, I sigh from happiness when I pull away, confident I'm wearing a silly grin. "I love you, Asher Charming."

"I love you too, soon to be Ella Charming."

Smiling he dashes away to tend to his task and seconds later there's a knock at the door. Grabbing the cash out of my purse to pay for the food, I open the door and to my surprise, it isn't the pizza. "Ella Barrie?"

"Yes?"

"Delivery for you, ma'am."

He hands me a large light blue box, "Thank you," I say taking it from his arms and closing the door behind me.

Curious, I sit down on the couch with the box in my lap and untie the white bow, and remove the lid. A note sits on top. Unfolding the paper, I begin to read.

Fairytale Vacations

Dear Ella,

Congratulations on your happily every after. We're thrilled to have had a hand in making your dreams come true. I enjoyed getting to know you on your wedding day and after. Keep believing in magic, Ella, and love.

Here's to your happiness,
Your Fairy Godmother (haha!) Faye
CEO Fairytale Vacations

"What?" I mutter and set the note aside, my brain trying to wrap around the words. Unwrapping tissue from an object, I take out a photo frame and gasp when I see the photo inside. It's Asher and me. We're standing at the altar in the church where we were "married" in Mexico. He's holding my hands and we're looking into each other's eyes. In the center, a book in her hand and a smile on her face is Faye. Our wedding officiate was Faye. The CEO of Fairytale Vacations.

Oh. My. God.

"Asher!" I call, "You're never going to believe this!"

And then they lived happily ever after

The End

Acknowledgements

Ever since I can remember I've been enchanted by princesses. When I was a little girl I'd imagine myself as each one as I would watch them find their true love. It's always been my dream to write a book that was my own version of "Once Upon A Time," and with Charming I feel like I have. The feeling is surreal, and my heart is full.

While writing Charming, I experienced some intense writer's block. The story was there, but the words wouldn't come. I am so incredibly lucky to have friends in my corner that ALWAYS cheer me on and do their best to motivate me and encourage me when I need it. With their help, I was able to keep pushing through. Georgia aka Gypsy, you're my person and I can't imagine doing this without you, I hope I never have to. Until we're old and gray, right?

Mayra Statham, thank you for your pictures of Sam Heughan, messaging me constantly to see how my writing is going, for always telling me that you want another Jennifer Miller book and most importantly for being my friend.

Angela Corbett, thank you for helping me work out a big plot issue I was having. Thanks for not minding when I sent you text messages or Facebook messages at all hours and for letting me pick your brain. You made me feel like you were as excited for me to write this as I was to get it out of my brain, and that motivated me to keep going. Also, thank you for my new favorite phrase, "deep fried fucks."

Glorya Hidalgo, Stephanie Brown, Vanessa Rohbock – I'm so lucky to have found friends in you. Our banter and laughs have added so much to my life and you are always right there with a kind word or telling me just what I need to hear. I waffle you.

Mom, thank you for loving me enough to take this journey with me. I'm lucky to have you, and appreciate your feedback and edits more than you could possibly know.

To Robin Harper with Wicked by Design, we make an amazing team. I am SO in love with this cover. We knocked it out of the park. Elaine York with Allusion Book Formatting, you always make me feel like I matter any and every time I contact you. You have a whole list of clients, but you always make me feel like you drop everything for me. I imagine we all feel this way about you, and it says so much about how amazing of a person and businesswoman you are. Amber Garcia with Lady Amber's Reviews and PR, you are killing it. I'm so glad we are finally working together.

To my agent, Sarah Hershman, thank you. Here's yet another one to add to your list of things to do. Ha!

To Jake and our girls, thank you for your patience, helping me name characters, telling everyone you know about my books and for dealing with me when my mind is somewhere else. I love you madly.

To you, my reader, thank you for taking this journey with me. Your unwavering support, notes, messages, and comments do not go unnoticed or unappreciated. I read and hold close to my heart all of your words. All I've ever wanted is to offer an escape for you the same way that books have always been one for me. Thank you for continuing to take a chance on me, and I hope that you've all found, or are taking life's journey toward your own happily ever after.

About the Author

Author Jennifer Miller was born and raised in Chicago, Illinois but now calls Arizona home. Her love of reading began when she was a small child, and only continued to grow as she entered adulthood. Ever since winning a writing contest at the young age of nine, when she wrote a book about a girl with a pet unicorn, she's dreamed of writing a book of her own. The important lesson she learned about dreams is that they don't just fall into your lap – you have to chase them yourself. Most importantly, she is a wife and mother, and is very lucky to have a family that loves and supports her in all things. She also has an unhealthy addiction to handbags and chocolate covered strawberries, neither of which she cares to work on. For more information about Jennifer Miller, please visit www.jennifermillerwrites.com

Facebook – https://www.facebook.com/JenMillerWrites?ref=hl
Twitter – https://twitter.com/JenMillerWrites
Pinterest – http://www.pinterest.com/jenmillerwrites/
Sign up for my newsletter – http://goo.gl/JNRarK
Instagram - http://instagram.com/jenmillerwrites
Goodreads - https://www.goodreads.com/author/show/7019978.Jennifer_Miller
Amazon Author page - http://amzn.to/1DzbfUH

Other books by Jennifer Miller

Pretty Little Lies

Pretty Little Dreams

Pretty Little Vows – A Novella

Perfect Little Plan

Whispering Wishes

Fighting Envy

Fighting Wrath

Fighting Lust